Praise for Lost and Found

"This charming romance is propelled by winsome, endearing characters and digs into rich questions about tradition, progress, and loyalty. Fisher's fans won't be disappointed."

Publishers Weekly

"This story is very entertaining and engaging, with lots of surprises and even a bit of suspense."

Interviews and Reviews

"An Amish romance at its very best, author and storyteller Suzanne Woods Fisher's latest novel, *Lost and Found*, is a fun read from cover to cover."

Midwest Book Review

Praise for *Anything but Plain*

"Readers will be won over by the delightful leads, and the nuanced treatment of Lydie's ADHD and crisis of faith brings depth to the narrative. This is another winner from Fisher."

Publishers Weekly

"*Anything but Plain* is a heartbreaking yet beautiful Amish journey. Suzanne Woods Fisher tackled so many themes beautifully in this novel."

Urban Lit Magazine

"Suzanne Woods Fisher is the master at telling historic tales."

The Stand

A Healing
Touch

★

Novels by Suzanne Woods Fisher

A Healing Touch

SUZANNE WOODS FISHER

R
Revell

a division of Baker Publishing Group
Grand Rapids, Michigan

Published by Revell
a division of Baker Publishing Group
Grand Rapids, Michigan
RevellBooks.com

Printed in the United States of America

Library of Congress Cataloging-in-Publication Data
Names: Fisher, Suzanne Woods, author.
Title: A healing touch / Suzanne Woods Fisher.
Description: Grand Rapids, Michigan : Revell, a division of Baker Publishing
    Group, 2024.
Identifiers: LCCN 2024005085 | ISBN 9780800745288 (paperback) | ISBN
    9780800746353 (casebound) | ISBN 9781493447145 (ebook)
Subjects: LCSH: Amish—Fiction. | LCGFT: Christian fiction. | Novels.
Classification: LCC PS3606.I78 H43 2024 | DDC 813/.6—dc23/eng/20240206
LC record available at https://lccn.loc.gov/2024005085

Scripture used in this book, whether quoted or paraphrased by the characters, is taken from the King James Version of the Bible.

Cover photograph: Ildiko Neer / Trevillion Images
Cover design: Laura Klynstra

Baker Publishing Group publications use paper produced from sustainable forestry practices and postconsumer waste whenever possible.

24 25 26 27 28 29 30   7 6 5 4 3 2 1

To AJ,
who helped me push this book
out of the stall and into
the exciting arena!

"A doctor can treat, but only God can heal."

—Dok Stoltzfus

Meet the Cast

Ruth "Dok" Stoltzfus (age late fifties), doctor to the local Amish of Stoney Ridge as well as non-Amish patients, sister to Bishop David Stoltzfus, married to police officer Matt Lehman. While in her teens, Dok left her Amish upbringing to pursue higher education and a medical career. In the book *The Devoted*, she was reunited with her family.

Annie Fisher (age 20), Amish, office assistant to Dok, daughter to Sally (a raging hypochondriac). Her mother's many unusual ailments have given Annie a keen interest in the medical world.

Bee Bennett (age 51), former Olympic elite equestrian, now a horse breeder of Dutch Warmbloods. Over a year ago, Bee moved to Stoney Ridge when her husband Ted retired from his medical practice to start a hobby farm. (But then he died.)

Damon Harding (age 60), former Olympic elite equestrian, now a high-level horse trainer. Had once competed with Bee on the US Olympic Equestrian Team. To Bee's surprise, he's missing his left arm.

Sally Fisher (age 58), Amish, mother to Annie, wife to Eli, diagnosed by Dok to have hypochondria. Sally rejects that label. She's convinced she's not well.

Eli Fisher (age 61), Amish dairy farmer, father to Annie and long-suffering husband to Sally.

David Stoltzfus (age midfifties), bishop to the Amish church of Stoney Ridge, husband to Birdy, brother to Dok, father to many—both his own children and his flock.

Fern Lapp (age late sixties), Old Order Amish, the type of no-nonsense, kind but firm woman whom everyone needs in their life. First arrived in Stoney Ridge in *The Keeper*.

Matt Lehman, husband to Dok, police officer. Met and wooed Dok Stoltzfus in *The Devoted*.

Hank Lapp, one-of-a-kind elderly Old Order Amish man. Readers first met Hank in *The Keeper*. Even then, he had one volume: loud.

Edith Fisher Lapp (won't reveal her age), married to Hank Lapp. An interesting love match, because no two people could be more opposite. As Dok says, "There's a lid for every pot."

Sarah Blank (early twenties), Old Order Amish, friend of Annie's, works at Bent N' Dent store. Has a huge interest in others. Some call it nosiness.

Amish EMT . . . well, you'll just have to read on to find out more about him.

One

The workday had barely begun and Dok Stoltzfus was already running behind schedule. Levi Yutzy, an Amish farmer, had been waiting for her at the office, his hand wrapped in a blood-soaked towel. Half of one finger had been nearly severed while chopping wood. As Dok gathered clean bandages to wrap Levi's hand so she could get him to the hospital for reattachment, he asked her how much the surgery might cost him. "Doesn't matter," she said firmly. "You need your finger."

Levi's big body spilled over the edges of the exam table. "But how much, do you figure?" he said, peering at his hand while Dok bandaged it. "Might be best to just cut off the rest of it. You could do that right here, couldn't you?"

Those were the moments when Dok had to remind herself that the goal was to get this man to the hospital for reattachment of a severed digit. She had to handle this in a way that made sense to this Amish farmer, even if it made no sense to her. "Levi, if you were a few decades older," she said, "I might give you an option. But you're a young man, with a big family. You need your hands in working order to farm well."

Levi seemed unconvinced. "Besser einen Finger als die ganze Hand verloren." *Better a finger than the whole hand.*

"Besser zehe Finger." Dok sighed. *Better ten fingers.* "God gave you ten fingers for a reason, and if we hurry, you still have a good chance to keep all ten of them."

Levi looked down at his hands, and she knew he was considering her words. Slowly, his long beard wiggled up, then down. A nod. Still, Dok had insisted on driving him to the hospital's emergency room, just to be sure he got there and stayed there.

And as soon as she had a moment to spare today, she would march over to the Bent N' Dent to complain vigorously to her brother David, the bishop, about Levi's flawed logic. Dok complained to David quite a lot about the people in his church. Imagine putting a price tag on a finger!

They were her people too, David would quietly remind her. So right. For all the frustrations she had with the Plain People, she also loved and admired them. They were her people too.

Dok had been raised Amish, though she hadn't gone through baptism like her brothers David and Simon had. There was a deep hunger inside her for higher education, a longing to become a doctor. That desire won out over conforming to her family's expectations, though it came with a price—losing her family. She'd gone through medical school, become a doctor, and in an unexpected turnabout, ended up back among the Amish.

Having been raised Plain, she understood them in a way few others in her profession could. Frugality and practicality were baked into them, part of their DNA. Yet while she understood it, reluctance—like Levi Yutzy's—to take advantage of what modern medicine had to offer simply out of penny-pinching, well, those moments could try her patience.

Dok stayed with Levi in the ER's waiting room until he was admitted and taken in to be examined. Glancing at her watch, she weighed the cost of adding one more unexpected errand into the morning's time-crunched schedule. Annie Fisher, Dok's office assistant, had just called to tell her the lab results from

Bee Bennett's recent biopsy. If Dok took a shortcut through the back roads, she would drive right past Bee's. House calls beat a phone call or video call, every time. Most doctors would disagree, but Dok thought a house call even beat an office visit.

Especially with this kind of news.

When Bee Bennett answered the knock at her front door to find Dok Stoltzfus, her stomach clenched in a knot. Bee's husband Ted had worked with Dok before she left the hospital to buy a practice of her own in Stoney Ridge. They'd stayed in touch over the years; Bee and Ted had even been invited to Dok's wedding to Matt Lehman. Bee and Dok were more than doctor and patient, though not quite friends. Somewhere in between. But she sensed that Dok would let any patient know, face-to-face, if something was wrong. That's just the kind of doctor she was. Dok developed a bond of trust with her patients, the same kind of bond Bee sought with her horses.

Bee invited Dok in and they sat in the living room, Dok on the couch, Bee on the seat of the large bay window. "I'm pretty sure you didn't drop by for a cup of tea," Bee said with a nervous laugh. "So my guess is you have some news to tell me."

"I do. Not the news that I had wanted for you, Bee." Dok clasped her hands in her lap. "But it's not the worst news, either. Your breast cancer was caught . . . and caught early."

So, there it was. Bee'd had a sense, all along, that the biopsy report would be positive. She'd braced herself for this moment, dreading it, yet she felt strangely detached to hear the actual outcome said aloud. She blew out a puff of air as she visibly stiffened her spine. "So, what comes next?"

"I'll get appointments set up for you with a surgeon and an oncologist. The oncologist will make further decisions about treatment."

"What kind of treatment?"

"Those decisions will be made postsurgery."

"Dok," Bee said, in a "you know the answer to that" tone.

Dok sighed. "Most likely, you'll need a course of radiation. But, Bee, all of that will be decided by specialists. You can trust their decisions. And, Bee, you've got an excellent prognosis."

Bee shifted on the seat to look out the window at two of her horses, Echo and Willow, in the snowy pasture that lined the house. Two of her favorites, though they were all her favorites.

Dok wasn't quite finished. "You're very fortunate. Catch cancer early, while it's easy to treat."

Bee turned to her with a scoff. "Easy?"

Dok rose to join her on the window seat. "This will end up as a blip on the radar. You'll get through this. You're strong, Bee."

Was she? Bee used to think of herself as strong, but that was before her husband died so suddenly, so unexpectedly, shortly after he had retired from a demanding career as a vascular surgeon. They'd sold their home in the suburbs of Lancaster and moved to twenty acres in Stoney Ridge to start an official horse breeding farm, a lifelong dream for Bee. She'd been an unofficial horse breeder for years, trying to carry on the lineage of Ozzie, her magnificent mare. Ted had never begrudged the costs of keeping Ozzie stabled, or later on, her progeny. He was the one who found a "retirement" property that had a barn and a covered arena. He teased Bee that since she had found a way to collect horses, it would be cheaper to house them than to keep paying their board.

Happily, Ted was all in with the notion of becoming a gentleman farmer. He was eager to spend time developing skills for his interests, like gardening and carpentry, all the hobbies he had postponed for retirement. He had relied heavily on his fine motor skills for intricate surgeries and took care not to do anything that could injure his hands—even avoiding typical husband-tasks like chopping firewood or fixing a broken garbage disposal. The day after he retired from his practice, he went to Home Depot and spent a fortune on tools. Lining one garage wall in the Stoney Ridge house was a stack of boxes of unused tools, still in their original packaging.

Barely sixty. Ted had just had his sixtieth birthday when he died. Bee had gotten what she had wanted for the next chapter of life, but Ted never had time to get what he had wanted. Over a year had passed, yet Bee still felt his loss like a fresh wound.

"You know, Bee," Dok said softly, "over the years, I've noticed that many newly diagnosed cancer patients have experienced recent trauma."

Bee blinked. "What exactly are you trying to say?"

"That trauma, like loss, takes a tremendous toll. There's even a book about it called *The Body Keeps the Score*."

Bee turned her gaze back to the window. "In other words, we're all doomed, because sooner or later, no one gets by in this life without hardship."

"No, no, that's not what I mean. I'm not saying we're doomed. I've just seen a correlation between trauma and disease in my practice. Research is starting to pay attention to this, to the toll that elevated cortisol levels take on a body. It's why, after Ted passed, that I've been after you to take care of yourself, to not skip or postpone any appointments, to get up to speed with all your tests."

This last year, Bee had been overdue for just about everything related to body maintenance—dentist, doctor, even regular haircuts. She just didn't have the energy for them. She gave Dok a wry smile. "And here I thought you just liked to meddle."

Dok burst out with a surprised laugh. "I do! I do like to meddle. A trait I inherited from my mother. The family had a nickname for her, though I'm not sure she ever knew it. Mammi die Nasiche. Mammi the Meddler." She chuckled. "Anyway, lately I've been thinking that there's another component to caring for my patients, especially those who've

17

experienced recent trauma." She patted her heart. "Healing the heart, the soul." She turned to Bee. "I think it would help you."

"Oh no." Bee shook her head. "I went to a grief group at a church and came home feeling even more depressed."

"What?" Dok's blue eyes went wide with surprise. "How? Why?"

"Because the leader invited everyone to share their feelings, and so they did. I discovered that there's a lot of people walking around who feel just as bad as I do."

"But didn't the leader make any effort to help people heal?"

"He talked about how happy our loved ones are, and that was supposed to bring us great comfort." Bee lifted a hand. "Don't get me wrong. I'm a big fan of the hereafter. I believe Ted's there. But how does that help me in the here and now?" She clapped her hands on her knees. "Tell me, Dok, what does it look like to heal from losing your spouse and best friend? Give me some idea of what you mean, because I can't figure it out. I'm only fifty-one years old and I don't know how I'm going to get through the rest of my life." She hadn't meant to spill so much. She hardly knew Dok! But since she'd gone this far, she might as well go all the way. "I've wondered if . . . maybe . . . with your news today, maybe the rest of my life isn't going to be all that long."

Dok reached her arm around Bee to pull her close in a side hug. "I know it doesn't seem like it, but today's news is a gift. Because you were willing to get a mammogram—"

"But I wasn't willing. You made me go. You picked me up and drove me to the appointment."

"—it caught a potential threat to your health. You don't give up on your body because a few errant cells are multiplying. Your body just needs a little help from you. First, we're going to deal with this breast cancer . . . and then we're going to work on healing from grief."

Bee pulled back from Dok. "You didn't answer my question. What does that truly look like?"

"To be perfectly honest, I'm not sure I have a satisfying answer. Because . . ."

"Because you've never lost someone, have you?"

"I have, but not like Ted's sudden death. Both of my parents have passed away. My mother died just last year, in fact. But I wasn't surprised by her passing, not like you were."

Boy, was she ever. Bee had gone to the grocery store to pick up a few things for dinner, and when she returned, she noticed the front door had been left wide open. Very unlike Ted. He was an attention-to-detail kind of guy. She set the bag of groceries on the porch and took a tentative step into the house, calling Ted's name. That was when she saw her dearly loved husband on the hallway floor, clearly gone. A myocardial infarction, the coroner ruled. A fancy way to say heart attack.

"It seems to me," Dok said, "that a sudden death might be what we all want for ourselves, but it is particularly brutal on those left behind."

Brutal? Not even close. Shattered into a million sharp fragments was more like it.

"That reminds me. Do you stay in touch with Ted's son? Tyler, right? I remember meeting him at Ted's memorial service. He seemed like a very warm young man. A lot like his dad."

Tyler, Ted's son from his first marriage, was grown and married. And yes, he resembled Ted in many ways. "He's a doctor at NYU and married to a doctor. Super busy, as you can imagine. Plus, they're having a baby."

"Bee," Dok said, with wonder in her voice. "*You* are going to be a grandmother."

"No, I'm not," Bee said flatly. "His mother is."

"You could be in that child's life. Ted certainly would've been."

"But he's not, Dok. His death changed a lot of things." Like

Bee's connection to her stepson. Without Ted, they'd lost that impetus to stay in touch.

Out in the pasture, one of the horses lifted its head with a loud neigh. "Bee, how many horses do you have right now?"

"Seven."

"Hmm. Seven is a lot. You're going to need extra hands around here for a while."

Bee knew Dok was trying to be helpful, but these horses weren't exactly trail nags. They were Dutch Warmbloods, strong and athletic, bred to be show jumpers. Besides, Bee didn't let just anyone near them. They were too valuable. And then there was the bond between a rider and horse. It took years to develop, and that partnership was what made jumping seem like dancing.

Of course, Bee didn't expect Dok to know that. All Dok knew was that Bee had once ridden in the Olympics on a horse named Ozzie.

Dok's phone had been vibrating. Bee could tell that she was needed elsewhere and rose to make it easy for Dok to leave. "Speaking of horses, I'd better get these two into their stalls and deliver their lunch."

But Dok wasn't quite ready to go. "Last night, Matt said something about a friend of his who trains horses. I have to admit that I was only half listening." She squinted. "Something about having time on his hands. Anyway, I'll find out more and let you know. Matt invited him for dinner tonight." She walked to the door. "And my assistant Annie will get those appointments scheduled. You've met Annie, right?"

"I do remember Annie. Very cute. Very bashful."

"Yes, both. She's an excellent assistant. One of the best I've ever had. You'll see. She'll get your appointments set up by day's end. And I think she's making some progress with her shyness." She knotted her forehead. "I hope so. That's the plan, anyway."

Bee smiled. She had a hunch that Annie was one of Dok's

projects, like she was. "You're a wonderful doctor, but you don't need to worry about me or my horses."

Dok reached out and put her hands on Bee's shoulders. "Can't help it. Comes with the territory." She gave Bee a quick hug and hurried out the door.

Bee waved until Dok's car turned onto the road and disappeared. She wasn't surprised by the biopsy's result. But what did take her off guard was that she didn't feel anything. Nothing at all. Dok could've told her that she was coming down with a cold. Bee felt utterly indifferent to having cancer. And that, she knew, was no way to live.

Although painfully shy, Annie Fisher had decided long ago that she wanted to work for Dok Stoltzfus. Her admiration first began as a result of how Dok had managed Annie's mother as a patient.

Annie's mother Sally always had a myriad of physical complaints, one after the other. Some of Annie's earliest memories were accompanying her mother to a doctor's office. Those visits were probably how Annie's shyness—which she self-diagnosed as "social anxiety" after reading one of Dok's medical magazines—went from mild to severe.

Her mother would insist that Annie be allowed in the exam room to be a witness to testify to her most recent symptoms. A typical scenario went like this: "I'm real sure," Mom would tell the doctor, "it's a case of rheumatoid arthritis. Tell him, Annie. Tell him how red and swollen my hands looked yesterday."

But they hadn't. They had looked just fine to Annie.

The doctor or nurse would turn to Annie for confirmation and her mind would go blank. Absolutely empty. She had no idea how to respond. She didn't want to deny what her mother said to the doctor, but she just couldn't lie, either. She was a terrible liar. So Annie wouldn't say anything. Not a word. In that awkward silence, she could feel her cheeks heat to scarlet, so she would look down at her shoes and her mother would say, "See? See that? She can't even speak. She's overcome with worry for me."

Not exactly. Mostly, Annie was trying to be invisible.

And the unsuspecting, well-intentioned doctor would refer Mom to a specialist who did all kinds of tests that never found anything wrong. When Mom didn't like what that doctor had to say, she would move on to another one.

But Annie didn't move on. Her curiosity about her mother's current disease—whichever one it was—would be piqued. Having never heard of it, she would head off to the library and read all about it. This kind of scene repeated itself many, many times, with a variety of diseases. Whenever her mother heard someone speak of a new ailment, most often her cousin Gloria who lived a few towns over, she became convinced she had it too.

Little by little, Annie became quite knowledgeable about serious illnesses.

It wasn't until Dok Stoltzfus started her practice in Stoney Ridge that Mom was properly diagnosed. On the very first visit, Dok had asked Annie's mother if she had brought her medical records with her.

Mom said no.

From under her black cape, Annie pulled a four-inch stack of records and handed it to Dok.

Mom gasped. "I've never seen those folders before." From the look she gave Annie, she wasn't happy about it. "Where did those come from?"

"After each appointment, I always kept the paperwork. I've brought them to each doctor visit. It's just that . . . Dok Stoltzfus is the first doctor who asked to see your medical records."

Dok had her eyes on them, listening to their whispered conversation. She spent a few minutes reading through the top few folders. "They're in chronological order?"

Annie nodded.

Dok held up a paper of handwritten notes. "Annie, you took these notes?"

Again, Annie nodded.

"Well, Sally, you certainly do have an unusual assortment of ailments." Dok closed the folder and held the stack against her. "I'll give you an exam today and get some blood work, and then I'll let you know when the results come in."

A few days later, Dok asked for the family to come to her office—Mom, Dad, and Annie, all together. Dok explained that she was convinced Mom had a type of anxiety disorder called *hypochondria*.

"So," Mom said, "you're saying that if I think I'm sick, then I will get the symptoms?"

Dok nodded, like *Bingo*.

"But I do think I'm sick."

Dok sighed. She looked right at Annie's father. "Eli, it's time to stop doctor-hopping. Sally needs counseling to overcome her health anxieties and she needs lots of reassurance from family, but she does not need to be going from doctor to doctor."

Dad left Dok's office full of relief and resolve.

Mom left Dok's office offended. She was unwell, she was just sure of it.

Annie left Dok's office fascinated with the anxiety disorder of hypochondria.

She went straight to the library to read all about it. She would never forget that moment—like a lightning bolt out of the sky. The diagnosis described her mother to a T! For years, the family all assumed Mom wasn't well, and if she could just find the right doctor who could make an accurate diagnosis and provide treatment, then she could finally get better.

In a way, that was true. Dok was the right doctor. Mom finally had an accurate diagnosis of her condition. But she sure didn't like it. In fact, she refused all of Dok's suggestions for treatment. That, Annie read, was typical of hypochondriacs. They didn't want to get better.

But knowing Mom's true diagnosis was incredibly helpful for the family. Dad, especially. He insisted Mom remain a patient at Dok's practice. Dok was convenient, she gave a discount for cash, and she was the bishop's sister. Even better, Dok wouldn't refer Mom to specialists for expensive, futile tests like so many other doctors did.

Grudgingly, Mom remained with Dok only because she had no other options. She still insisted that Annie come along with her as her witness to symptoms. So on a regular basis, Annie was in Dok's office. Her admiration for Dok grew and grew, as did her determination to work for her. On the day she'd heard that Dok's assistant was getting married and moving away, Annie wrote a letter to Dok that she'd like to be considered for the job as her new assistant. Sadly, she didn't hear anything back.

Not until the October day when Dok drove to the Fisher house and offered Annie the job. She didn't even interview her. She sat at the kitchen table with Mom and Dad and Annie, sipping a cup of coffee, chatting about nothing in particular. Through the window, Mom saw the mail truck and hurried outside to post a letter in the mail. And no sooner had the screen door slammed shut behind Mom than Dok turned to Annie and said she'd like her to come work for her as her assistant. No interview necessary, she said.

At first, Annie stared at Dok in confusion, not believing what she'd just heard. She scooted forward in the chair, her fingers curled around the edge of the seat. Could she be dreaming? No! Dok was right here, waiting for an answer. If Annie didn't hurry and say something, her mother would be back in the kitchen and decline the offer. The clouds parted and from deep inside Annie came a "Yes!" She said it in such a loud, clear voice that Dok nearly spilled her coffee.

But immediately, a glitch arose. Dad said Annie could only work for Dok until the end of March. Come spring, he needed her help on the farm. Annie's brothers had married and moved away to start their own dairy farms. That left Annie as her dad's main farmhand because he couldn't afford to hire on for seasonal work, like spring planting. Crushed, Annie had dropped her chin to hide her tears.

Dok didn't seem at all concerned about that limitation. "That sounds doable."

Annie's head snapped up. Was this really happening?

Dok smiled. "Anyone who can take notes and keep track of records like you, Annie, is just the person I need for this job. It's all about scheduling and billing." The only thing she asked of Annie was to memorize a bunch of Bible verses. "A prescription for extreme shyness," she said, handing her a list of verses.

Annie tucked the list in her Bible and, in her excitement, promptly forgot it.

Working for Dok was all Annie dreamed it to be. Nothing seemed to bother Dok, except for one thing—those times when Annie didn't interrupt her for an important phone call if she was in an exam room with a patient. It was the only part of Annie's job that was a constant challenge for her. She would stand outside the exam room door, frozen. What if the patient was in the middle of undressing? What if the patient was a man? What if the patient was *naked*?

It didn't take long for Annie to realize that Dok had a certain tone she used when she was growing exasperated. She would spell out all the reasons she wanted Annie to knock on the door to the exam room and interrupt her: "I want you to do this, Annie. It doesn't matter what the patient might think. It doesn't matter if the patient is half-dressed or stark naked.

It doesn't matter who the patient is. Male or female. Young or old. When phone calls come in from other doctors or the lab calls with test results or the hospital calls with a patient update, you need to come get me."

Annie hated the feeling of disappointing Dok. Yet just yesterday afternoon, a call came in from a doctor for a consult about a patient, and Annie couldn't make herself knock on the exam room door. This time, the patient in the exam room with Dok was the bishop. No way, no way. Annie couldn't open that door and risk seeing the *bishop* partially undressed.

No way.

Later, after the bishop left the office, Annie handed Dok the phone message to return the call from the doctor about the patient consult.

Dok looked crestfallen. "Annie," she said, holding the slip of paper in the air, "we've been over and over this."

Annie knew she needed to work on her social anxiety. For Dok's sake, for her own sake.

Last night, Annie skimmed through her Bible and found the list Dok had asked her to memorize. No, she had *told* Annie to memorize these verses. She looked up the first verse: "Let us therefore come boldly unto the throne of grace, that we may obtain mercy, and find grace to help in time of need."

She wrote the verse down on an index card and repeated it to herself over and over and over until she had it committed to heart.

The next morning, a phone call came in from the lab with a test result. Annie closed her eyes and repeated the verse to herself. She walked down the hall, "Boldly approach the throne of grace. Boldly approach the throne of grace," and took a deep breath before knocking on the exam room to interrupt Dok and her naked patient. (Annie was never sure if the patient was naked or not. She had kept her gaze on her shoes.)

As Dok breezed past her to get the phone call, she gave Annie an encouraging squeeze on her arm.

Annie had done it. There was *not* going to be a need for another crestfallen look of disappointment from Dok. She'd done it!

The bishop often said that God worked with us in little steps, one at a time, to get us where he wanted us.

Little steps, Annie thought. Little steps.

Heit waar der Daag en woch lang. *Today was a week long.* Dok tried to explain that Penn Dutch saying to her husband Matt when she arrived home at nine o'clock, after missing the dinner he had planned with his horse trainer friend. "I was doing everything I could to get home in time for dinner. I really was. But I was running behind all day. I probably shouldn't have stopped by Bee Bennett's—but a cancer diagnosis isn't something to hear on the phone."

"Of course. I told you it was the right thing to do when you called on your way back to the office. But you also told me you were going to make it home for dinner, no matter what."

"And I was trying! But right at closing time a mother brought in a three-year-old boy who had swallowed a penny and it had lodged in his throat. He was having trouble breathing. I took them over to the emergency room and . . . well, you know what that's like."

Matt shook his head. "I do know, Ruth. I realize how many patients depend on you. I know how much you give to your patients. You never stop. But something's got to change."

"Matt, I said I'm sorry."

"I want you to consider getting a partner."

This wasn't a new conversation between them. Dok bristled at the thought of sharing her practice. She had yet to meet another doctor who shared her views, especially on the importance of house calls. To her way of thinking, a joint practice was like a marriage.

"You can't keep going like this. *We* can't keep going like this."

"What does that mean?" She had thought things were sailing along smoothly between them. Maybe sailing *smoothly* wasn't the right word. Maybe the waters were a little rough at times, a bit choppy. "I didn't realize you've been feeling so frustrated," she said, trying to hide the hurt she felt.

"Not frustrated," Matt said. "I just feel as if we could be doing more with our lives."

Oh, come on! It wasn't like Dok spent her downtime as a couch potato. And it wasn't like Matt didn't thoroughly devote himself to his career as a police officer. He did! But she knew she needed to keep the conversation going. "More in what way?"

"Like . . . we haven't really been back to church regularly since the pandemic."

"We watch online." Most of the time.

He gave a scratchy, disbelieving laugh. "Not the same."

No, not exactly. It was a lazy way to worship. But Dok did appreciate what a time-saver it was.

"Ruth, we had talked about joining a small group. About getting more involved."

He had talked about it. She hadn't. She couldn't imagine fitting one more thing into her schedule. How could she when her patients needed her twenty-four hours a day? "I am sorry about missing dinner with your friend tonight. But it doesn't seem fair to expect me to add things to the calendar."

"I'm asking you to prioritize balance, for my sake as well as yours. Can you even remember the last time we went somewhere together? The last time we went on a date? You work six days a week and you're exhausted on the seventh. That's if you haven't gone to see patients in the hospital on Sunday."

Now Dok was getting steamed. She was hungry and tired and knew she should watch her words. Did she? No. "This is a doctor's life, Matt. You knew what you were getting into when you married me."

"Maybe so, but it seems . . . as if you take me, us, our marriage . . . especially our marriage, for granted. And that's a pretty lousy way to feel."

Dok's mouth fell open. "You think I take our marriage for granted? You can't be serious."

And then Matt brought up marriage counseling.

"Oh," she whispered, stunned.

Two

There was just something about Dok Stoltzfus that made a person start longing for more. Reaching for more. After a few months as Dok's assistant, Annie had studied, tested, and qualified for a GED, the equivalent to a high school diploma. When patients weren't in the waiting room, she read through Dok's medical magazines and texts, writing down vocabulary words that were new to her. The more she knew, the more she wanted to know . . . though she didn't really know what "more" might look like because Annie was, in her heart and soul, Plain.

Annie was the youngest in her family by quite a few years. The caboose, her dad liked to call her. She was also the only girl. Her four brothers had married and moved out of state to be closer to their wives' families, and Annie's mother was eager for her to hurry up and get married and give her grandchildren.

But marriage wasn't something Annie thought much about. She refused to go to the youth gatherings—too much pressure for an acutely shy girl—which caused her mother much wringing of the hands.

Just this morning, over breakfast, Mom had tried and tried to talk her into going to a hymn singing on Saturday afternoon with the other youth. "Annie," Mom said, "you'll never meet anyone if you don't socialize. You don't want to be single."

"I might," Annie said, which only worried her mother all the more. But it was true.

Her mother's face pinched. "I hope it's not a mistake. You working for Dok Stoltzfus, I mean. Dad thinks it's good for you to have to talk to strangers—"

"Most of Dok's patients aren't strangers, Mom. Everyone in our church goes to her."

"—but Edith Lapp warned me that working for Dok might influence a young girl to leave the Amish—"

Annie had jumped from the chair and said she forgot to feed the dogs or let the cows out of the barn or maybe both— she just wanted to end this conversation. She knew that if she weren't the youngest, she probably wouldn't have been allowed to work for Dok. Her parents had softened much over the years. Her older brothers liked to tell stories about how strict Mom and Dad had been on them, and complained at how easy they were on Annie. Maybe so, but being the youngest meant that nothing you did was of much interest to anyone. It had already been done.

And right now, Annie was living an incredibly interesting life. Every single day in Dok's office was full of the unexpected.

Take today. On this winter afternoon, Annie had been waiting for Dok to return to the office to see one last patient. As soon as Dok walked in the door, Annie handed her a patient file. "Nora Miller and her thirteen-year-old daughter, Riley. They've been waiting over an hour. The mother refuses to leave until she sees you."

Dok started down the hall, then pivoted. "Which one is the patient?"

"Both, I think," Annie whispered.

Dok was finishing up paperwork for the day before heading home, but her mind was still on a patient she'd just seen. Thirteen-year-old Riley Miller had been brought in by her mother who was concerned about her daughter's odd behavior. Dok had given Riley an exam, asked her some questions that didn't get many answers, and decided to meet with her mother privately. She had sent Riley out to visit with Annie, hoping the girls might strike up a conversation. Probably not. Annie wasn't much of a talker, to say the least.

"So, Nora," Dok said, "Riley's pulled her eyelashes out."

"Yes. If it's not her eyelashes, she's pulling her eyebrows out."

"When does this behavior usually occur?"

"Mostly at night." The mother leaned forward in her chair and tapped her head. "Is something wrong with her? Mentally? My sister's daughter has started cutting herself."

Dok wasn't entirely sure how to answer Nora, but she vaguely remembered skimming through a recent medical journal on behavior disorders that had an article on this very thing. "I'd like to go check on something. I'll be right back." She went to her office to look for the journal, searched high and low, but couldn't find it. Finally, she went out to ask Annie if she had any idea what had happened to it.

Annie blanched. Seated at her desk, she reached into a drawer and pulled out the journal.

Dok took it from her. "Why do you have it?"

"I've been reading it."

Dok glanced through the table of contents, then pointed to the title of an article. "Did you happen to read this?"

Annie nodded.

"Come with me," Dok said. In her office, she pointed to a chair for Annie to sit in. "Tell me what you learned from that article about body-focused repetitive behaviors."

"BFRBs? Let's see . . ." Annie looked up at the ceiling.

"They're more common in females. Behaviors usually start in puberty. They can include hairpulling and skin picking. Nail biting too. They're . . . hmm, how did the article describe them?" She squeezed her eyes closed, then opened them wide. "Self-grooming behaviors that can cause damage to the body."

"Would cutting be considered a BFRB?"

"No. The article said that BFRBs aren't the same thing as self-harm or self-loathing."

"So what triggers them?"

"The article said there could be a lot of reasons. Genetics, stress, habits, hormones . . . but the bottom line is anxiety."

"Anxiety," Dok said. "Which tells me a lot about how to treat it."

"Actually, the last few paragraphs of the article have some specific suggestions."

Riffling to the last page, Dok sent up a silent word of thanks to God for this remarkable assistant. Shy little Annie, easy to overlook, yet so much was going on in that head. Astonishing. Finding what she needed, she glanced up. "Thank you."

With that, Annie caught the cue to head back to her desk. After Dok finished the article, she returned to the exam room to explain BFRBs to Riley's mother.

Nora narrowed her eyes. "But you can give Riley something to stop it, can't you?"

"There's a lot that can be done to help, starting with focusing on the amazing aspects of Riley."

Nora's jaw dropped. "I do. She *is* an amazing girl. But the eyelash-pulling behavior is not amazing. That behavior needs to stop."

"Do you tell her that?"

"All the time."

Yep. That's just what the journal article had described. "Parents often contribute to the cycle of anxiety."

Nora clasped her hand to her chest. "Me?!"

"Yes. The best advice about BFRBs is to 'release, don't police.' Don't mention the behavior at all. Instead, focus on everything Riley is doing that's right. That's how you can help her." Dok took out a pad of paper. "Here's a website with a lot of good information about BFRBs. And I'll add a name of a good counselor."

"A counselor? Wait a minute. You aren't going to give Riley anything for this?"

Dok shook her head.

Nora scowled. "Do you have children of your own?"

"I don't." Dok handed her a slip of paper with the name of a counselor.

Nora gathered up her purse. "I didn't think so." She left the office without taking the paper.

Dok couldn't shake off Nora Miller's response. More and more pediatric patients were coming into her office with anxiety disorders, and a common refrain from parents was to expect a drug to be the solution, like a magic elixir. Sometimes, Dok did see the need to prescribe medication for anxiety, but never without adding a therapist. Anxiety in a child or teen had to be addressed more holistically.

She rested her elbows on the desk. These patients weren't Amish ones. Anxiety in children was not a common problem among the Plain People. It wasn't that the Amish were perfect—they weren't. Dok was well aware. But anxiety disorder? Rare among the Plain people. She rubbed her face, discouraged. It was too bad that friendships were few between Amish and non-Amish. Sometimes she thought that English mothers could learn a few things from seasoned Amish ones.

And suddenly an idea popped into Dok's head. It wasn't just mothers who could borrow some life strategies from the Amish. Bee Bennett came to mind.

Bee led a mare and her yearling, two of her favorites, to the pasture to let them get some fresh air. As soon as the yearling, Dusky, was unhooked from the lead, he dashed off in a gallop around the large pasture, delighted to be out of the barn. His mother, Twilight, looked on with interest, as if to say, "Ah, to be young."

It was a sight that never failed to pull at Bee's heart.

She watched Dusky's enthusiastic romp for a few minutes, until she heard the sound of a car. She turned around to see a police car in her driveway. When the officer got out of the car, she closed the pasture gate and walked over to meet him, wondering what had brought him here.

"You're Bee Bennett, aren't you? I'm Matt Lehman. Dok Stoltzfus's husband."

Oh, right! She'd met Matt only once before, at his and Dok's wedding. From a distance, he looked rather intimidating in his white uniform shirt and crisp black pants, radio clipped to one hip, gun holster on the other. But his was a friendly face, warm and approachable. She did remember that kind face from the wedding, as well as the adoring way he had looked at his bride. Like he couldn't believe the prize he had won. "I didn't recognize you in full uniform and a squad car."

Smiling, Matt closed the door of his car. "I'm here on unofficial duty. Dok might have told you I have a horse trainer friend who's offered to help out while you're . . . um . . ." A streak of red started up his cheeks.

"Recovering from surgery for breast cancer."

Matt's cheeks went even redder. "I'm sorry. Ruth . . . I mean, Dok takes patient confidentiality very seriously. Normally, she doesn't tell me anything. Not much, anyway. Honest, she doesn't."

"Not to worry." Bee waved that off. It didn't bother her for Matt to know her diagnosis. But setting up a stranger to care for her horses bothered her immensely. "I do appreciate the offer, but I don't need any help with the horses."

Matt turned to look at the pasture where Twilight was grazing. Dusky had settled down and joined his mother. "For some reason, I thought Ruth said you had a stable full."

"Well, I do, but I don't need help. Not just any help, I mean. These horses, you see, are Dutch Warmbloods."

"Yeah, Ruth said something about the horses being fancy." He grinned. "Pretty sure my friend can handle them."

"I'm sure your friend knows horses. It's just that these particular horses require special care and training—"

"Right. That's what he does. He trains horses. He used to ride a lot until, well, he couldn't anymore. So now he just trains."

"Training . . . as in . . . basic riding skills? Or a specific discipline?"

Matt blinked. "A little bit of everything, I think. To be honest, I'm not the one to ask. I'm embarrassed to say that I'm afraid of horses. But I know my friend is good at what he does. Really, really good."

She narrowed her eyes. "But he has time on his hands?"

"Well, sure. To help you out. You know, as a favor to me."

If this guy was any good, he shouldn't have time on his hands. High-end trainers were in great demand. One of Bee's eyebrows arched. *Something sounds fishy.* "And how do you know him?"

"We grew up together. Even way back, when we were kids, horses were always his thing. His whole family was into horses." Matt turned at the sound of a vehicle approaching. "Here he comes now."

In a pickup truck. *Great, just great.*

"Maybe you could just . . . talk to him and then decide." He grinned. "I did promise Dok that I'd find help for you."

Bee cringed. She hadn't asked for help! Why did Dok feel the need to fix everything for her? She could manage her own life. The horses could go without exercise for a day or two. Besides,

Matt's vague description of his childhood friend did nothing to persuade Bee to consider hiring this weekend cowboy.

As the man emerged from his truck, Bee felt an odd flicker of recognition. Then it hit her full on, like a big splash of cold water on a winter day.

"Bee," Matt said, "this is—"

"Damon Harding," she said in a low, monotone voice. Or, as she thought of him, Damon the Demon. "We go way back." All the way to the Olympics.

"No kidding?" Matt said, though his voice held a tinge of sounding not surprised. "Well, isn't that a coincidence?" A squawking sound came out of Matt's police car. "Dispatcher. Gotta go. I'll let the two of you talk horses." He hopped in his car and drove off, leaving Bee and Damon to stand together in the driveway. Awkwardly.

Damon regarded her for a long moment before breaking the silence. "You look well, Bee."

Him too. He looked like the Damon she remembered. Thirty years older, but much the same. Sculpted. Chiseled. All sharp cheekbones, square jaw, remote dark eyes, his athletic body lean and fit, his hair black as coal. Still handsome in a distinguished way that left a lasting impression. She opened her mouth to say something but clamped it shut.

His left arm was gone. His coat sleeve was pinned up.

He noticed that she noticed. "Had a little accident."

Hmm. She'd like to know the story behind that. "Can you still ride?"

He looked away. "I can train just fine."

As uncomfortable as she was at the unexpected appearance of Damon the Demon—this man, whom she'd held a silent grudge against for decades—she couldn't help but feel a twinge of pity for him. This last year, her horses were the only reason she was able to get herself out of bed. If she couldn't ride, she'd wither up and die. She dropped her chin. Would tomorrow's surgery impact her ability to ride? Dok mentioned they'd be taking a few lymph nodes from under her arm, just to be sure the cancer hadn't spread. Would that hinder her movement, her flexibility?

He cleared his throat. "So I hear you need a little help."

She lifted her head and smiled, a forced smile, meant to convey that she was in charge here. "Look, Damon, I don't know what Matt told you, but I'm just having a minor medical procedure. In and out on the same day. I've got a neighbor boy who can muck the stalls and feed the horses."

"Your horses will need more than that. Turnouts, exercise, training."

"Well, I don't really train."

"If you aren't training," he said, thick black brows furrowing, "you're untraining."

Every muscle in Bee tightened. "I only meant to say that I don't do high-level training. I do groundwork, flatwork, under-saddle training. But I stay in the breeder lane."

"These horses are high quality. Every day matters."

She knew that! "Well, it's just a day or two. Then, I'll be back in the saddle, so to speak." When he didn't respond, she folded her arms across her chest and tried to look as commanding as possible. "Look, I just prefer to handle my horses myself."

She could've bet the farm that he wasn't listening to her. He was completely absorbed in watching Twilight and Dusky in the pasture. "They're from Ozzie's line, aren't they? I can see her in them. Such balanced conformation. Well proportioned, powerful topline. The yearling will have potential as a stud."

She didn't answer him, but he didn't seem to expect an answer. It almost hurt to hear her beloved horse's name said out loud, much the way it hurt to hear someone talk about Ted. Grief felt so private to her, so personal. It belonged to her and no one else.

"Ozzie was the best. The finest show jumping horse I've ever seen."

With considerable restraint, she stopped herself from asking: So is that why you sabotaged her?

No proof, she reminded herself. No evidence. Even in her own head, she sounded like a sore loser who'd been nursing resentment for over three decades . . . which she had.

"How many horses have you sold?"

Only one. There could've been two—she'd had a verbal agreement to sell two-year-old Strider, one of Ozzie's grandsons, because she didn't think she could manage a stallion. But at the last minute, she backed out. She couldn't bring herself to let him go. Not after Ted died; she couldn't handle any more goodbyes. However, she didn't want to talk about her horses with Damon. Before he could ask another question, she backed away. "Look, I really don't need any help. Thank you for coming." She went to the house and paused to unlock the front door.

To her annoyance, Damon followed her, stopping at the threshold of the open door. His gaze swept the living room to the left of the entrance hallway. "Matt didn't tell me that you had just moved in."

"I didn't. I've been here about a year and a half." She turned to see what he was looking at. "What makes you think I just moved in?"

"There's nothing on the walls."

Seeing the house through his eyes, it did look bare, unfinished. She hadn't gotten around to hanging anything up—it was a task Ted had always done. All the mirrors, the framed pictures, and a few pieces of art were still in boxes, buried somewhere in the garage. But she certainly didn't need to explain her lack of decorating to Damon the Demon. "So long. Thanks again for coming." She reached a hand to grab the door.

"Hold it. When exactly is your, uh, minor medical procedure?"

She had started to close the door, but stopped, surprised by his interest. "Tomorrow morning."

His dark eyes met hers. "Good luck, Bee," he said.

As she closed the door behind her, she remembered that he'd told her the very same thing just as she headed into the Olympic arena with Ozzie for her final round in the show jumping event. Up to that moment, she'd been in the lead. First place. Gold.

No proof. No evidence. Sore loser. She'd had to repeat those words over and over to herself on a daily basis for months after the event.

"Good riddance, Damon," she whispered.

Three

After yesterday's brilliant sunshine, today's morning sky was full of heavy gray clouds that threatened snow. Dok drove into the small parking lot she shared with the Bent N' Dent and noticed something on the front step of her office. She turned off the car and squinted. It was a good-sized basket, bigger than the ones Amish patients normally left on the stoop for her. In the summer, they'd drop off excess produce from their garden. In the fall, canned fruits or vegetables. In winter and early spring, baked goods. It was the Plain way to say thank you, but they always wanted their baskets returned. Dok knew their ways well.

Before getting out of the car, she turned to see if her brother David's buggy was at the Bent N' Dent. Not there. Too early for the store to be open. Too early for an Amish bishop to be up. She yawned. But not too early for a doctor to be making a house call. She'd just been on a predawn visit to Dave Yoder's, who thought he was having a heart attack but it turned out to be indigestion. Dave was a man who was wound pretty tight, but Dok wondered if his daughter Shelley was the reason for his severe heartburn. When Dok had gone to the kitchen sink to get a glass of water for Dave to drink down an antacid, she'd noticed the bottle of Shelley's prescription pills in the cupboard with the glasses. She picked it up and opened it. The seal hadn't been broken.

It didn't take much for Shelley to go off her antipsychotic meds, and when it did, the entire Yoder family would descend into chaos. Dok thought she might drop by again later today and follow up. Better still, she might stop by the schoolhouse during lunch recess and talk to Shelley's sister, Trudy. She was the most forthcoming of the Yoder family, the only one who understood the gravity of Shelley's mental illness. The only one in the Yoder family, Dok had found, with any common sense.

This was one of the reasons Dok believed so strongly in keeping up the practice of house calls. While house calls were far more convenient for the patient than the doctor, Dok found she learned a great deal about her patients when she was in their homes. Especially among the Amish, who were reluctant to go to a doctor unless it was unavoidable, like an artery was spurting blood.

But Dok had given a lot of thought to the difficult conversation she'd had with Matt the other night. Finding a partner to share the practice seemed like the ideal solution to Matt, but he had no idea what he was asking. The main reason Dok hadn't wanted a partner to join her practice was because she had yet to meet another physician who was willing to make house calls.

As she opened the car door, she heard a mewling sound come from the basket and she let out a groan. No! Not kittens. Not again. Some people around here considered her a vet as well as a people doctor. Finding sickly animals on her doorstep wasn't common but not unusual. She remembered the first time she had met Hank Lapp—he had brought his mule to her office door and asked her to drain an abscess on its ear. When she told him no, that she was a doctor only for humans, he had said, "But DOK, a LIFE is a LIFE. And a SUFFERING life is NO LIFE at all!"

She had drained the mule's abscess. It was hard to say no to Hank.

She grabbed her medical bag from the trunk of her car and walked to the office, wondering if she could leave the basket in front of the Bent N' Dent for David to deal with. But the closer she drew, the more the hair on the back of her neck stood up. This wasn't the mewling sound of a kitten. Of any animal.

She crouched down to lift a light cloth off the basket and gasped at the sight of a newborn baby, wrapped in a blanket. She looked around the parking lot to see if someone was watching her. The mother, she hoped. But she saw no one, no movement. She unlocked the office door and picked up the basket to go inside and get the baby out of the bitterly cold morning air. Carefully, before lifting up the baby, she looked in the basket for a note, but found nothing. The infant must've been born within the last few hours, with vernix still coating his skin. His umbilical cord, about a foot long, looked like it had been severed with a dull knife.

Hearing the front door creak open, Dok spun around, hoping it might be the baby's mother, coming to retrieve her baby, but it was only Annie. "Thank God you came early! Annie, I need your help. In the storeroom, you'll find packages of infant formula for new mothers. I need a bottle prepared, right away."

Cucumber calm, Annie hung up her bonnet and coat on the wall peg and followed instructions. So typical of her, she could pivot on a dime. It was one of the qualities Dok liked most about working with her—she was remarkably calm under pressure. While Annie was getting a bottle ready, Dok took the infant to an exam room. She gave the baby a brief exam, noting his respiratory rate, heart rate, muscle tone, reflexes, skin color. Though he barely weighed in at five pounds, he seemed healthy and alert, and she saw no obvious signs of abuse. When Annie brought the bottle to her, she pointed to the chair. "Could you please try to feed him while I call Matt?"

Again, Annie seemed to sense this was not the time to ask questions. She sat in the chair, arms held up to receive the infant. Dok handed her the baby and, for a moment, was distracted by the sight. Annie was so comfortable with a newborn, holding him snug but slightly tilted as he nuzzled for the bottle's nipple. Although Dok had been raised Amish, she had never seemed to have a natural maternal instinct, not like Annie. She paused so long that Annie looked up at her. "Just checking to see how easily he latches on. That's another indication of the infant's condition." His appetite seemed robust.

Dok turned away to call Matt. He answered on the first ring, and she quickly explained the situation. "So can you come and get him? Off the record?"

"Nope. Ruth, you're going to have to call 911."

"Why?"

"Because that's protocol. It's the right thing to do."

"I was hoping you might be able to find out who the mother is. Maybe we could return her baby and help her out and keep the social workers and endless paperwork out of this."

"Can't. You need to call 911 to get paramedics involved. They'll take custody of the baby."

Lowering her voice, she said, "Matt, I'm sure I could find an Amish family to care for him. That would buy some time while we look for his mother. That's the goal, right? To find his mother and get her the help so she's able to care for her baby. That's the social worker's goal too. So what if we just . . . you know . . . go around the system?"

"Honey, this isn't a lost puppy. This is a little human being. Who knows if this birth mother had received any prenatal care? Or if she might've used drugs? The baby will need to be tested. You can't expect an Amish family, or any family, to provide care for a baby without knowing what you're asking of them. That's not fair to them, and it's not fair to the infant."

Dok let out a long sigh. He was right. "Fine, I'll call."

"Okay. Give the paramedics everything you found with the baby. I'll stop by your office later this morning to start a report on an abandoned newborn."

She hung up with Matt and called 911, insisting to the dispatcher, twice, that this was *not* an emergency. Minutes later, she heard the wailing sound of an ambulance racing through the countryside.

Settled in Annie's arms, the sweet little boppli's eyelids grew heavy before he finished his bottle. Into the exam room walked Dok, followed by two men in uniforms, one wearing a black hat. Dok took the baby from Annie and turned to face the two men, giving them details about the baby's condition and his circumstances. Annie slipped out of the room and returned to her desk, all the while wondering about the man in the black hat. His head was down the whole time, focused on the newborn babe, so she never caught a glimpse of his face. Was he old? Young? She couldn't tell. All she really wanted to know was why he was wearing an Amish hat.

She'd never known any Amish who worked as a paramedic. Volunteer firefighters, yes, but not as ambulance drivers. No, impossible. He couldn't be Amish. Mennonite, perhaps?

But that was an *Amish* hat, identical to her father's winter hat.

A few minutes later, the man in the black hat strode past her desk to head outside, leaving the door open. She watched from the open door to see him lift a stretcher from the ambulance and head back into the office. Head still tucked down, he hurried right past her. Another minute or so later and the newborn was wheeled out. Annie was so struck by the sight of the helpless, motherless baby on the tiny stretcher that she forgot to get a look at the man. Dok and the paramedic followed the stretcher out, but Annie stood at the open door, watching. The man in the black hat sat in the back of the ambulance with the baby. He glanced up, as if he sensed he was being watched, met Annie's eyes, and held them—it couldn't have been more than five or ten seconds, but Annie felt a jolt run through her whole body—before he turned his attention back to the boppli.

He was young, Annie realized, and shockingly handsome, with sparkling blue eyes, full of merriment. They actually twinkled.

Dok turned toward Annie. "The paramedic wants to know if you are aware of any unmarried pregnant Amish girls."

What a question! Her mother would be horrified that Dok would ask such a thing of Annie. She shook her head in response. She couldn't think of any, but such conditions weren't spoken of. Besides, she couldn't imagine any Amish girl abandoning a baby, under any circumstances. An unmarried Amish girl would be forgiven for a transgression, and the baby would be welcomed.

Dok and the other paramedic finished talking and he returned to the ambulance to close the double doors. "Take good care of the baby," Dok said.

"Of course," the paramedic said. "We take good care of everybody. That's our job." He saluted Dok like she was a general and drove off, siren blaring, scaring a roost of crows right out of the trees.

They watched the ambulance disappear from sight.

"Dok," Annie said, as they turned to walk to the office door. "Was the other fellow Amish?"

"Amish?" Dok scrunched up her face. "I didn't notice. What makes you think so?"

"He wore an Amish hat."

"Maybe he is," Dok said. "Or maybe he just likes a black hat."

Maybe, but Annie didn't think so. It was definitely an Amish hat. "How could he drive an ambulance if he's Amish?"

"He didn't, though. The other one did."

"Can you be a paramedic and not drive an ambulance?"

"Not sure. But the one wearing the hat might've been an EMT."

"What's that?"

"An emergency medical technician."

A small spark flared inside Annie's head, or maybe her heart. "What do they do?"

"They're certified in essential skills to help with life-threatening situations. A lot of EMTs go on to become paramedics. Actually, a lot of doctors and nurses started out getting certified as EMTs." Dok walked through the open door and stopped at Annie's desk to examine the basket more closely.

Annie remained rooted to the spot where she was. The spark ignited into a flame. A voice as clear as a bell told her, "This is it, Annie. This is what you were born to do."

Annie looked around for who had spoken to her, but the whole world suddenly seemed to have fallen silent. No cars, no horses, no planes overhead, no birds in the trees. Utter silence.

Yet it was so vivid, so real, that Annie was sure Dok had heard the voice too. When she turned to Dok, she could see that her mind was elsewhere. She was turning the basket on its sides, examining it from every angle.

Annie felt a fine trembling going on inside her. Could this have been a calling . . . from God? She'd heard about that kind of thing but had never experienced it herself. It seemed audible, and yet not. More like words spoken to her heart.

"Annie," Dok said, "would you go through the patient files and give me a list of those who are due to deliver a baby this month?"

As Annie shut the door behind her and walked to her desk, she noticed a small handkerchief on the ground. She picked it up and held it out to Dok. "Could this have fallen out of the baby's basket?"

Dok took it from Annie. "It must have been under the baby."

She fingered some small initials embroidered in the corner. "Matt's going to drop by this morning to start a report. I'll give the handkerchief to him. He'll know what to do with it."

Annie stared at the handkerchief. "I've never heard of an Amish person being an EMT."

"First time for everything," Dok said. "Like today. A newborn baby abandoned on the doorstep is a first for me."

"For me too," Annie said, wondering what steps were required to become an EMT.

All day, Dok tried to keep her mind on her patients, but it kept circling back to the abandoned newborn. When Shelley Yoder and her parents came to the office, she forced herself to stop thinking about the baby. They sat in her office like three children called into the principal's office. That's how it felt to Dok, anyway. After speaking to Trudy and finding out that Shelley had indeed gone off her meds, Dok called them to her office for a reprimand. Keeping Shelley on those important meds was critical for her well-being, for the whole family's well-being. "If I have to come out every day to your farm and give the medication to Shelley myself, then that's what I'm going to do." She held Dave Yoder's gaze as she spoke, a stare-down, until he finally bent in a nod, conceding.

As soon as the Yoders left her office, her thoughts returned to the infant. She wondered where his mother was, who she was, and what was keeping Matt. She checked her phone for a text from Matt but nothing yet.

Her next patient, a man in his midforties, cleared his throat.

Dok slipped her phone back into her pocket, embarrassed. "I'm sorry. I'm a little distracted. Tell me one more time what has brought you in today."

The patient repeated his complaint. "I can't seem to get my contact lenses out at night."

"Soft contacts, right?"

"Yes. I feel like I'm almost scratching my eyes to get them out."

Dok looked through her notes. Last summer, she'd given this patient an annual physical and his blood panel showed nothing to be alarming. She turned on the exam light to examine his eyes with the ophthalmoscope. "And this happens at night?"

"Yes. Only at night. I have no problems getting contacts out during the day."

Dok sat on the stool, puzzled. She took note of some visual clues. The patient's shoes were flip-flops, which told her that, most likely, especially considering it was winter, he didn't exercise much. He wore no wedding ring, which might indicate a lot of time spent alone. And he had a rather pronounced belly. She thought about ordering a hemoglobin A1C to rule out diabetes. But then a thought occurred. "Do you have a habit of drinking alcohol in the evening?"

The big man reddened and looked away. "Perhaps a wee bit."

A lot more than a wee bit was Dok's guess. "Pretty sure you're dehydrated. You're going to have to cut down on alcohol consumption. Way, way down."

"Maybe I could just drink more water."

Dok raised an eyebrow. "Do both. Drink more water and less booze." She rose. "Plus, I want you to start taking a walk each evening."

"A walk?" His bushy eyebrows shot up. "Every night?"

"Yes. Every night. Call me in a week and let me know if there's been any improvement." She opened the door and nearly jumped to find Annie standing there, waiting patiently. "Annie, I've told you to just knock on the door if you need me."

"Yes, but—"

How many times did they need to go over this? "Part of your job description is to interrupt me. I want you to."

"It's just that—"

"The patients will understand. When there's something I need to know, then knock on the door and tell me what it is. Got it?"

"Got it," Annie said.

Dok knew this part of the job was a stretch for Annie, but she needed to stretch. Her shyness was nearly crippling, and yet there was so much potential in her. Dok had been watching Annie for years, knowing she'd be an excellent assistant, and she was . . . but for this shyness. More specifically, but for the avoidance that came out of her social anxiety.

Most everyone experienced social anxiety to some degree—walking into a roomful of strangers, for one example. Public speaking, for another. Dok knew that the way to overcome anxiety was to repeatedly expose oneself to that fear, to take away its power. When you no longer avoided that which you feared, eventually the anxiety would dissipate. That was the lesson she'd been trying to teach Annie. "So, what did you want to tell me?"

"Your husband is here. He said he wasn't in a hurry so not to interrupt you."

"Oh. Oh, sorry." She handed the patient's file to Annie and walked down the hall toward the waiting room. Matt was sitting next to Edith Lapp, telling her a story that actually had her shoulders shaking as she chuckled. Imagine that! Edith Lapp . . . chuckling. A rare sight. She was the archetypical dour Amish Hausfrau.

Matt saw Dok at the door, lifted his eyebrows in a wordless hello, finished his story, and patted Edith on the shoulder. "Excuse me, Edith. Gotta check in with the doc."

Matt followed Dok into her office and closed the door behind them. She picked up the handkerchief from the baby's basket and handed it to him. "I didn't notice this until after the paramedics left."

He took it from her. "I just heard over the scanner that a

young female was picked up not far from here. Sounds like she recently delivered a baby, but no baby is with her."

"She *must* be the mother." What a relief. She knew that if they could find the mother, she could be helped. "What's her story?"

"Not sure. But there was evidence of recent drug use."

"Oh no." Dok had been hoping this story would have a happy ending. The baby's life might be forever altered because of his mother's drug use. She exhaled a sad sigh. These kinds of situations weighed on her.

"Do you have any patients who were due about now?"

"I had Annie check the files. There's one or two Amish women due this month, but they're all married, with multiple children. No one fits the profile. I can't figure out why the baby was left here."

"What do you mean?"

"The fire station has a Safe Haven box. Why didn't the mother put the baby there? She must have come here for a reason."

Matt turned over the handkerchief and startled at the sight of the embroidered initials. "Whoa. Whoa, whoa. Hold the fort. This belonged to my mother."

"What? Are you sure?" Matt's mother died years ago, long before Dok started her practice in Stoney Ridge.

"Mom always added her initials to these little hankies. See? ERL. Elizabeth Rachel Lehman." He lifted his head. "Are you absolutely sure this was with the baby? Any chance it could've been in your purse?"

"Annie found it on the ground near her desk. I just assumed it had been in the basket. Honestly, Matt, I've never seen it before. Could you have left it here sometime? How else would one of your mother's handkerchiefs get into my office?"

"She used to give them as gifts to people." He shrugged. "Maybe one of your patients dropped it." He stuffed it into his pants pocket. "I'd better get going."

"You'll let me know when you hear news about the infant?"

"You know the drill, Ruth. A social worker will place him in a foster home."

"I meant about his condition. If drugs are in his system."

"I'll see what I can find out." He lifted a hand. "Here's some good news. I just left my horse trainer buddy at Bee Bennett's house. Turns out they know each other."

"Really? That is good news. It's not easy for Bee to accept help, especially when it comes to her horses. She's *very* particular."

"Yeah, I caught that. Hopefully, she'll accept his help." Matt's pager beeped. "Gotta go." He kissed her on the forehead and started out the door.

"Hey! It's amazing to think that Bee knows your friend."

One hand on the jamb, Matt popped his head back in. "Small world, huh?"

Small horse world, Dok mused. And then her thoughts returned to the handkerchief. Just how small a world was it?

Four

Bee Bennett's chest was wrapped so tightly after surgery that she had trouble getting a full breath. She could barely lift her arm. She'd taken an Uber to the hospital but was told she could be released only if a family member or friend came to pick her up. So frustrating! The surgery had been delayed for two hours. The neighbor boy had flaked on her, so the horses were still stuck in their stalls. She needed to check on them, to turn them out, to make sure they had water. It was past their lunch and they'd be hungry. She could imagine the sounds coming from the barn—a chorus of whinnying complaints. Strider, her most opinionated horse, kicking at his stall door. The very thought of her horses in distress made her shudder.

She was chomping at the bit to go home . . . with no way to get there. As she started to make a case for releasing her to an Uber driver, another nurse came into the recovery room and said that a friend had arrived to take her home.

Thank God, was her first thought. *Sweet*, was her second. Dok had come for her, Bee assumed. Maybe her husband Matt. That's the kind of people they were.

An orderly wheeled her out to the front of the hospital. There was Damon Harding, waiting by his pickup truck. "Damon. What are you doing here?"

"Matt asked if I could get you home, safe and sound."

Not ideal, but Bee was eager to get home, eager to get this event behind her. Damon opened the truck's door for her, and Bee got out of the wheelchair to climb in. She hoped he could drive well with one arm. She also hoped he didn't want to talk. She remembered him as the quiet type. Happily, he said nothing all the way to the house, and to her relief, he handled driving the truck easily for a one-armed man. Her curiosity was growing about how and when he had lost his arm, and if that's why he had time to spare, but she didn't ask. She didn't want him to think she had any interest in him. She just wanted to get home.

As they pulled into the driveway, she saw some horses in the pasture. "Why are they out?"

"Matt had called the hospital to find out what time to come get you and was told the surgery had been delayed. I wasn't surprised. Surgeries can back up like airplanes on a runway. So I stopped to check on the horses and fed them, turned two out for a while, then brought them in and turned out two more." He pointed to another paddock. "I did the same with the others. Took turns turning them out, I mean. I hope you don't mind."

She did! But she didn't. "Thank you, Demon." Her eyes went wide. "I mean, Damon. Thanks for your help, *Damon*."

He laughed. "I knew that's what the other teammates called me behind my back. Didn't bother me."

No? Bee wondered why it wouldn't have bothered him. It should've. Damon was the most competitive rider on the team. He was at the Olympics for gold and everyone knew it.

He was out of the truck and around to her side, opening the door for her. She just wanted to get inside and lie down for a long binge of Netflix. "Thanks again for the ride. I'll be fine now." She climbed out of the truck and went to her front door. He followed her, which was annoying. She didn't need his help! She unlocked the door and turned to say goodbye, just as a gust of wind took her paperwork every which way. Damon scooped it all up with remarkable one-armed coordination and handed it to her.

Then he didn't let the papers go. "Is that a prescription slip? How about if I run over to the drugstore now and get it filled for you?"

"No, no. That's not necessary." Though it was. The pain meds from the hospital were wearing off and she was starting to hurt. She'd intended to stop at the drugstore on the way home to get meds but completely forgot. Damon's unexpected appearance distracted her.

He lifted the slip in the air. "You know, I'm going anyway. Back in a flash." And off he went.

He moved so quickly that she didn't even have time to shout at him to stop, that she didn't need his help! But she did.

She set down her purse and went right out the back door to head to the barn, just to make sure he hadn't botched anything up with her horses. But as she walked up and down the aisle, she saw that all was well. The stalls had been mucked and replaced with fresh straw, water buckets were full, and it looked like the right amount of hay had been given to each horse. The equipment had been replaced slightly different than she'd left it yesterday, and she realized that he must've exercised the horses in the arena. She even noticed that the grooming brushes had been used.

What is up with him? Why is he here? What does he want? Why is he trying to be so helpful? Damon Harding's presence unnerved her. And yet, grimly aware of how sore her body felt, how stiff and swollen her underarm was where the lymph nodes had been removed, she was in no condition to refuse his help.

As soon as Annie had time to spare, she went to the library to look up everything she could find out about what was required to become an emergency medical technician. She needed a GED. Check. She grinned. Done.

She learned that the EMT course lasted about twelve weeks, and then passing a test was required to be certified. An EMT, she read, couldn't do all that a paramedic could do—EMTs couldn't put in an IV or "break skin" or intubate a patient. She discovered that paramedics, typically, began their careers as EMTs and progressed from there with additional training. But EMTs could do much as trained first responders—they could assess injuries at an accident site, they could provide CPR, administer oxygen, manage basic emergencies. They could even deliver babies.

She wrote down the names of places not too far from Stoney Ridge that provided EMT certification. Her mind bounced back to the Amish EMT in the ambulance who had come to get the abandoned baby. If he was Amish, what church did he belong to? Was it more progressive than Stoney Ridge's Old Order Amish church? She wondered how she might be able to find him. The Amish world wasn't *that* big. Maybe, if she went to a youth gathering and asked the right people—like chatty Sarah who worked at the Bent N' Dent and knew everything about everybody—someone might know of him. She'd like to ask him questions about being an EMT that only another Amish person would understand.

The more she learned about being an EMT, the more she felt she'd heard a clear call from the Lord. This, she felt, was the kind of work she'd been made to do while still remaining in her faith. The question was, would the bishop allow it? Would her parents? Even if a miracle occurred and the bishop said yes, and her father said yes, she was pretty sure her mother would strongly object. More than just pretty sure. Absolutely sure.

Well, she'd worry about that later. Annie checked out every single book she could find on careers as a first responder. She'd keep them tucked away at Dok's office and study them when the waiting room was empty. When Dok was out of the office.

Little steps. Little steps.

Today, during lunch, Dok answered the phone call of an Amish mother who was very worried about her eight-year-old daughter, but she didn't have any way to bring her to the office. The girl had acute pain on her side and was having trouble swallowing. Dok listened to the Amish mother and asked a few questions. It sounded like appendicitis, but that would be unusual in a young child. Typically, appendicitis presented during teen years and early adulthood. Pneumonia could be the culprit—it could mimic symptoms like appendicitis in children.

A familiar hitch in her gut made Dok decide to drive out and see the girl. She left a note taped to the door for Annie, who'd gone to the library during the lunch break, to let her know she'd be back as soon as she could.

As Dok pulled into the driveway and the mother came out to meet her, she quickly realized by her clothing and prayer cap that she belonged to the Swartzentrubers—one of the most conservative sects of all the Old Order Amish. The mother explained that she and her daughter had come to Stoney Ridge for a funeral.

Dok's eyes widened when she saw the little girl in her bed. During the funeral, the mother explained, the girl started complaining of abdominal discomfort and a sore throat. Her chin and throat were swollen. The child was suffering, but not from appendicitis. She had a full-blown case of mumps. Dok gave thanks to God for that hitch in her gut. For the circumstances that kept this mother from bringing her daughter into the office this morning while newborn twins were getting their six-week checkup.

It had been years since Dok had seen a case of mumps. "Do you have other children with you?"

The mother shook her head. "They're at home."

"Good." Swartzentruber families were larger than those in Stoney Ridge, with often as many as twelve to fifteen children. "You'll need to stay right here until your daughter is no longer contagious."

The mother's eyebrows shot up. "How long will that take?"

"Viruses can last a while. She was contagious a few days before the swelling started. Then once her salivary glands started to swell, she's contagious for another five days or so."

The mother started to tick off days on her hands. "So, maybe three more days, then? Or two? I really need to get home."

"Let's hold off on that decision for a while." Dok didn't miss the disappointed look on her face. "Mumps is a serious illness. Side effects can be quite severe. The last thing you want to do is to give the rest of your family back home a case of the mumps."

As Dok drove back to the office, she mulled over how many inconsistencies there were among the Amish. Over two-thirds of the Amish vaccinated their children, but nearly all the Swartzentrubers chose not to. Reasons were varied—distrust of the safety of vaccinations, skepticism over government claims, and ignorance. Surprisingly, religious conviction did not top the list. Even among the Stoney Ridge church, Dok made a priority of giving tetanus shots to nearly every patient who came to her office. They just didn't see the need for it, not until Dok described, in great detail, the kind of gruesome death that could result from tetanus. That convinced most of them.

In the distance, she saw the red windmill of Windmill Farm and realized she was close to Bee's house. She had planned to call her today to find out how she was feeling after the surgery. Since she was nearby, she decided to drop in and see for herself.

Bee had just made a fresh pot of coffee when Dok arrived unexpectedly at her door. She knew she was here to check up on her. She poured two cups and handed one to Dok, now seated at her kitchen table.

Dok took a sip of coffee. "So, Bee, how are you doing?"

"Fine," Bee said, lying through her teeth. "Just fine."

"You don't look fine. You look sore and tired and sick of feeling bad. Which is exactly how I had expected you to feel three days after a lumpectomy. Surgery is hard on a body. Third day is usually the worst day."

Bee let out a half sigh, half laugh. "You're right. I feel terrible. Sore and achy. Like I've been riding all day and need a massage but I can't lie face down on a table."

Dok laughed. "Oh, ouch. That sounds painful." She set her coffee down. "How's it going with Matt's trainer friend? I hear you've met him before."

"Briefly. A long, long time ago." Bee had no interest in explaining the history she had with Damon. "He's been . . . helpful." More than helpful. Too helpful.

"Matt said he's quite a horseman. I thought he would be a perfect match for you—"

"Match?" Bee stiffened.

"Horses. A match for your horses, while you're under the weather."

Relaxing a bit, Bee nodded. "I thought I'd be able to keep up . . . but . . . ." She tried to lift her arm. So sore. "That's why you're here, isn't it? You knew I'd cry uncle by day three."

Dok smiled. "Asking for help isn't such a bad thing." She leaned her elbows on the kitchen table. "So I've been mulling over this idea for you. A grief counselor."

Bee shook her head. "I told you. I went to a grief group and came home feeling worse."

"This is different. She's just . . . a really good person to talk to. In fact, I already spoke to her and she said she'd be willing to take you on."

"Take me on?" Like Bee was a stray puppy?

"Yes. Take you on." Dok slapped her hands on the table. "So consider Fern Lapp to be your new grief counselor."

"Fern Lapp. Isn't that an Amish name?"

Dok nodded. "Fern is Old Order Amish. She wants you to come to Windmill Farm some afternoon."

"Windmill Farm?"

"It's that farm down the road with the red windmill. You pass it all the time."

She did? She'd never noticed a red windmill.

Dok misread Bee's silence. "Winter is the perfect time of year to spend time with someone who's Amish. Come March, the chores start piling up. I'm sure you remember seeing Amish farmers plowing fields last spring."

Nope. Bee hadn't noticed them. She had been in a complete fog last spring. Summer and fall too.

Dok let out a happy sigh. "I can't wait for the weather to warm up. Spring is my favorite time of year around here. Driving through the farmland, seeing an Amish farmer walking behind those huge horses as they plow the fields in even, straight rows. Such a time of promise."

Bee's mind wasn't on the weather or the seasons or the Amish. "Look, Dok, I have to be honest with you. I've never been all that great with people to start with. I'm much better with horses. I've never even spoken to an Amish person other than exchanging cash at a farm stand. I remember seeing them at your wedding, but I didn't speak to any of them."

"Actually, you have. Me. I was born Amish."

"You?" How had Ted never mentioned that vital piece of information? Then again, knowing Ted, he'd probably never asked about Dok's upbringing. To Ted, a person's past wasn't pertinent, only who they were now. The opposite way Bee thought of people's past. She thought it had everything to do with who they were now.

"I was raised Old Order and left to go to college, then medical school, then started my career in Ohio. I never imagined I'd be a country doctor to the Amish in Lancaster County, with my brother as the bishop."

"Your brother?" Bee's eyes went wide. "Your brother is an Amish bishop?"

"David Stoltzfus. He runs the Bent N' Dent near my office. That Amish store. Stop in sometime and meet him. He's a wonderful man. The store is a great place to stock up on spices too."

Bee had seen the little signless building when she'd been to Dok's, and had even noticed horses and buggies at the hitching post, but she had no idea it was a store.

Dok's cell phone chirped and she answered it. "Yep, yep. On my way." She clicked it off. "I need to head back to the office." She rose. "So, Windmill Farm, Friday afternoon. Fern's expecting you."

Oh, come on! "What in the world could I learn from this Amish woman about grief? We come from different worlds."

Dok smiled. "I think this particular Amish woman will surprise you."

Later that afternoon, Bee went out to check on her horses and saw Damon in the arena with one of her favorites, a two-year-old mare named Firefly. He was introducing Firefly to ground poles and cavalletti, and she hurried to stop him. "That's not necessary," she told him. "I'm a breeder, not a trainer."

"Your horses are ready to do more. Everything has to have a purpose, Bee." Ignoring her, he went back to training the horse.

She didn't have the energy to argue with him. Frankly, she knew she didn't have much substance for an argument. He was right. She took excellent care of her horses, but she provided only basic groundwork, flatwork, obedience. Just green horse training. If she started to train, she could command a higher price tag. A well-trained competition horse could get over six figures. But training meant showing and competing, and that's what stopped her cold.

All because of Damon Harding.

Five

All evening, Bee's thoughts kept returning to when she had first met Damon, over thirty years ago. Bee had heard of Damon Harding, everyone in the show jumping horse world knew of him, but she'd never met him until they both secured a spot on the same US Olympic Equestrian Team for show jumping. There were only six spots for American riders on the Olympic team, only sixty riders in the entire Olympics.

Damon was older than Bee by a decade or so, and had much more experience competing as an elite equestrian. He had earned a spot on several Olympic teams but had never medaled as an individual, only for team events. Bee remembered Damon as serious and unsmiling, somewhat aloof. Handsome, though. And not unkind. He was very helpful to the other team members, and more than helped the team win a medal.

Bee was only twenty-one years old when she'd been selected for the team. She'd been training her mare Ozzie for two years, competing in shows, winning medals in nearly all of them. Bee and Ozzie understood each other in a way that she'd never had with another horse. Riding Ozzie, Bee never felt the typical nerves that hit before showing. Not once.

The year leading up to the Olympics had been a stellar year

for Bee and Ozzie, and yet when she was notified that they'd been offered a spot on the Olympic team, she had walked around in a daze for days. She had assumed her show jumping career was just getting started, with a long future ahead. That was something she loved about being an equestrian. You didn't age out, you only got better. Even today, there were Olympic equestrian athletes in their sixties who were competing. Unlike racehorse riders, a show jumper could compete at an older age. And something else Bee appreciated about the sport—it was one of the few where men and women competed together.

So Bee had gone to the Olympics with an attitude of wide-eyed appreciation, grateful to represent her country, eager to help her team medal, ready to do her best, but with low expectations for an individual medal. Ozzie had a different frame of mind. Winning for the US team rounds came first and seemed like just a warm-up for Ozzie. That mare was here to win it all.

Damon had done extremely well in both of his individual rounds, clearing every jump, beating the clock. He was in the lead for a gold medal . . . until Bee and Ozzie's first flawless round. If the second round was like their first, that small margin could win Bee the gold.

And still, Bee wasn't at all nervous. She had complete confidence in this magnificent mare.

They were waiting outside the Olympic arena for the second round to begin, and Bee had asked Damon if he would hold Ozzie's reins for a moment as she checked the saddle cinch one more time. It was a very common request among riders, helping each other in those kinds of ways. As she tightened the cinch, she let the stirrup down and took the reins back from Damon.

"Good luck, Bee," he said in his serious way.

She had barely started into a canter when she sensed something was bothering Ozzie. The mare kept lifting her head, tossing it. She seemed distracted, which alarmed Bee. The round was only two minutes long. The moment you entered the arena, the clock started.

Scores for show jumping competitions were based on a combination of factors, including time, faults, refusals, and knockdowns. In show jumping, when a horse makes contact with a rail or obstacle, causing it to fall to the ground, it's called a "knockdown." Knockdowns result in penalty points or faults, and these faults can affect a rider's overall score and placement in the event.

Bee made the last pass around the arena before heading to the jumps—hoping she'd find that sweet moment of "loving the canter"—when she and Ozzie were completely in the zone. But it never came.

Bee knew she'd lost it as she left the arena. As soon as she could, she dismounted and ran her hands over and under the saddle, and then the bridle. That was when she felt the hook of the buckle on the noseband, digging a sharp edge into the horse's chin. Horses like Ozzie were highly sensitive—something that small could disturb her concentration. Bee couldn't believe she had missed it. The most important ride of her life, and she'd overlooked a small hook.

Bee put her forehead against the horse's withers. "I'm so sorry, Ozzie."

It was odd how many thoughts ran through your head in moments like that. *Had* she overlooked it? She had checked and rechecked and triple-checked every piece of equipment while she was waiting for her rounds. She had never left Ozzie's side. Except for that one moment when Damon held the reins . . .

Damon.

It must have been his doing. Or undoing.

She had no proof. No evidence.

Damon ended up winning the gold medal. Bee won the silver. She'd been ahead of Damon by a small margin as she went into that last round. She should've won the gold.

But she couldn't accuse Damon of intentionally sabotaging her round without sounding like a poor loser. Doubt gnawed and gnawed at her. She couldn't let it go.

If this was the kind of thing that could happen in elite equestrianism at the global level, then she wanted nothing to do with it. No more showing. No more competing.

Bee didn't give up Ozzie, though. She used her magnificent mare to start a breeding program and keep her lineage going. Breeding horses suited Bee nicely—her responsibilities were significant, as these horses were highly valued. But she did only groundwork with them. She didn't train them at a high level to compete. That was an entirely different career path.

Ozzie lived to be twenty-seven years old, and putting her down was the worst day of Bee's life. She'd thought so, anyway, until her husband Ted's death.

Dok walked into the house and smelled something wonderful cooking. Simmering tomato sauce, she guessed, hoping Matt had made his famous marinara and meatballs. Her favorite. She set her purse down and breathed in the comforting aroma of a home-cooked meal. He was a great cook.

But normally, Matt cooked only on his days off. It was unusual for him to have the time or inclination to cook on a workday. He took cooking very seriously. Dok teased him that he used up every single dish and utensil when he cooked, and she wasn't entirely teasing. His cooking was worth the mess.

Matt was in the kitchen, apron around his waist, stirring a pot. She wrapped her arms around him from behind and peered at the marinara sauce. "Just what I was in the mood for."

"How was your day?"

"Long. Long but good. I stopped by Bee's on the way home. She's got that third-day postsurgery hit-by-a-Mack-truck feeling."

"Hopefully, Damon can lighten the load for her until she's back on her feet. He's determined to help her, whether she wants it or not. On the morning she had surgery, he even called me to make sure she had a ride home from the hospital. Worked out well because you had just texted to see if I could pick her up, but I was stuck at work."

"How does he know her?"

"They were in the Olympics together."

"No kidding?" She wondered why Bee hadn't mentioned that fact. It was kind of a big deal. "And how exactly did Damon know that you knew Bee?"

"Oh, that? Turns out they were both at our wedding."

Really? Dok had no memory of him, but she hadn't known most of Matt's friends. Besides, that whole day was a blur.

"When Damon came for dinner, he asked me how Bee was doing. It was crazy timing—the very day you'd told me she'd been diagnosed with breast cancer."

"Hold on. Matt, did you tell Damon about Bee's diagnosis?"

A guilty look came over his face. "I know, I know. I shouldn't have. I just . . . felt sorry for her. You know, widowed, then hit with a cancer diagnosis." He turned back around to stir the marinara sauce. "Anyway, it all worked out. Damon wondered if she had planned for someone to take care of her horses while she was recovering, and I knew, from you, that she didn't. When he offered to help her out, I set up a time to connect with Bee."

Nice. Knowing Matt's friend was there had made Dok feel less worried about Bee's reclusiveness. She sat at the kitchen table and went through the mail. "Any update on the abandoned newborn? Or the mother?" She noticed Matt's whole body stilled.

He turned off the burner and set the spoon down. "I was going to tell you more over dinner."

An oddness filled the room, almost like a vibration. "Tell me more about what?"

"Do you remember my cousin Laura?"

"No."

"I'm sure I've talked about her. She has a couple of kids and the youngest one, Monica, was wild. Crazy. Always giving Laura a run for her money."

"Is there a reason you're telling me about her now?"

"Turns out Monica the wild child . . . well, she's the mother of that newborn."

Dok's jaw dropped open. "So it *was* your mother's handkerchief. Amazing." She shook her head. "Such a small, small world." She let out a sigh. "Well, best of luck to Laura. I hope the mother and baby are with her soon."

"Not possible." He filled up a glass with wine and handed it to her. "Laura moved to Florida a few months ago because her husband has been having health problems."

Dok took a sip of the wine. She didn't know where he was going with this, but something made her feel like she should brace herself.

"So apparently Monica slipped out of the hospital."

That funny feeling grew stronger. "With the baby? Or without?"

"Without." Matt sat down across from her and folded his hands together. "I got a call today from the baby's caseworker. A lady named Sandra. She asked if we would consider providing emergency foster care for the baby."

"Oh no. No, no, no, no, no." Dok was floored he would even bring it up. "Matt, be realistic. Newborns take a lot of work. We're not exactly spring chickens. We both have demanding careers. Our house is constantly under renovation. Just think of how complicated this would be in our lives. And why? We could find all kinds of families who would be wonderful at fostering this baby. Look at Luke and Izzy Schrock."

"The caseworker wants the baby with a relative, and I'm the only relative left in the state of Pennsylvania. Ruth, this baby belongs to my people. I feel a sense of responsibility to him."

Dok wasn't wavering. "If you don't want to consider an Amish family, then why not ask someone in your extended family to step up?"

"Who could we ask? I'm not like you. My family is small. No one else can take him."

"Can't? Or won't?"

"Both. They all live in another state." He put his hands on her shoulders. "I know this is a big ask. But I feel the right thing to do is to take the baby in."

"You're really serious about this?"

"I've never been more serious. I've even thought of taking a leave of absence from work if I can't get vacation time."

Dok swirled the wine in her glass, watching the way it coated the sides. Saying yes to fostering this baby would create enormous disruption in their routines. But she wondered if saying no might drive a permanent wedge between them. "Matt, what kinds of drugs did the baby have in his system?"

"Amazingly, nothing was detected."

Dok let out a relieved sigh. *Thank you, Lord, for protecting this child.*

He glanced at the two-by-fours that divided the kitchen from the dining room. "I was even thinking that when the baby sleeps, I could finish a few things up."

Right. As if the sounds of construction work wouldn't wake up a baby. Had Matt ever really been around babies? "But this would only be a week or so, wouldn't it? Just until the caseworker finds a more permanent placement, right?"

"Yeah, sure. Just a short time. For as long as the baby needs us." He took in a deep sigh. "I've been thinking that this could be good for us, Ruth. We haven't exactly made *us*"—he waved his hand between them—"much of a priority these last few years. I know that work demands a lot out of us, but it seems as if we've let work get out of balance. It's all we do. It's all we think about, or talk about."

She knew he was being kind. He was describing Dok's absorption with work, not his.

"Sometimes," he said, "it seems like we're . . . like two trains on different tracks. I just feel as if we need to do this. For the baby's sake, but also for our sake."

She felt a tightening in her stomach. "Are you saying you're unhappy in our marriage?"

"Not unhappy, not exactly. I just think . . . we could do more with our marriage. We could be more to each other. I guess I just feel like . . . we're missing something."

"Missing something?"

"Yes. Like . . . fun."

Fun?

"We haven't even gone on a vacation in . . . I don't know how long."

"We went to that medical conference in Miami last spring."

He rolled his eyes. "Not sure I would classify hanging around with a couple hundred doctors as *fun*."

Dok felt differently. She'd had a wonderful time. "I don't see how fostering an infant could be considered fun. Babies are a lot of work. And who knows what kind of prenatal care this baby had? He might have all kinds of residual issues from his mother's drug use." She thought back to the rudimentary exam she'd given him after she'd found him on the office steps: good heart rate, good reflexes, good muscle tone, good pink color. Small but healthy, considering the start to his life.

Matt let out a sigh. "Seems like this could be good for us, sharing this kind of role."

"You mean, as parents."

"Yeah, I guess that's what I mean."

Dok and Matt had met while in their late forties. It was the first marriage for them both, as they'd both been devoted to their careers. Neither of them had a strong desire for children. Maybe a twinge now and then, but a visit to David and Birdy's house usually cured that. There were plenty of nieces and nephews to give Dok, at least, a sense of family and belonging and connection to the next generation.

But Matt . . . he didn't have those kinds of familial connections. He would've made a wonderful father, though he had always insisted that his life was full enough. "Matt, when we talked about marriage, we both agreed that we just weren't the traditional parenting types. That was one of the things that drew us together. Are you changing your mind?"

"I'm not saying that we're missing something because we don't have children. I'm saying we're missing something because . . . work is the main priority. The only priority. And as far as this baby goes, well, maybe we aren't the traditional parenting types. But he's not asking us to be traditional. He's asking us to provide a loving home for him, just the way we are."

"You can't be naive, Matt. Babies don't exactly fit into a two-career household like ours. After all, you're taking vacation time to be a full-time caregiver."

"It's emergency foster care. That's all. One week. Two, tops."

She was quiet for a long moment, knowing he was waiting for her response.

Finally, he left his chair and came around to hers, crouching down in front of her. "Ruth, I want you to be on board with this. I won't say yes unless we're both on board."

"Short-term. You promise?"

"Absolutely," he said with a big grin. He kissed her and went back to the stove, turning on the burner to get the marinara sauce simmering again. "Just short-term."

She wondered, though.

Six

To her mother's great delight, Annie agreed to attend a youth gathering to ice skate at Blue Lake Pond on Saturday afternoon. She tagged along to the gathering with Sarah Blank, who had started working at the Bent N' Dent about the time Annie had started working at Dok's. Sarah, a big girl with an even bigger personality, knew just about everyone in town and even more about their personal business. Not the EMT, though, which was why Annie had decided to go to the youth gathering in the first place. As soon as she asked Sarah if she knew of him, she wished she could rewind her words.

Snapping the buggy horse's reins to pick up the pace of his trot, Sarah cast a sideways glance at Annie, positively beaming. "So you're sweet on him, right?"

"What? No!" How mortifying! "Sarah, I've never even met him. Honestly, I barely remember what he looks like." Those twinkling blue eyes . . . she did remember those. "I just wondered if you knew who he was. That's all. I've never heard of any Amish who became EMTs."

"Don't you worry, Annie. I will find this fellow for you. You can count on me." Sarah gave her a big wink, and Annie wondered how much it would hurt if she jumped out of the fast-moving buggy right now and into a snowbank. Would she break a bone or two? Would it be worth the risk? She didn't want to go ice skating. She didn't like to ice skate. She hadn't even thought to bring skates. She came along only so she could ask Sarah about the EMT, and that was an instant backfire.

Sarah, being Sarah, kept up a one-sided conversation for the rest of the drive. As soon as they arrived, Sarah dashed off to join friends, leaving Annie to tether the reins to the hitching post and cover the horse with a blanket.

Down on the beach, Sarah had stopped to lace up her skates. Her friends were calling to her to hurry, waving to her from the ice-covered pond. The mid-January storms that had blown through had been bitterly cold, freezing the pond solid so far out that skaters glided back and forth, from one snowy edge of the pond to the other, sailing right across the center. Boys raced each other in their attempts to get girls to notice them. Girls bunched together in circles toward the center of the pond, giggling at the boys. Annie watched for a long moment, feeling like an outsider. She was never one of them. She was never the kind of girl who spent time thinking about the boys, other than how ridiculous they seemed. She still thought they seemed ridiculous.

This, feeling awkward and alone, was why Annie didn't go to youth gatherings. If she didn't have a task to do, like she did when she served meals after church, it meant she stood around the fringes of the gathering. She used to have a few friends who would scoop her along with them, but they'd since gotten married. At that point, she'd stopped going to gatherings altogether.

She walked toward the large fire on the beach, a safe spot. Cooking help was always needed, and it gave her something to do besides stand around self-consciously. Ellie Schmucker, one of the Amish mothers who supervised the gathering, directed Annie to get paper cups ready to be filled with hot chocolate warming in a huge pot near the fire. As Annie lined up paper cups on a tray, a loud crackling sound filled the air. Time stood still as everyone stopped to see where the sound was coming from. And then the screaming began. Annie saw it unfold—the ice beneath Sarah had started to break and she had fallen to her hands and knees, scrambling desperately to stay out of the water. The more she scrambled, the more the ice collapsed, and soon she was slipping into the water.

Annie turned to Ellie and said, "Call 911."

Ellie's eyes went wide. "But how?"

"Somebody around here is hiding a cell phone." Annie grabbed a long stick of wood that was set aside to feed the fire and bolted to the ice. "Get back!" A couple of boys had drawn close to Sarah to try and help, but their combined body weight was only cracking more ice, enlarging the hole where Sarah was flailing. "Move far away," Annie said, in an authoritative voice that she barely recognized in herself.

Sarah had sunk under the water, then popped partially up, gasping, thrashing her arms. Annie looked around for the most solid part of the ice and carefully lay down flat on her stomach. As she did, Sarah slipped below the surface again. Annie inched her way toward the broken ice, holding the stick in front of her, praying for Sarah to pop her head up again. *Please, please, please*, she prayed. She knew, from reading a book on first responders, how dangerous this could be. It would take only a minute or two before Sarah might become too weak to survive. The cold shock of immersion caused a person to gasp, which could create a drowning emergency if they inhaled water. She also knew that often rescuers became victims.

Slowly, Sarah's head emerged, but this time she wasn't gasping. Her lips were blue and her eyes looked stricken, like she was in shock. "Sarah, keep floating, keep your head above the water. Reach for this stick. Hold on to it. Don't let go."

Sarah looked at Annie but didn't move her arms.

"Sarah, grab the stick. GRAB IT!"

With effort, Sarah reached one hand out to grab the stick. Annie pulled Sarah toward her, moving carefully, hardly aware of anyone or anything around her. Suddenly two hands reached around Annie's ankles and held them firmly. "Okay," a deep voice said. "I'm going to pull you back, slow and steady, while you hold on to that stick. Don't let it go. Then I'm going to change places with you and take hold of the stick."

Annie let herself be slithered backward until she was confident she was on solid ice. The man took the stick from her and exchanged places with Annie. She sat on her knees, watching. He had brought a rope and made a lasso out of it, tossing it to Sarah, guiding her to put the circle of rope around her waist. He carefully pulled Sarah out of the water. As soon as Sarah had been tugged far from the broken ice, the man picked her up in his arms and hurried toward the beach. Annie followed close behind. Another man was waiting on the edge of the pond with a stretcher. Sarah's face and hands were a blue color, and when asked questions, she responded in slurred, unintelligible words. Annie knew that the color of Sarah's skin meant that her body was trying to protect its core. Blood flow had slowed down. Annie wondered if there was concern about frostbite, and she didn't have to wait long to find out.

The two men spirited the stretcher up the beach toward the open back doors of the ambulance. Annie trotted behind, listening carefully. One paramedic spoke in staccatos. "Cold water shock. Hypothermia. Weak pulse. Cold incapacitation. Dilated eyes. Confusion."

Annie felt as if she were reading one of Dok's medical books.

The other one put a hand on Annie's shoulder. "Sollscht du kumme. Will helfe ihr dreeschde." *You should come. You'll help her feel more comfortable.*

She nodded, and slowly it dawned on her that this one had spoken to her in Penn Dutch. Everything had gone so fast, and she'd been so focused on Sarah, that she hadn't noticed. Her head jerked up. *Him.* It was him! The Amish EMT.

She waited outside the ambulance while they removed Sarah's wet clothing, covered her in warm blankets, and hooked her up to some machines. The paramedic hopped out and helped Annie in. She sat down, holding one of Sarah's ice-cold hands. Bright screens surrounding them beeped and whirred. Suddenly Sarah let out a gasp, then her whole body started to shiver.

"Schauder," the Amish EMT said in a low voice. "Gut." *Shivering. That's good.*

Annie's eyes flew to his, those beautiful, twinkling blue eyes. She felt a zing down her spine, then through her whole body, so shocking that she had to quickly look away.

The paramedic—the driver—turned on the siren and flashing lights and barreled down the road toward the hospital. Annie kept her eyes on the EMT as he monitored Sarah's pulse and blood pressure. Now and then he would adjust a dial on a machine, and Annie wondered why. She would've loved to ask what all these machines were doing and tracking, but she didn't want to interfere. Besides, this was no place to talk. She could barely hear herself think over the siren's loud scream.

But her eyes could soak up this man. They kept wandering away from Sarah on the stretcher, traveling to the EMT. Hatless, his honey-colored hair was thick and curly. Unruly. He had a cleft in his chin, and high cheekbones that had a natural blush to them. Despite winter, his skin had a buttery-tan look, like he spent most of his time outside.

The way he picked Sarah up on the ice, like a rag doll, revealed astonishing strength. She wondered if some Amish father were wishing his son were helping him on the farm instead of sitting in the back of an ambulance.

As Annie watched him, her fascination grew and grew. He spoke comforting words of reassurance to Sarah in their own language. Such a calming voice. Relaxed yet confident. Whenever he checked Sarah's vitals, the action was carried out with confidence, precision, purpose. The way he worked, the way he held himself, struck her as professional and competent. Like he knew exactly what to do, when to do it, and how.

Where did he get his training? How was he able to become an EMT? She had a million questions and no opportunity to ask them, even if she could muster her courage to voice them. In what seemed like minutes, they'd arrived at the hospital, the back door of the ambulance had been opened, Sarah's stretcher was eased out and whisked off to the emergency room.

Alone, Annie climbed out of the ambulance and walked to the doors of the emergency room, unsure of what to do next. She should call Sarah's parents, and maybe Dok. Better still, she could let Dok call Sarah's parents.

No sooner had she thought it than she looked up to see someone watching her. The Amish EMT had left the emergency room and stopped about five feet away from her. "Du bischt en schmaeder Maedel." *You're a smart girl.* He pointed to his head. "Schnell." *Fast.*

He waited for her to say something, but she couldn't string two words together in her head. Usually, Annie would automatically avert her eyes when she was spoken to by a stranger. A lifelong habit. But for this man? She couldn't make herself look away even if she tried. She stared at him, wide-eyed, speechless. She took in the sight of him, and he did the same right back to her, for what seemed like a good full minute. Maybe an hour.

She wished she had words to thank him. He had saved Sarah's life! She wondered how many lives he saved in the course of a week. She wished she could let him know how much she appreciated the work he did.

This was her chance! She had so many questions for him— *How did you convince your bishop to let you become an EMT? What about your parents? How long have you been an EMT? Do you like your work? Is it as fulfilling as it seems to be? Did you get "the call" from God to do it, like I did?*—but her mind kept overriding those questions with overwhelming thoughts of how beautiful he was. Seriously handsome.

Finally, he broke their stare with a grin. "Und friede." *Quiet.*

His grin broadened into a full smile before he turned to join his partner in the ambulance and off they went. Once again, Annie watched until the ambulance rumbled out of sight.

Standing there, she basked in the memory of the EMT's brilliant smile. Slowly, sadly, it dimmed, overshadowed by the realization of how awkward she'd been. Why couldn't she just talk and act like a normal human being? A wonderful opportunity had just been handed to her and she missed it. While she should have been, could have been, asking the Amish EMT about his work, all that filled her mind was an absurd thought: his smile was so wide, his teeth so straight and white, that he could've been featured in one of those orthodontist advertisements in Dok's medical magazines.

Hey, Annie! She could suddenly hear her own voice hollering inside her head, as loud as Hank Lapp's bellow. *Pull it together!*

What was going on with her?

Seven

Last night, Bee googled the Amish, just so she wouldn't appear as ignorant as she truly was about them. Just so she wouldn't ask stupid questions. She felt embarrassed that she didn't even realize some of her own neighbors were Old Order Amish! True, the farms were large, houses were far apart, but it had more to do with how reclusive she'd become since Ted died. She hardly ever left her home or her horses, and when she did, she kept her head down. Errands were quick, purposeful. Antisocial.

Feeling a little better each day from the surgery, Bee decided to go visit Fern Lapp at Windmill Farm on Friday afternoon and just get it over with. She anticipated a painfully quiet visit. She assumed that Fern Lapp, being Amish, would be similar to Dok's assistant Annie—meek, mild, reluctant to talk. Would Fern have an accent? Did Annie? Bee hadn't noticed one if she did.

It was the first time Bee had driven since the surgery, and it felt good to reclaim some independence, though her left arm felt stiff and the seat belt harness was uncomfortable over her sore breast. If the weather were warmer, she would've walked to get some exercise. But it was bitterly cold, and the roads were icy, and she decided to drive herself. As soon as she saw Damon lead a horse into the arena and knew he was preoccupied, she made a dash to her car. She didn't want him to insist on driving her. Thanks but no thanks.

The combination of Dok, her husband Matt, and Damon meant that Bee was constantly getting "overhelped." Damon, in particular, didn't seem to grasp that she didn't need him to come anymore. She'd told him that very thing for the last two days, handing him an envelope with a generous check for his day's work, and he always nodded as took the check, like he understood. The next morning, back he'd come, like clockwork, heading straight to the barn to feed her horses. He spent the entire day working with her horses—feeding, turning out, exercising them. He didn't leave until the last horse was back in its stall and the barn was closed for the night.

If Bee had a little more fight in her, she'd be more forceful about it. But the truth of it was, the surgery was harder to recover from than she'd expected. She couldn't deny that she didn't have the strength to manage basic care for her horses, not yet, and even less to exercise them. Plus, there was still treatment to face. Radiation, according to Dr. Google, took a cumulative toll. Prepare to be exhausted, she read. Prepare for some body parts to smart like a bad sunburn.

Irksome! Damon Harding, of all people, was the ideal person to step in to help her sensitive, highly valued horses. And yet Damon, of all people, was the *last* person she wanted near her beloved animals. It's not that she thought he would harm any horse—she knew he wouldn't. He handled her horses with skill and expertise. He seemed to instinctively know what each one needed . . . or wanted. But still, this was *Damon Harding* in her barn. And he was missing an arm!

At first, Bee was highly skeptical that a one-armed man could get the work done—exercising the horses, in particular. The neighbor boy, when he wasn't being flaky, could handle the manual labor around the barn, but Bee never let him work with her horses. She didn't even let him turn them out to the pasture. To Bee's surprise, Damon didn't let a missing arm stop him; he had figured out how to get tasks done. Whenever she watched him lunging a horse in the arena, she forgot all about his arm. He was still Damon—demanding, authoritative, yet respectful.

Still the same Damon, yet different. Softer. Maybe . . . humbler?

But why was he here, anyway? Why now? She assumed his missing arm had something to do with why he had time on his hands. The man volunteered no more than he absolutely had to about himself. She'd kept in touch with a few other Olympic team members, and over the years, they'd mentioned Damon now and then, so she knew a few facts about him: He had retired from showing to become a trainer. He'd never married, nor had a family, but that wasn't unusual for elite trainers—they were married to their sport, traveling constantly. Not the family type.

Maybe Dok might know what had happened to Damon's arm. Could Bee ask her? Or would that be considered breaking doctor-patient confidentiality? Even though Damon wasn't Dok's patient, Bee wasn't exactly Dok's friend. It was a little messy, all these overlapping connections.

Bee blew out a puff of air and gave up thinking about Damon and why his arm was missing. It wasn't any of her business.

Finding the red windmill at Fern Lapp's farm wasn't difficult. As she drove up the long driveway that led to Windmill Farm, she tried to decide on what seemed like a reasonable amount of time for a visit between complete strangers. Maybe thirty minutes? She'd already planned on a solid excuse to get up and go: she needed to take her pain medication and forgot to bring it with her. True, in fact. Intentionally true.

Bee stopped the car at the top of the hill and sat for a long moment, looking at the spacious, white farmhouse set against a grove of now leafless trees, the row of birdhouses that lined the yard, the immense barn to her left, the snow-covered pastures, the flock of sheep huddled together. Such a lovely setting.

Bee jerked. Someone was outside her car window! She pressed a button and the window glided down. A small bespectacled gray-haired woman peered at her. Where had she come from? She didn't wear a prayer cap or bonnet on her head but a thin, woven gray scarf, tied under her chin. There was an unusual alertness behind her eyes that startled Bee, as if nothing could surprise her.

"You must be Dok's widow lady," the woman said.

Bee cringed. What a terrible way to be identified. "I am," she said, smiling tightly. "I'm Bee Bennett."

"Bee like the buzzing kind?"

"Bee . . . short for Beatrice."

"Well, Bee, you'd better get out of that car and get inside before you freeze to death." And off she scurried toward the farmhouse.

So. This was Fern Lapp.

One thing was clear—Fern was not meek and mild. She was the one in charge of this arranged meeting. Not Bee.

She rolled her window back up and got out of the car, locking it with her key fob.

Fern was waiting on the porch steps, watching her with those piercing eyes, shaking her head. "Every Englischer locks up their car like there's bandits hiding in the barn."

"Out of habit, I suppose," Bee said, though it did seem like a silly thing to do. This farm radiated peacefulness. She wondered if that was because of winter, when the land was resting. Dok had told her that Windmill Farm was originally made up of orchards of fruit trees. There was more to it now—a buggy repair shop and a knitting shop. She turned to ask Fern a question and realized she had disappeared. Already in the kitchen.

Whoa. That woman moved fast. Silently. Stealthily.

Assuming Fern expected her to come inside, Bee opened

82

the door to pop her head in. The day was gray and the room was dimly lit. Only one hissing lantern hung overhead, and it took a moment for Bee's eyes to adjust. Her first impression was how spotless this house was, hospital clean, neat as a pin, with a slight scent of Pine-Sol in the air. Braided rugs scattered across gleaming linoleum floors, a couch rested against one wall, a desk next to it. And on the opposite wall was a floor-to-ceiling bookshelf, full of titles. The walls were painted a pale green. Near the desk hung a calendar with a large picture of Yosemite's famous Half Dome on it. A long rectangular wooden table and chairs claimed the bulk of the space. The big room was comfortably warm, heated by a polished black woodstove in the corner. So this, Bee realized, would be the Amish version of a great room. Kitchen and family room all blended together. Nothing new, nothing fancy. But it held a certain comfortable charm.

In spite of the reluctance she had upon arriving, Bee felt herself slowing down, wanting to take her time, to examine every inch of this house.

She caught a faint whiff of something sweet baking in the oven. "Shall I come in?"

Fern didn't even look up. She was rolling a hunk of dough on the counter. "Grab a rolling pin." She jutted her chin in the direction of a rolling pin and another hunk of dough.

Bee set down her purse and took off her coat. A little non-plussed, she picked up the rolling pin and tried to press down on the chilled dough. She didn't even make a dent in it.

Fern's eyes flicked up. "Harder. You need to put a little oomph into it."

Bee pressed harder on her right side and finally made an impact on the dough. "You live here alone?"

"No. Luke and Izzy Schrock live here with their brood. Luke's a buggy repairman and Izzy runs that knit shop down near the bottom of the driveway. Luke has a cousin down in

South Carolina, but he had to have some kind of back surgery and asked Luke to help out with his own buggy repair shop for a few months. Luke and Izzy jumped at the chance. They were happy to skip out on a Pennsylvania winter like the one we've been having."

Such a big farm for such a small, elderly woman. "You didn't want to go too?"

"No. Somebody needs to make sure the animals are cared for. Besides, I'm a homebody. I like my routines . . . and my own bed at night."

"Me too."

Bee was about to turn the dough around when Fern said, "So your left side was where the . . ." She mimicked scissors cutting.

So much for doctor-patient confidentiality. "Yes."

"Then don't turn the dough. Get that arm working."

Bee paused, annoyed. What would Fern Lapp know about recovering from breast cancer surgery? About anything in Bee's life? This was turning into overhelping by yet another person. She didn't want to be here. She wanted to go home . . . so maybe she should do just that. "Fern, I appreciate the invitation to your home, but perhaps I could come another day. I'm not really feeling up for a visit today."

Fern stopped rolling and peered at Bee. "Three years ago, my husband died suddenly, right up there in the orchards. You're not the only one in this world who has had a few hard blows. So how about if you stop feeling so sorry for yourself and pick up the rolling pin?" Back she went to rolling out the pie dough. Her movements were confident, well-practiced, and in less than a minute's time the dough was transformed from a lump into a flat, perfectly shaped circle.

And while Fern had been rolling that dough, Bee had been trying to absorb the shock of her sharp words. All kinds of bristling emotions raced through her—anger, self-pity, indignation, embarrassment. She'd hardly said more than a few words of greeting! What made Fern think Bee felt sorry for herself? She did, but she didn't think it was *that* obvious.

Fern Lapp was *not* the Amish woman whom she had expected her to be. Part of Bee wanted to walk right out the door. And part of her wanted to see what else Fern had to say.

So Bee picked up the rolling pin and started to roll the dough, pressing a little harder on her left side.

After the last pie went into the oven, Fern and Bee sat down with coffee and dug into a piece of cooled-down pie. Bee had a sense that this sit-down time would be quick, that Fern wasn't one to linger. So Bee decided to not waste any time. "You said your husband died three years ago. Tell me, what does grief look like for you now?"

"What does it look like for you right now?"

Frustrating! Bee wanted answers, not questions. *But OK. Here goes.* "It's been a little over a year since Ted died. At some point of every day, I cry. I still can't look at his picture. I can't bear to listen to his old messages on my phone's voicemail. Losing Ted like that . . . it's like the sun has gone out of my life. Like every day is gray and cloudy." Her voice cracked a little, and she knew that a wave of emotion was starting to swell up. "It wasn't supposed to be this way. Ted was young. He had just retired, and we had so many plans for this time of life. I just ache for all the time we lost. I feel so . . . robbed. So blindsided. Disoriented. I feel like, well"—she pointed to her chest—"like I've had surgery without anesthesia and it still feels like a raw, open wound."

Sipping coffee, Fern kept her eyes on Bee. "And now you have breast cancer to deal with."

"Yes. Dok said she thinks my heart broke when Ted died, and when a heart breaks, the body can start to break down. It keeps score, she said." Bee let out a long sigh. "There's a part of me that wishes the cancer hadn't even been caught. Dok is just so . . . persistent. She wouldn't leave me alone. She made me go get a mammogram. She gave me no choice. She *drove* me there."

A slight smile tugged at Fern's lips. "That's why she's a good doctor."

Yes, but Bee wanted more from Fern. "I'd really like to know, what does grief look like for you? Is it different, being Amish? Is it easier? If so, how?"

Fern took a sip of coffee, as if gathering her thoughts. "Yes, I think grief is easier for the Plain People. But we're also warned to not overgrieve. There's a saying among our people—'Wann der Gaul dod is, drauere batt nix.'"

"Meaning . . ."

"When the horse is dead, grieving does no good."

That stung.

Bee dropped her chin. She had shared more about her feelings of loss with Fern than anyone else, and in doing so, she was told to stuff her grief down. "I hope you won't feel offended if I tell you that sounds like denial. Pretending feelings aren't there to feel."

"You asked me about the Amish and grief. You can't pick and choose what you want to hear." Fern polished off the last bite of her pie. "When an Amish woman has a stillborn baby, do you know what is said about it?"

Bee shook her head.

"That the baby's life was complete."

Stilling, Bee tried to wrap her head around that. It was a strange thought.

"When you understand *that*, you'll understand how the Amish grieve." Fern scooped up her pie plate and Bee's. "Hank and Edith Lapp are coming by to pick up these pies and deliver them to shut-ins." She went to the sink and started rinsing the dishes.

More bluntness. Clearly, that was Bee's cue to leave. She'd been dismissed.

Putting on her coat, Bee felt more than a little miffed. She was leaving with more questions than answers. She walked to her car, got inside, closed the car door, when suddenly, there was a knock on the window. *Fern.* Bee lowered the car window.

Fern handed her a pie through the window. "Bring me back the pie plate at our next visit."

Bee looked at the pie. It was her own clumsy-looking pie with crust that was patched together. When she lifted her head to say thank you, Fern was gone. In the distance, she saw the door to the farmhouse close shut. *Wow.* That woman moved like lightning.

So there was to be a next time? Maybe there were answers to come. Maybe this odd little Amish woman might have something to teach Bee about grief, if she could only get her to slow down and give a straight answer. The thought of more visits with Fern cheered Bee.

So did the berry pie. The first pie she'd ever made. She felt rather proud of it, though it didn't look anything like Fern's. She drove home from Windmill Farm as carefully as she could so that the berry pie on the seat next to her didn't jiggle and spill. As she handled the steering wheel, she realized her left arm felt less stiff, less uncomfortable. So maybe Fern was right about the benefits of oomph. Using her arm instead of coddling it, making it work.

The pie smelled heavenly. She smiled. She might even give Damon the Demon a slice to take home. And then she'd tell him not to come back tomorrow.

Eight

Dok had never seen Matt act so decisively. For as long as she had known him, he was a rather slow-moving, thoughtful man, who took his time to carefully deliberate over decisions. A good starter, a slow finisher. That's why their house remodel had taken four years and was nowhere near completion. Matt liked to ponder every single decision—right down to the perfect light switch—and a whole house remodel required thousands of decisions. Dok's work required so much out of her that it was easy to let Matt take all the time he needed, to do whatever he needed to do. That kind of accommodating attitude made their marriage work. She gave him space; he gave her space. She'd thought so, anyway.

Last week Matt had promised Dok that he would handle everything for the baby, all the paperwork, and there was a little part of her that thought (hoped!) his follow-through might fizzle out. When no updates arrived from the caseworker assigned to the baby, she was sure he'd dropped the ball. So, so wrong. The slowdown came from the Bureau of Child and Family Services. Apparently, Matt had filed everything necessary to be emergency foster parents. This morning, after receiving word that they'd been approved as emergency foster parents, Matt filed his own request for vacation time to start immediately, followed by a trip to Walmart to buy a crib, formula, diapers, car seat, baby clothes, stroller, and on and on and on. He even bought a sound machine because the saleswoman at Walmart suggested it.

And this afternoon, he brought home the abandoned infant boy from the hospital.

Dok came home at the end of a long day and found Matt sprawled out on the sofa, shirtless, holding the sleeping newborn against his bare chest. On the floor next to the sofa was a stack of books about baby care.

"Skin to skin contact is supposed to be best for a baby," he said, a little embarrassed. "For the bonding, and all."

"True," Dok said, trying to sound calm, accepting, professional, though inside she fought a rising panic. Life at home, she sensed, had just radically changed. And she had liked her life the way it was.

Annie's dad had just dropped her off in front of Dok's office when she heard a shriek coming from the Bent N' Dent.

"Annie!"

She turned to find Sarah Blank flying toward her, arms wide. Sarah enveloped Annie in a smothering hug, rocking her from one side to the other. "You rescued me from drowning!"

Annie couldn't breathe. She peeled Sarah's arms off her. "When were you released from the hospital?"

"Saturday night. They just kept me for observation for a few hours." She glanced back at the store. "I had to rest at home for a few days before starting to work again."

Annie could see Sarah was back to her loud, boisterous self. "No frostbite?"

Sarah held up her fingers and wiggled. "All is well, thanks to your quick thinking." She grabbed Annie for another smothering hug. "How can I ever repay you?"

"No need!" Annie said, gasping for breath as she wiggled out of Sarah's embrace. "I'm just thankful you're all right."

"There must be something I can do for you." Her eyes went wide. "I know! On the way to Blue Lake Pond, you asked me to find you a boyfriend. Don't you worry. I'll find just the right someone for you!"

"No! No, I didn't. That's not what I said. Nothing like that. I had asked you if you knew of any Amish EMTs."

"Oh, that's right. That is what you had asked me." Sarah's face scrunched up. "So why were you asking about him?"

"Um, well, it's better if I don't say." Annie cleared her throat. "Dok's work requires a lot of confidentiality." A vague response, but Sarah seemed to accept it.

"Well, I am going to find this EMT for you if it's the last thing I do. It's the least I can do for you. After all, you saved my life!"

"No, no, I really didn't," Annie said. "It was the paramedics who saved your life. They're the ones who fished you out of the water and whisked you off to the hospital."

Sarah, naturally, wasn't listening. A buggy had arrived at the store, full of women, so she scurried across the shared parking lot to return to work.

A gust of cold air swirled past Annie and she hoped Dok would arrive soon. If she was on a house call, she usually found a way to let Annie know. If Dok missed catching her at home, she would leave a message at the Bent N' Dent. There was a bulletin board near the door where messages could be left. Annie waited on the front step as long as she could, until standing in the cold was just too much to bear. She went to the store, hoping Sarah would be busy with customers and not notice her arrival.

"ANNIE!"

Sarah had noticed.

"Attention, everyone! This is the girl who saved my life!"

All eyes in the store went to Annie, and she felt her face turn a shade of hot red. Being the center of attention was painful to her. Excruciating. "I didn't, really," she mumbled. "The EMT did."

Sarah cupped her hands around her mouth. "Does anyone here know of an Amish boy who is an EMT? Anyone? No? Well, if you hear of anyone who knows him, Annie needs to find out his identity. For a private, personal reason that she can't talk about. Dok won't let her. It's not because she's sweet on him."

Mortifying. Absolutely mortifying.

Where was Dok? Annie went to the bulletin board, hoping there was a message from Dok. Nothing.

Annie sat down in a spare rocking chair by the fire and waited, trying to be as inconspicuous as possible. Invisible. Just as the door blew open and in walked Hank Lapp, followed by a half dozen graybeards.

His face lit up when he saw her. "ANNIE FISHER!" he bellowed. "I HEAR"—cough, cough—"excuse me. Got a little TICKLE in my throat." He coughed a few more times. "I HEAR you PLUNGED into FREEZING WATER to rescue our SARAH!" The more excited he got, the louder his raspy voice would get. "GRABBED HER FROM THE CLUTCH OF DEATH!"

"No," Annie said meekly, shrinking in the chair. "No, nothing like that."

Sarah came bustling up. "Hank, do you know of an EMT who's Amish? Annie's desperate to find him."

Annie shot out of the rocking chair. "No! Not desperate. Not at all. Just curious. That's all." She started sliding toward the door, weaving between the graybeards.

As she grabbed the knob to open the door, she heard Hank say, "Why, YES. I believe I DO."

Slowly, Annie closed the door and turned around.

Nine

Hank Lapp was full of hot air. While Annie waited in the Bent N' Dent for him to remember the name of the EMT, he hemmed and hawed until he realized that he thought Sarah had asked about Auntie Em's Dog Grooming Service. That confusion took a full ten minutes to unravel. Annie was exasperated with Hank *and* with Sarah, both of whom never stopped talking. Every customer who walked in the door was treated to a dramatic retelling of Sarah's near drowning, and it grew bigger with each telling, along with Annie's desperate need to find the identity of the Amish EMT. There was no stopping Sarah.

Until suddenly, an Englisch mother called out in the back of the store for help. Annie went to see if she could help and saw that her little boy was having an allergic reaction. Hives were forming on his hands and arms, his face was red, and he tugged at his throat as if it was bothering him.

"Is he allergic to anything?" Annie asked.

"Peanuts," the mother said. "But where would he have found a peanut?"

From those old graybeards who tossed the shells into the fire and missed half the time! "I think he might have found one on the floor and started to eat it."

Annie peered around the aisles to look out the window, hoping to see that Dok's car had arrived at her office. Still no sign of her. "Sarah, call 911."

"I can't!" Sarah said. "The old phone's not working. The bishop's out getting a new one now."

Annie turned to the mother. "Do you have an EpiPen?"

The woman rummaged through her purse, panicking. "I'm sure it's here somewhere . . . Here!" She handed it to Annie. "I've never had to use it."

The EpiPen came with instructions on how to use it. Annie read them, held her breath, and gave the child the injection. The response was immediate, like magic. The child started to breathe normally, and as Annie watched, his face drained of that red-hot color and turned a normal shade.

"Thank you," the mother said, hugging her boy. "Thank you, thank you, thank you."

"He needs to go straight to the emergency room," Annie said.

The mother looked up in alarm. "But he's feeling better."

"Doesn't matter," Annie said. "He has to be seen. Right now."

"But—"

"Listen to Annie," Sarah said. "She saved my life the other day."

The mother nodded, picked up her little boy, and headed to her car. Everyone in the store quietly watched them leave, then turned all eyes on Annie.

Sarah's hands were clasped over her heart. "Annie Fisher, you have saved two people in one week. How do you have the presence of mind to act in a crisis? So calm."

"CALM as a CUCUMBER," Hank bellowed.

"Unflappable," Sarah said.

"Our ANNIE can NOT be FLAPPED," Hank said.

Sarah frowned, pointing a finger at him. "And you, Hank Lapp, you and your friends are always dropping your peanuts and shells all over this store. I've told you and told you to clean up after yourself."

As Hank sputtered away in self-defense, Annie quietly slipped out of the store and scurried across the parking lot to wait for Dok. Enduring the cold was better than having to listen to Sarah and Hank.

Ten minutes later, Dok pulled in, nodded to Annie, unlocked the front door, and went straight to her office, closing the door behind her. Not a word. Something about the look on her face told Annie not to bother her.

So Annie sat at her desk, preparing for the day, and thought about Sarah's near drowning at Blue Lake Pond and about what had happened just now at the store with the little boy. She had known what to do in both situations because she'd been prepared. But she wanted to know more. She wanted to help people in need, yet her knowledge was so limited.

Could these two experiences be confirmation from the Lord that she was on the right track to pursue becoming an EMT? Maybe so. The other day at Blue Lake Pond was a little step. Today was another one.

She wished she could ask Dok about becoming an EMT, but she didn't want to raise concern that she might quit. Working in Dok's office was a dream come true, and even though her parents expected her to stop working in the spring, she had a hope that, somehow and someway, she might be able to stay in the role. If that were to happen, it would be a miracle. So if being Dok's assistant was as far as Annie could ever go in the medical field, then it would have to be enough.

She dropped her head into her hands. Who was she trying to fool? It wasn't enough.

Exhausted didn't come close to how Dok felt after being up most of the night with a newborn. Matt had promised, several times, that he'd get up during the night with the baby, but that man slept like a bear in hibernation. After so many years working on call, the slightest sound could yank her out of deep sleep. Whenever the baby squeaked or moved in his crib, Dok stirred awake. And then her doctor-ness kicked in and she got up to check on him. She would glance at the clock and realize there was no point in going back to bed now. The baby needed to be fed every two to three hours to get some weight on him. So she'd feed him a bottle, put him back in his crib, and then lay wide awake, worrying if he was cold, or if his diaper needed changing. Or how soon a foster family would be available for him and if they were kindhearted people. She squeezed her eyes shut. Of course they'd be kindhearted, she scolded herself. Of course.

And all this worry came to her without much of any real attachment to this child other than duty. Imagine what ran through the minds of tired new mothers. Dok had a new empathy for them.

As tired as she felt this morning, she couldn't wait to hand the care of the baby over to Matt—who apologized profusely for sleeping so soundly but Dok was so mad she hardly looked at him—and get to the office. As soon as she unlocked the door, she went straight to her office, closed the door, and sat in her chair, leaning back, closing her eyes. It was nice here, in the quiet before the day started, before patients arrived.

Lord, I can't do this. It's too much. No matter what Matt says, this is hard on us. I'm asking you for help to get out of this situation, as fast as possible. Please help.

She thought she might call the caseworker today and see if they could speed up the process of placing the baby in a permanent foster home. She dreaded facing more sleepless nights, and Matt shouldn't be using vacation time to sit at home.

"Um, excuse me, Dok? Excuse me."

Dok jerked, blinking. "Annie, good morning. I didn't hear you come in. What do you need?"

"I waited as long as I could, but your first patient is here."

Yawning, Dok sat up. "How long . . . have I been asleep?"

Annie looked at the wall clock. "Over forty-five minutes. I figured you must have had a hard night and needed the nap."

"You guessed right." She got up and stretched, then reached for her white coat. "Who's the first patient?"

"Your husband. He has a question. And he's brought a baby." Annie tipped her head. "Is there any chance that it's the same baby who was left here?"

"An excellent chance." Dok buttoned up her coat. "I would've told you sooner but, to be perfectly honest, I didn't think it was actually going to happen." She let out another yawn. "Matt and I are providing emergency foster care for this baby, just until a permanent home can be found." She glanced at Annie, almost amused by the shocked look on her face. "I can tell what you're thinking."

"What am I thinking?"

"That there's got to be a family connection we have to this child—because we're way too old to care for a newborn. Way too busy. And if that's what you're thinking, then you're absolutely right. The baby's mother is a second cousin to Matt, is a current drug user, and has disappeared. No one has any idea where she is, or if she'll ever return for her child. Miraculously, the baby doesn't seem to be adversely affected by his mother's use of drugs during pregnancy." She buttoned the last button. "And yes, I am way beyond the age of providing full-time care for a newborn baby."

Annie blushed and looked down at her shoes. "Actually, I wasn't thinking any of that."

"Then what were you thinking?"

"That this little boppli must have a very special purpose in life."

As Annie left to get Matt and the baby, Dok paused by the door, resting her forehead on the jamb. This, she realized, was

God's answer to her plea for help. Not exactly what she asked for, but a very direct response. As clear as a bucket of cold water tossed in her face.

Bee sat in the waiting room of her surgeon's office, trying to distract herself from feeling anxious. Bothered. About everything.

This morning, she'd caught Damon introducing her three-year-old horse Echo to low cross rails and small verticals. Such a sight told Bee that he'd been steadily training the horse to become comfortable with jumping obstacles, despite her objections. She did not want Damon to do any high-level training with her horses. Did he listen? No.

She didn't want to be here, sitting in a doctor's office. She didn't want to have cancer. Didn't want to have to face it without Ted.

Her mind circled and landed on Fern's parting remark about how the Amish considered the death of a stillborn baby, that his or her life was complete.

That way of thinking didn't make any sense.

But it did.

Bee knew Fern was making a point that our lives were not in our hands. She agreed with that thinking; she had faith in God. And yet it was hard to grasp what that really meant from this side of Heaven. A stillborn baby never took a single breath of life. How was *that* a complete life? From any way you looked at it, that baby was cheated out of life.

She wanted to ask Fern about it, and wondered how soon she could visit her again without being a bother. She sensed that Fern had answers that Bee needed.

"Beatrice?"

Bee looked up at the sound of her formal name. Only her mother had ever called her Beatrice. She went into the exam room, had her blood pressure and temperature taken by the nurse, and changed into the paper gown. The doctor came in and sat on the stool. Bee's stomach tightened.

"How are you healing from the surgery, Bee?"

"Fairly well, I think."

"And your arm? Are you using it? Doing a lot of stretching?"

"Trying." She kept her eyes on the file in the doctor's hands. "Good news from the results, I hope."

"Yes," the doctor said, drawing out the word. "Estrogen receptor positive, the more common postmenopausal cancer. We took two lymph nodes out. One clear. One had a tiny trace of cancer."

Oh. "That's not good, isn't it?"

"Your lymph node was doing its job." She glanced at her chart. "You're seeing the oncologist this morning, too, I see. He'll explain next steps."

"You mean, treatment."

"He's an excellent oncologist. You'll be in good hands."

"I'm sure he is, but . . . what if I don't want any more treatment? I thought my prognosis was excellent. Maybe surgery is enough."

The surgeon paused to gather her thoughts, and Bee knew she was probably trying to sound logical and professional when she wanted to shout at Bee to stop whining. "It's all about statistics, Bee. All about reducing your chances for recurrence."

"Is the risk of recurrence really that high?"

"Yes," she said firmly. "Cancer should never be underestimated. Especially once your body has learned how to make it."

With that, the surgeon examined Bee, admired her own stitching, and sent her over to the oncologist. "My work is done," the surgeon said, sounding pleased.

But Bee felt as if her work had just begun. The oncologist explained the process of what was to come: meeting with the radiologist. She would face six weeks of radiation, given Monday through Friday. Treatment loomed over her head, along with frustration at how interrupted her life had become with this diagnosis. She just wanted her life back. She wanted her energy back. She wanted Damon the Demon to go away.

On the way home from these morning appointments, Bee drove straight to Windmill Farm to see Fern Lapp.

Bee found Fern in the kitchen. She didn't seem at all surprised to see Bee at her door. "Good thing you came. It's bread-making day."

"I thought I smelled fresh-baked bread as I got out of the car."

"There's another bowl of dough ready to knead," she said, as if Bee had asked.

Kneading bread was another thing Bee had never done in her life. Not once. She and Ted had eaten out in restaurants quite a bit. Neither of them had the time or the inclination to cook. She washed her hands at the sink, dried them on a dish towel, and peered into the bowl. "Fern, what should I do?"

"Sprinkle some flour on the counter, get the dough into a ball, and start pushing and pulling."

"How will I know when it's done?"

"See how craggy it is now? It needs to be smooth and elastic." Fern looked at her over her glasses. "You might want to take off that ring."

"Right." Bee took off her wedding ring, pausing for a moment. She'd never removed it since Ted had passed. Not once. Her finger looked naked without it. Sad. Empty.

"The thing about bread dough," Fern said, "is that the more it gets worked, the better it will be. I like to call it the Romans 8:28 method of making bread."

"As in . . . from the Bible?"

"'All things work together for good to them that love God,'" Fern quoted. "I like to knead it longer than most think is necessary. Extra kneading ends up with the best bread of all—light and airy and delicious. A little like life, I've always thought. Difficult times end up making us the best we can be."

Fern's fists started hammering the dough. Bee sprinkled flour over the counter, dug her hands in the bowl, and started to bring the dough together into a ball. Then she copied Fern—pushing and pulling, whacking away at the dough with her fists.

It felt good. Really, really good. She pounded out all her frustrations on that poor lump of dough—her anger at having breast cancer. *Smack!* At having to undergo treatment. *Bam!* Her annoyance with Damon's out-of-the-blue arrival. *Slap!* At his insistence on training her horses. *Punch!* Her irritation that she *needed* his help with her precious horses. *Whack, whack, whack!* That bread dough took it all.

By early afternoon, she was heading home with a loaf of bread, still warm from the oven. She and Fern hadn't really had much conversation, yet Bee felt like a different person.

The drive home was surprisingly pleasant.

During an office lunch break, Dok went over to the Bent N' Dent to talk to her brother the bishop, so Annie used the quiet time in an empty office to call the community college to ask about an EMT course. It took three tries. She spoke so softly that the registrar kept hanging up on her, thinking no one was there.

"I'm here," Annie said in her boldest voice.

"Speak up," the registrar said. "I can't hear you."

Annie cringed. She could tell that the registrar was the impatient type. She took in a deep breath. "I want to become an EMT."

"How old are you?"

"Twenty. Almost twenty-one."

"Really? You sound like a child."

Annie frowned at the phone. "When will the next course begin?"

"You just missed the deadline for winter quarter. Next one will be spring quarter. If you want to apply, fill out the online application."

"What if . . . what if I don't use a computer?"

"What? You mean, you're low-tech?"

"More like . . . no-tech."

"Say *what*?" The registrar let out a deep sigh. "How are you going to be an EMT if you don't know how to use basic technology?"

"I . . . I'm not sure." It was one of the many questions Annie had.

There was some tapping on a keyboard, then the registrar said, "There's an informational meeting about becoming paramedics and EMTs this Saturday afternoon at the fire station in Gordonville. Starts at one o'clock. Honey, if you're serious about this, then *be there*."

Annie stared at the receiver. Saturday afternoon could not be more ideal! Dok's office closed at noon. Her mother had been putting pressure on her to go to another youth gathering, but this would give her a solid out. She would be attending an informational meeting that related, somewhat, to her work at Dok's office. It was the truth. Annie might not volunteer everything to her parents, like getting her GED, but she wouldn't lie to them.

Annie hung up the phone, grinning. Little steps, little steps.

Ten

Dok had always appreciated Matt's ability to sleep soundly. She'd even considered it an asset because of her frequent night calls. She never had to worry that interruptions would bother him, because they never did. Right out of high school, Matt had joined the navy and spent months deployed overseas, assigned to some kind of naval ship in which the bunk room was next to the engine room. He attributed his sleeping ability to that time in his life. He could sleep through any sound.

This week, his ability to sleep deeply infuriated her. If she didn't think it would've traumatized the baby, she would've used a bullhorn to rouse him.

Four days had passed and Dok hadn't slept more than a few hours here and there. Matt promised and promised that he would get up during the night to care for the baby—whom he named Gabriel after Dok complained that they couldn't keep calling him *that* baby—but she could not rouse him out of his deep slumber. She tried! The man was a champion sleeper.

This just couldn't keep going on as it was. This was meant to be emergency foster care. Hadn't they done enough?

Each morning as Dok arrived at the office, and each evening just before she left, she put in a call to the caseworker to see if there'd been any progress in finding a foster family for baby

Gabe. She'd left so many messages on voicemail that the case-worker had stopped returning her calls.

To be fair, Matt felt terrible about continually bailing on his promise for night duty. He even slept on the floor in the baby's room last night, yet still snoozed away through the baby's every-two-hour feedings—and such a small baby needed those regular feedings. Dok heard every peep the baby made, even with a sound machine turned up as loud as it could go—and her bedroom was down the hall!

And yet, she couldn't overlook two things that made this lengthening emergency foster care survivable—this baby was a dream baby. During the night, she had to wake him to feed him and then he'd go right back to sleep. He was content and curious and rarely cried. If he did cry, he wasn't unreasonable the way some babies could be—working themselves into a crying jag. If baby Gabe cried, he had a good reason. It was like he knew he was a houseguest who was on the verge of overstaying, so he tried to be extra polite.

The second thing Dok couldn't ignore was Matt's over-the-moon delight with fostering baby Gabe. Once Matt did actually wake in the morning, he sprang into action. He held the baby all the day long, fed him diligently, changed his diapers, cared for every need. Matt was a big, muscular man, a seasoned cop. To most people, he seemed like a tough guy. Dok knew better. He was a fire-roasted marshmallow—crisp on the outside, tender and gooey on the inside. He was the romantic one in their marriage. He left little notes for her around the house, brought her flowers for no reason, cooked elaborate homemade meals on Sundays.

The gentle way Matt handled the baby touched Dok's heart; it even made her feel a little sad. He would've been a wonderful father. Sometimes she wished they'd met when they were younger, but neither was ready for marriage until late in life. To be perfectly frank, she doubted they would've chosen each other had they met in their twenties or thirties. More candidly, Matt might have chosen her—he said the moment he had met her, he knew she was *the one*. He never wavered from that single-minded devotion. Dok, on the other hand, had been attracted to the wrong kind of men. Handsome, successful, and selfish. Even in her midforties, when she first met Matt, she dismissed his pursuit of her. He was too kind, too good to her, treated her too well.

It took a wake-up call—getting fired from her job as an ER doctor. She'd taken the blame for an error made by the man she thought she had loved. A selfish man who had none of Matt's integrity or kindness. That bitter experience opened her eyes to Matt and his patient, persistent courting. They'd been happy together. She'd thought so, anyway.

She sighed. She couldn't stop thinking of Annie's remark that this baby must have a special purpose in life. That child landed on her doorstep for a reason. She needed to be open to this, from her heart, not just going through the motions. The baby deserved as much from her. Matt deserved it from her.

During the day. Not during the night. Tonight, she planned to spray cold water on Matt's face and see if that might wake him up.

On Saturday afternoon, Annie slipped into the room at the Gordonville Fire Station and took a seat in the back row. There were all kinds of people at the meeting, men and women, old and young, but none wore bonnets. Just her.

She untied her bonnet and held it in her lap to be less conspicuous, but her prayer cap was just as obvious to others. She kept her eyes down but felt the stares of others. Knew the questions circling in their mind . . .

Why is she here?

Amish can't be EMTs, can they?

*She looks too small to be an EMT. Too young. Too shy. Too
. . . everything.*

But maybe those questions were circling only in her mind.

Right at one o'clock, two men in crisp white shirts and black
trousers entered the front of the room to start the informational
meeting. Annie's heart started to pound. She hadn't expected
him to be here . . . but there he was! The Amish EMT. He sat
down in an empty chair in the front row as the other man in
uniform welcomed everyone. Annie recognized him as the paramedic who drove the ambulance. She could hardly believe she'd
found them. No wonder they answered calls for Stoney Ridge
emergencies—Gordonville was just a few towns over. Now it
made sense that Annie had never crossed paths with the Amish
EMT. Lancaster County was full of farming towns, sprawling
and spread out. Some had volunteer fire stations, like Stoney
Ridge, but few had both fire and emergency medical services.

As the paramedic welcomed everyone and outlined the meeting, Annie found herself unable to concentrate. The Amish
EMT was sitting only *ten rows* away from her. If she leaned
slightly to the right, she could see the back of his head. A
beautiful head of thick blond hair.

Leaning back to the left, she squeezed her eyes shut. *Notes.*
She should take notes. She grabbed her pencil and notepad and
wrote down today's date. Then, her thoughts reined in and
under control, she added bullet points and explanations from
the paramedic's informative talk.

Here was the best, most wonderful thing she learned from
him: She could probably keep working for Dok and attend
EMT school at night and/or on Saturdays. There were all kinds
of programs available to suit a working schedule.

She'd love to keep working for Dok if she could. She learned
so much from Dok, plus it helped her grow comfortable with
the world of medicine, as well as with talking to and manag-
ing all kinds of people. And it was probably the only way her

parents could be persuaded to let her attend classes. *If* they could be persuaded. Assuming the bishop could be persuaded. Assuming Dok would be okay with it.

She decided to put those worries off for another time.

The paramedic had been talking. She snapped back into the conversation to hear him describe the difference between BLS ambulances—Basic Life Support—staffed by EMTs, and ALS ambulances—Advanced Life Support—staffed by a paramedic and EMTs with higher training. While both ambulances provided transportation, the ALS personnel could do more things like "break the skin" by starting an IV or administer medication. The BLS personnel did a lot of transfers, such as delivering patients from one facility to another. Annie hadn't realized that there were so many options as an EMT.

A woman up front had been asking a steady number of questions. "Can you describe some recent calls?"

"Well, let's see. It was an auto versus a bicyclist. The patient was knocked down by a car that didn't stop behind the line at a red. We assessed the patient, found him to be stable."

The Amish EMT said something to the paramedic in a low voice—something Annie couldn't overhear, though she craned forward to try to listen.

"Right. Good point! Thanks for reminding me." The paramedic clapped his hands. "Here's one that'll separate the men from the boys. Just last week, we got a call about an unconscious male, aged nineteen, and when we arrived at the scene, patient was nonresponsive. Overdosed on fentanyl. I administered Narcan and the patient revived. Then came the typical response—the patient kicked, hit, and vomited everywhere." He chuckled. "You learn how to duck fast when you're in this business."

Now the paramedic was on a nostalgic roll. He sat on the edge of the desk and crossed his arms against his chest. "I'll never forget my first call. Vehicle versus bicycle. Thirteen-year-old boy, no helmet, massive trauma to the head. As we log rolled him onto the backboard, his skull collapsed in my hands. That was over twenty years ago and I still remember that moment like it was yesterday." He sighed. "Let that be a reminder to everyone. Wear a helmet."

The room was silent. The woman in the front row picked up her purse and left the room. The paramedic watched her go. "That's why we have these informational meetings. This line of work isn't for the faint of heart." He looked over the audience. "Any more questions?"

Another woman, seated in the middle, raised her hand. "Are most of the calls all life-and-death moments?"

The paramedic shook his head. "Most aren't, in fact. They're usually nonemergency, often prescheduled IFTs—interfacility transfers. Dialysis transports alone are a huge chunk of the IFT business. Those transports keep a lot of private ambulance companies in business. BLS does more assessment over treatment. I'd even go so far as to say BLS acts as a Band-Aid. Get the patient safely transported from one spot to another. So, to answer your question, the average EMT doesn't face a lot of life-and-death moments. That said, there are some calls that'll leave you with rattling teeth."

The woman raised her hand again. "Have you ever been afraid when you're out on a call?"

"Absolutely," the paramedic said. "Everyone is afraid, especially at first. Perfectly normal. But with great training, great equipment, you will end up with great courage. There's nothing wrong with being afraid. EMTs are trained to control their fears. Better still, to carry on despite fears."

Annie took in a sharp breath. That phrase hit her like a punch in the stomach. *To carry on despite fears.* She'd never been easily frightened, not squeamish or fussy, not like her mother was. Annie's fears were just as real but very different— she felt crippled with shyness around people she didn't know, and especially around those who held authority, like the bishop. Or even those who *thought* they were in charge. Edith Lapp came to mind.

The paramedic reassured everyone with the information that an experienced EMT or paramedic would always be matched with a rookie. That came as a relief.

Annie wondered if the Amish EMT was a rookie. Whenever there was a pause to allow for questions, her thoughts wound their way back to the Amish EMT in the front row. She wondered what his name was, and how long he'd been an EMT, where he lived . . . and if he had a girlfriend. How could he not?

She would correct those thoughts to get her mind back where it belonged—on this informational meeting. And then her doubts would kick in. Would the bishop allow her to pursue this? If the bishop did, would her parents? Or would it be better to approach her parents first, and then the bishop?

She didn't know!

She had so many questions about being an EMT and she had come determined to get her questions answered. She was *not* going to let her reticence win today. She'd written her questions down ahead of time. She'd practiced saying them aloud. Most questions, happily, had been asked by others.

Like, was there an age limit? Only that you had to be over eighteen years old. There was no cap on a person's age, only on their fitness.

Were jobs available? Yes. There was a constant need.

A few of Annie's questions remained unasked: Can I still become an EMT if I don't have a driver's license and never will have one? Will an eighth-grade education plus a GED suffice? Do I need to be proficient on a computer? Because that's out of the question. Is a uniform required of female EMTs? Because that wouldn't work for her, either. She was sure the entire room would turn to see who was asking such odd questions.

She was a grown-up. She could do this. Taking a deep breath, she tentatively lifted her hand just as someone else's arm shot up high in the sky, waving to get noticed.

And then it was over. The paramedic clapped his hands together. "If there aren't any other questions, then we'll give you some paperwork and wrap up the meeting."

But Annie still had questions to get answered! She was just about to raise her arm boldly when the Amish EMT stood up to pass out paperwork to each row, handing the first person a stack to pass back. She froze, watching every move he made, gathering identifying details. Dumb things, nothing important. Like, he was left-handed, same as she was. He wore a watch on his right wrist, and whenever he looked at it, he tossed his head to the side to get his hair out of his eyes. Blond hair, thick and shaggy, curled around the back of his shirt collar, and needed to be cut. Very, very nice blue eyes that drooped a little at their outside corner.

She wouldn't mind looking at that face for the rest of her life. It was a beautiful face.

And just at that moment, he noticed her sitting far off in the back corner. For a split second, their eyes locked, and Annie could tell that he recognized her. His face broke into a big grin and she smiled back, hesitantly.

Blushing, she tucked her chin and turned her attention to the papers she'd been handed to take home. She was glad she'd come, and not just because of finding the Amish EMT, whom she now knew worked in nearby Gordonville. She had learned a great deal and was leaving with a folder of paperwork to study thoroughly before she broached this with her parents or the bishop or Dok.

She was frustrated with herself that she didn't have the courage to get her specific questions answered—not a single one! Seeing those twinkling blue eyes again had distracted her, melting away her resolve.

But not her desire to be an EMT.

Bee had opened the garage door to let some light in as she looked through boxes, so many boxes, waiting to be unpacked. She turned and realized that Damon was standing in the driveway, waiting for her to notice him. "Are you leaving?"

That's about the only thing she ever said to Damon. She did her best to avoid him, going so far as to leave a chalkboard out in the stable with any details for a specific horse. Things like, *Marigold still needs stall rest. Dusty has a small cut on her fetlock.* Bee would even leave his now weekly paycheck taped to the chalkboard. Anything to avoid talking to him. A conversation might easily lead to an accusation. Hers. Damon Harding stole the gold from Ozzie.

She bit down on her lip, hard. *Allegedly* stole, she reminded herself.

No proof, no evidence, sore loser.

"Your treatment starts soon."

So? What business was that of his? Who told him, anyway? Dok probably told Matt who probably told Damon. Nothing felt private anymore. "I'll be fine."

"I'll drive you to the appointment."

Oh, no. He was *not* taking her to her radiation treatment. No way. "Thank you but no."

Typical of Damon, he ignored her. "And then I'll just wait for you. Getting zapped doesn't take long."

She looked up at him. Zapped? That was a rather casual way to describe high-energy gamma rays getting blasted at her poor breast. "Won't be necessary. I can drive myself." It came out a tad more irritated than it needed to be.

"I'll drop you off right at the front door so you don't have to hunt for a parking space. That entire section of Lancaster is full of detours. City's resurfacing the roads. It can get crowded."

She crossed her arms and stared at him. "I will leave plenty of time to find a parking spot." He was correct, though, about the detours. The radiologist's scheduler had warned her about the repaving of roads around the medical offices. She'd have to allow extra time to find parking each day. Which meant the whole *zapping* experience would take double the time. Argh! She hated this! Hated cancer, hated treatment, hated needing help.

"So I'll be here extra early to feed the horses and turn them out."

Her eyes snapped up to his. "No. Need. Regular time is fine. I'll drive myself." Her voice was thick with frustration.

He carried on, unbothered. "Don't want you worried if you hear noises in the barn while it's still dark." His gaze swept the garage. "Can I help you with"—he waved his right arm in a circle—"any of that stuff?"

Any of that stuff? Countless boxes, stacked floor to ceiling. An overwhelming amount of unpacked belongings. "No. It's a job only I can do." She turned to him, studying his eyes, searching his expression for signs of mockery. But she read only sincerity on his face. "Thank you, though, for asking."

With that, he said he'd see her in the morning and headed to his car.

Stop it! Bee wanted to shout. *Stop being so nice. In fact,* why *are you being so nice?*

Yesterday, she'd come into the barn to wrap Echo's right foreleg. Bee paid extra attention to her horse's forelegs. Most of the time, a horse's weight rested on their front legs; the back legs acted to propel them. If a horse showed lameness, Bee treated the injury immediately and took pains to find out what had caused it. In Echo's case, it was a stone bruise in her hoof. Not an uncommon problem, but one Bee took seriously.

As she had drawn close to Echo's stall, she realized Damon was inside with the horse. Bee stopped and listened, peering through the stall's bars at the back of Damon. He was stroking Echo's forehead in circular Tellington motions—known as

Touch. It was an equine therapy that could induce relaxation and improve behavior in a horse, even speed up the healing process. Bee wouldn't have thought he'd use such a gentle therapy, much less know of it. But then, a lot of things had been surprising her lately.

The sound of Damon's voice, calm and soothing, as he gently massaged Echo's forehead was touching to Bee. The horse acted as mellow as a purring house cat. Damon had been providing the kind of care to her horses that she normally gave to them. His knowledge and experience were what her horses needed. She did appreciate what he was doing for her horses. For her.

She reminded herself to stay bitter. They were not friends.

The dreaded daily radiation treatments started soon. Her incision had healed well, she was gaining back stamina, and now she had to get ready for another big wave to knock her off her feet. She'd made the mistake of obsessively researching symptoms of radiation treatment on Dr. Google and came across forums that described terrifying side effects: getting roasted, skin weathering, profound fatigue. She found a wide spectrum of opinions on how people coped with a cancer verdict. Some found it depressing, discouraging, frightening, while others thought it was nothing more than a blip on the radar. One woman went so far as to say a diagnosis of breast cancer had brought her a gift—of recognizing her limitations, of resetting her life while she still had time to make changes. She believed it wholeheartedly.

Huh.

Bee closed her eyes and tried to reflect on whether cancer had come bearing gifts.

No. Nada. Nyet. Nothing but an exasperating, unwelcome nuisance.

The winter sun was dropping low, so Bee turned her attention back to looking through boxes. She'd been over at Fern's earlier today, something that had become a frequent habit whenever she was feeling down. She had helped Fern cut pieces of fabric for a comfort quilt. You couldn't walk into the house without being given something to do . . . because Fern was always doing something. That little woman was never still. Bee found herself enjoying the visits, and although Fern didn't exactly talk to her the way a friend might—there were no lengthy conversations, no chatty back-and-forthing—she always left Windmill Farm with something to ponder.

Today, for example, Bee was complaining to Fern about starting radiation treatments. She felt this was a reasonable complaint. Who would choose to be radiated nearly every day for six weeks? No one!

Fern had listened as they cut triangles out of different colors of cloth—all solid colors—and when they finished one color, she set her scissors down and said, "Do you know what God's first spoken words are in the Bible?"

Bee had no idea.

"Let there be light," Fern said. She gathered up the cloth triangles and the scissors to pack up, a clear sign that their visit was over. Bee had grown accustomed to Fern's dismissals. It was just her way.

As soon as Bee had gotten home, she'd gone to the garage to hunt for her Bible, somewhere in an unpacked box. After opening several boxes marked BOOKS, she found it, dusted it off, and opened it up to the book of Genesis. At least she knew that much—the first book in the Bible. And there it was. *"Let there be light."*

Bee sat back on her heels, holding the Bible against her, like a shield. Once again, Fern's pithy words altered her entire perspective. She'd been dreading the cumulative effects of radiation, focused on the damage it would cause. She hadn't thought about the power of light to heal.

Eleven

Magdalena Riehl's bloated ankles worried Annie. The middle-aged Amish woman had come to Dok's office to get her blood pressure checked, which she'd been doing every week during this pregnancy, just as a precaution. She was a generously figured woman, jolly, always laughing. She liked to tease Annie about the boys in their church, asking which ones she thought she might be sweet on. Annie would shake her head vigorously, blushing, and then Magdalena would burst into peals of giggles. She found it amusing to embarrass Annie, whom she'd known since she was a girl. Sometimes Magdalena forgot that Annie wasn't a little girl anymore.

It was right after settling Magdalena into an exam room that Annie noticed the size of her swollen ankles. Huge veins stood out on Magdalena's feet like rivers. Were they quite so big last week? She wasn't sure.

Surely, Dok would notice.

But Dok was also exhausted from being up at night so often with the little foster baby in their home. So tired she was starting to make some mistakes. Saturday, she took a throat culture of a boy with strep throat and then wrote the previous patient's name on the test tube. Annie happened to catch the error before it went out to the lab. She could tell Dok was embarrassed.

Should she say something to Dok about Magdalena's ankles?

No. It wasn't Annie's place to point things out to Dok. Really, Magdalena was the one who should say something . . . although Annie knew she was the kind of person who would minimize any physical ailment.

She could tell Magdalena to point out her swollen ankles to Dok. Most likely, Magdalena wouldn't pay her any mind. To her, Annie was just a little girl.

Annie slipped the chart into the door pocket and went back to her desk. She heard Dok head into the exam room with Magdalena, and not much later, they both walked out, laughing over something. "Annie, please schedule next week's BP appointment for Magdalena."

Hank Lapp, sitting in the waiting room next to his wife Edith, a white bandage on his hand, overheard. "WHAT'S a BP?" Hank said.

Dok turned to him, pointing her finger at him. "Hank, du schteckt die Naas in alles." *You stick your nose in everything.*

Offended, Hank said, "I was only asking EDDY," before he coughed a few times.

Edith cast a side glance at him. "Blood pressure."

Dok noticed the white bandage on Hank's hand. "What happened to your hand?"

He held it up. "Got a little NIP from one of my birds. A FOUL fowl. Get it?" He laughed, which turned into a cough.

"Did you clean the bite well?"

"OF COURSE, Dok."

"Did he?" Dok looked to Edith for confirmation, who dipped her chin in a nod. Satisfied, she handed the chart to Annie.

Stilling, Annie didn't take the chart. Her eyes darted around the full waiting room, then down to Magdalena's ankles. "But what about . . . ?" she whispered.

Confused, Dok leaned in. "What about . . . *what*?"

Annie didn't feel comfortable in this position. First of all, modesty for Magdalena was in question. On top of that, she didn't want to sound as if she might be correcting Dok. Who did she think she was? Just an office assistant. A keeper of appointments. "Never mind."

"Annie," Dok said, slightly annoyed, "is there something you'd like to say?"

Yes, but not like this. Not in front of a roomful of nosy patients. Not in front of Edith and Hank Lapp. But Dok was watching her. Annie cupped her mouth so the other patients couldn't hear her. "What about her . . . you know?"

Magdalena drew closer. "What about my *what*?"

"Annie," Dok said, growing exasperated. "Speak up."

Annie whispered into Dok's ear. "What about her *ankles*?"

Dok stared at Annie for a moment, confused. "Ankles?" Then she pivoted, bent down, and lifted Magdalena's long blue dress to see her feet.

Hank gasped at the sight of those ankles—they were *that* big. "ENORMOUS! Eddy, what's that ELEPHANT MAN disease called?"

Dok dropped Magdalena's hem and scowled at Hank. "She's edematous, Hank. Not diseased."

"Ede . . . what?" Magdalena said.

Dok straightened. "Magdalena, please go back into the exam room." She took the chart out of Annie's hands. "Thank you."

Later, as Annie was cleaning up her desk, Dok came out, ready to head home for the day. She took her coat off the coat stand. "I'm grateful that you noticed Magdalena's ankles. Even more grateful that you pointed them out to me."

"They just didn't seem . . . quite right."

"No, they certainly did not."

"I was hoping she would ask you herself to take a look at them."

116

"She said she felt right as rain. Never better. But those ankles are a sign of a serious condition called—"

"Preeclampsia."

Dok stopped, surprised. "Where'd you learn about preeclampsia?"

Annie blushed and lowered her voice. "You know . . . my mother." Her mom knew a little about a lot, with symptoms for every possible disease. Over the years, Annie had learned a great deal about the human body and its diseases.

"Magdalena is starting to have symptoms of preeclampsia, which can be an extremely dangerous condition, both for her and the baby. I sent her home with orders to go straight to bed." Dok put a hand on Annie's shoulder. "You have good instincts, Annie. I just wish you'd have more confidence in yourself. Speak up when you see a problem. You have my full permission to point something out. I appreciate it." She yawned. "Speaking of, while Hank and Edith Lapp were in the waiting room, did you happen to notice if he coughed very much?"

"I didn't, actually." The appointment had been for Edith's itchy eczema. Annie heard plenty about that. Puh-lenty.

Dok yawned. "I need to get home."

As Dok put on her coat, Annie held her medical bag for her. "Is baby Gabe gaining weight?"

"He certainly is! I've been able to let him sleep for three-hour stretches now, which feels like Heaven. I have to admit that he is a sweet-natured baby. He's starting to smile. And lifting his head! Did I tell you?"

She had, actually. Twice. In fact, Dok arrived each day at the office with new baby updates. At first, Annie thought Dok talked about the baby the way someone described a dinner guest who had overstayed his welcome. Now, she reminded Annie of how women bragged about their babies. Like that saying "Every mother crow thinks their own crow is the blackest." "Still no sign of the mother?"

"No, thank goodness."

That, too, was a change in Dok's thinking. Not so long ago, she wanted the mother to show up, get clean and sober, and take responsibility for her child.

"No word from the caseworker, either." Dok yawned again. "Hopefully, it won't be long before she finds a permanent foster family for baby Gabe." She turned out the lights and locked the door behind Annie. "Well, thank you again for bringing Magdalena's ankles to my attention. And Saturday's strep throat patient. I don't know what I'd do without you."

If Dok hadn't yawned again, right at that moment, Annie was going to tell her that she was thinking of becoming an EMT. But Dok looked tired, like she just wanted to get home and go to bed, and Annie was catching a ride home with Sarah over at the Bent N' Dent, and the timing just seemed wrong.

That was the problem, right there. The timing always seemed wrong.

Damon positioned his truck smack-dab behind Bee's car in the driveway, effectively trapping her from leaving. He stood by his truck, prepared to chauffeur her to the first radiation appointment. Bee was furious! She told him to please move his truck, but the stubborn mule wouldn't budge. Faced with the looming specter of lateness, with the anxiety of starting Day One of radiation, Bee's resolve started to crumble.

Would it be so terrible to just let him drive her?

Fine, she decided with a long sigh. *He wants to help? So let him help.* What other choice did she have? Her car was trapped. *She* was trapped.

She slid into Damon's passenger seat, arms crossed, her gaze fixed outside the window. He appeared unshaken by her icy demeanor. He asked no questions, offered no idle chitchat. He dropped her in front of the building and reappeared again when she texted him after the appointment. It was a silent ride home.

As the day unfolded, Bee contemplated her choices. Parking near the building where the radiation treatments would take place would be a daily headache. The repaving project had turned the vicinity into a maze of congestion. If she insisted on driving herself, she'd need to budget an extra hour. Maybe more. And the bottom line was that she wanted to minimize the whole experience of "getting zapped." She didn't want to leave an hour early or have to walk a distance to get to her car. Get in, get out, get home. That was her goal. Minimal fuss, minimal interaction, minimal delay.

In the grand scheme of things, the act of getting zapped wasn't all that terrible. The technicians conducted themselves with utmost professionalism, their kindness evident in their swift efficiency. The actual zapping, the part Bee had dreaded most, consumed no more than a mere ten to fifteen minutes.

In the end, practicality triumphed. Bee decided she would accept Damon's role as her chauffeur—silent, solemn, brooding.

Or maybe that was her.

Dok was starting to feel like herself again. Baby Gabe was quickly gaining weight, which meant night feedings could be stretched out. She hadn't called the baby's caseworker for an update on a permanent foster home in three days. Besides, it didn't make any difference to call—the caseworker rarely returned her calls, anyway.

Those few times the caseworker did return her call, she assured Dok that she was looking hard for a home that might be open to adoption. In most of these cases, she told Dok, when a biological parent never appears for any court dates, the state moves to sever parental rights and take guardianship of the child. "That's why it's taking so long," the caseworker said. "I want to find the perfect forever family for this baby."

Right. And when would that be? After Dok voiced that question aloud, the caseworker ended the call with an abrupt, "As long as it takes."

Time was passing. Matt had used up his vacation time so he requested an unpaid leave of absence. Dok didn't object to that. If Matt wanted to take a break from work, he had every right to.

All in all, Dok felt pretty good about how they had given this little abandoned baby a good start in life after a very rocky arrival. Soon, she hoped, he would be transferred to a loving home, one which might be open for adoption. A forever family. And then Dok and Matt's life could go back the way it was. That's how Dok assumed things would roll out, anyway.

Until last night, when Matt brought up adoption.

Twelve

Dok came out of the exam room and handed Annie a file. "Why do boys stick things up their nose? Always boys. Never girls."

A smile lit Annie's face. "I thought Ethan Yoder put gum in his ear."

"Today, that's exactly what he did. But last time he stuck a bean up his nose."

Annie handed her a slip of paper. "How did you manage to get the gum out of Ethan's ear?"

"Tweezers." Dok rolled her eyes. "Long ones." She shook her head. "Always, always the boys."

And the bigger they grew, the more trouble they sought. Each summer, Dok could count on a boy who'd just graduated from high school getting seriously injured or even killed in a preventable accident. Every single summer. Teenaged boys considered themselves to be invincible. It was one of the many cons on the list she'd made about why they shouldn't adopt baby Gabe. Boys had a need for speed . . . and by the time Gabe would be of driving age, she and Matt would be slowing way, way down. A recipe for disaster.

She'd told him so when she stopped at home for lunch. Of course, Matt had counterattacked her con list. He accused her of lumping all boys together, of having a bias against boys' judgment (which she did), of borrowing trouble, of leaping forward two decades, and then he ended on a hard-to-dispute closing argument. He reminded her that a great God could be trusted with the needs of an eighteen-year-old boy despite his aging parents. Frankly, despite parents of any age.

Heading back to her office, Dok let out an exasperated sigh, thinking about this ongoing adoption discussion. Matt was determined. She was less so. Not entirely closed to it, but not at all convinced it was the right thing to do—for Gabe's sake as well as for theirs. She still had doubts about their ability to adjust to parenting, especially at their age, but she no longer had doubts about their capacity to love Gabe like he was their own. The longer the baby was in their home, the more attached they were growing to him.

From the first day, Matt had been smitten by baby Gabe. To her shock, Dok wasn't far behind. The baby continued to have a mellow, easygoing temperament. The thought of giving the baby over to be adopted by others, even to a forever family, had started to make her feel uneasy. She and Matt might be on the downhill side of middle age, but it also meant they were financially stable, able to provide for a child, to educate him, to expose him to a world full of possibilities. Just yesterday, Matt and the baby spent the day at a petting zoo.

Late in the day, gazing out her office window, Dok could see the light snow that had been predicted had started to fall, dusting the empty parking lot like talcum powder. The Bent N' Dent looked closed, no horses and buggies were at the hitching post. As she watched, a gust of wind blew snow sideways. She smiled. Amish farmers could forecast the weather better than satellites or Doppler radar. If the Amish weren't out and about, this storm was going to be a doozy.

The last two patients for the day had already canceled their appointments, so Dok closed the office early, dropped Annie off at home, and headed home herself, driving carefully through the swirling snow. She peered up at the gray sky through the windshield. When would spring ever arrive?

She turned on her headlights and picked up a little speed, eager to get home. A smile started slow and spread wide as she thought of the look on Matt's face when she would walk through the door. It was the second time this week that she had made it home in time for the baby's baths and she was rather proud of herself.

Such thinking was new to her. Dok had spent her entire adult life focused on her work—everything else came second. Relationships, especially. Work had always been enough for her. Until lately. She kept trying to get home early to spend the evenings with Matt and the baby.

This morning, Dok had caught herself thinking about growing a garden this summer and had no idea where that thought came from. She'd never had a garden. She certainly didn't need any vegetables. She never left a house call at an Amish farm without a basketful of tomatoes or squash. Even if she said no, they would insist, foisting the basket into her arms. Followed by a gentle reminder to return the basket.

Last night, Dok had brought up the idea of inviting Bee Bennett over for Sunday dinner sometime.

Matt had looked at her as if she might be coming down with something. "You want to invite someone over to our house for dinner?"

"Yes. Why? Don't you think she'd appreciate a home-cooked meal? I've bragged about your cooking."

"I'm not thinking about Bee. It's you. Ruth, you have never, ever, ever initiated having dinner guests. Not once. Each time I've brought it up, you've shot it down."

"Not shot it down! I just . . . thought we should wait until the house remodel was done."

"It's not done. Nowhere near done."

She looked around the family room. There'd been some progress in the last few weeks, and it was looking less like a construction site. But holding off until the house was completely done didn't seem important anymore. "I thought we might also invite your trainer friend who's helping Bee, but then I worried either of them might think it was an attempt at matchmaking. I stay far away from that line of work."

Matt seesawed his hand in the air. "I don't know the backstory between them, but I get the sense that they've got some history. Not the good kind."

"I've had that same feeling. Like, Bee appreciates this guy's help with her horses, but she's eager for him to move on." Or maybe Bee was just eager to move on from breast cancer and all that went with it. Dok really didn't know Bee very well, but she'd like to get better acquainted, as friends. She could use a friend.

That, too, was new thinking to Dok. Matt was much better at friendships than she was. Someone once described Dok as a woman with minimal social needs. It was such an odd thought, one that still rankled her. She'd grown up Amish, where community touched every part of life. You couldn't avoid being social, nor did you want to. Besides, when did "social needs" become a thing?

Still, it was true that Dok had never really cultivated friendships nor felt the need to. She worked alongside colleagues, she treated patients, plus her brother David often acted as her sounding board, as did her husband Matt. But she didn't have the kind of friend to call to see a movie together or do some shopping. Then again, she didn't do those kinds of leisure activities.

Maybe she should. Maybe this was the "fun" that Matt thought they needed more of in their marriage. Fun had never been a priority for Dok. After Matt had pointed that out, she started to wonder what fun might look like for her. And that's how the whole gardening/Bee-for-dinner idea got started. The more she thought about fun, the more fun things she thought of, the more longing she had for it. The sense that she'd been missing something kept growing stronger.

She turned onto Ronks Road, squinting through the fast-moving windshield wipers. The snow was piling up along the roadside. She let out a puff of air. Nearly home.

Pulling into the driveway, she saw that Matt had already turned on the exterior porch light for her. She paused for a moment, watching Matt framed in the kitchen window, baby nestled in a carrier against his chest, stirring something in a big mixing bowl. His famous chocolate chip cookies, she hoped.

It was good to be home.

Thick snow covered the countryside. Annie had gone down to the phone shanty as the sun started to light the sky and listened for messages. Just as she had thought, Dok called to cancel the day's appointments. Using her flashlight to go through her appointment book, Annie left messages for each patient and told them to call the office tomorrow to reschedule. By the time she'd finished the list, the sun was up. She clicked off her flashlight and left the shanty. The slant of the morning sun glinted off the snowy fields, so bright it made her eyes water.

Halfway up the driveway, Annie stopped and lifted her head, turning in a big circle. She loved the morning after a snowfall. The whole of Stoney Ridge seemed to have a heavy blanket spread over it, muffling all distractions. The air was so clean, the sky so blue, the farm so peaceful. And so, so quiet. It was stunning how silent the farm was after a snowfall. Any sound, like the whinny of a horse or screech of a hawk, was magnified tenfold.

Slowly, it dawned on Annie that she had a full day alone, all to herself.

But her mother didn't know that. Her father didn't know that.

While she'd been in the phone shanty, she'd seen them leave the house in the buggy fitted with skis. They'd finished morning chores early to spend the day over at Ben and Penny Zook's, to help them get their house ready for hosting Sunday church. If her mother knew that Dok had closed the office for the day, she would expect Annie to come to the Zooks' and help out.

And if her dad knew she wasn't at Dok's today, he would expect her help with the dairy. Milking a dozen cows twice a day, even with a generator-fed milking pump, was exhausting work. Morning and night, her dad carried out the same chores, over and over. The only shortcut he ever took was to leave the morning mess the cows in the stanchions left behind during milking. He'd get to it later in the day.

Most likely, Dad would've used that shortcut this morning. He would've been in a rush to get to the Zooks', intent on getting the milk cans emptied into the bulk tank. Today was pickup day for the milk company truck, assuming the roads would be plowed. If her dad knew she wasn't at Dok's, he'd expect her to shovel and haul the manure out to the pit. Horrible. An absolutely horrible task.

But Dad didn't know. Mom didn't know. And, most likely, they wouldn't ask. Right from the start, Annie had been extremely tight-lipped about Dok's office—zealously guarding doctor-patient confidentiality—so that her parents had given up asking anything other than if she'd had a good day.

So she wouldn't be lying. She just couldn't lie to anyone. But she wouldn't be volunteering the truth. That was how she justified certain things that were important to her, like getting her GED.

Annie hardly ever had a day all to herself. It happened once in a blue moon. And today, she knew just what she wanted to do. She cut a path right through the snow to the barn and went inside, breathing deeply of the warm scent of horses and cows and hay. She grabbed a bridle off the wall and went to the stall of her favorite horse, a giant Percheron with hooves the size of dinner plates. He nickered when he saw her, like he'd been missing her.

When her older brothers still lived at home, Annie would hop on a horse, bareback, to bring messages out to the fields, or deliver a jug of water. More often than not, she would take her sweet time getting back to the house, choosing the long way back through the woods. This morning, she wanted to go on a long ride. She knew all the shortcuts through farmers' fields, knew where each gate was and where there were no fences at all. On a horse as big as this one, she could ride for hours and hours, even in deep snow. The big horse dipped his head low so she could easily slip the bridle on.

A grin spread over her face, ear to ear. Today was turning into a perfect day.

Bee Bennett hung up the phone, so frustrated she slapped her hands on the counter. The Lancaster County snowplows weren't able to get to outlying towns like Stoney Ridge until later this afternoon. And that meant she would miss her radiation treatment this morning! She couldn't stand the thought of prolonging it by one more day. She called the scheduler to ask if her appointment could get pushed back a few hours, but the irritable-sounding woman said the afternoon was booked solid. Bee begged. The heartless woman was unmoved.

Bee could've cried. She knew in the grand scheme of things, it was a minor glitch. Still, it was a disappointing minor glitch.

From somewhere outside she heard the sound of a car door slamming shut. Hurrying to the living room window, she peered out to see Damon's truck in her driveway. In a flash, she was out the door. "How did you get through the roads?"

"Four-wheel drive," he said with a shrug, like it was no big deal. "I'll feed the horses. You better go get dressed."

"You think we can still make the appointment?"

"Not if you keep standing out here in your bunny slippers." His eyes swept her from head to toe.

Bee was wearing a big thick robe but suddenly felt as self-conscious as if she were in a skimpy bathing suit, like a line of intimacy had just been crossed. As she started to pivot to head back inside, something big and dark dashed behind Damon's truck. She lifted her arm and pointed, speechless. He spun around and saw it too. They watched until it disappeared. He turned back to Bee, his eyes wide and clear. "Was that what I think it was?"

She nodded. "An Amish girl on the back of a Percheron."

A smile broke over his face, and she couldn't help but smile too. They stood there for a while, grinning at each other, soaking up the moment.

Then he had to go and spoil it. "You're heating the whole outdoors." He headed off to the barn and she scurried into the house, closing the door behind her.

But she couldn't stop smiling. The day was looking up.

Thirteen

Over the years, Dok had delivered hundreds of babies. She might not remember all the babies she had helped to guide into the world, but she could definitely recall every time when a situation didn't end in the typical joy of welcoming a healthy newborn. Tonight felt like it might be one of those.

Dok had been woken out of a deep sleep by a phone call from a gruff voice, which said tersely, "Baby's coming. You'd better get on over here."

"Whose baby?" Dok had said, blinking to clear her eyes as she peered at the clock on the nightstand beyond Matt's snoring body.

"Magdalena's," the husband said and hung up.

Too soon, too soon. Magdalena wasn't due to deliver for six more weeks. This was her seventh child. Most likely, labor would progress quickly.

Wide awake, Dok bolted out of bed and called for an ambulance to meet her at the Riehls' home. Not a minute later, she was out the door. The car headlights shone on the dark, curving road as she drove as fast as she dared, hoping to get to the Amish farmhouse before the ambulance arrived. The roads had been cleared of snow, and the full moon reflected off white

129

fields so brightly that she hardly needed her headlights on, but the last thing she wanted to do was to hit a patch of black ice.

As she passed by the Fisher farm, she could see the swing of a lit lantern crossing from house to barn, as Eli Fisher headed to the barn to start the day's first milking. For a split second, she considered turning up the Fisher driveway to fetch Annie, but she didn't have a minute to spare. The ambulance was on its way to get Magdalena to the hospital, hopefully before this baby arrived. Dok didn't want to jeopardize this situation with a home birth. The baby would be premature; its lungs weren't fully developed. And then there was Magdalena's precarious condition.

Dok did her best to keep her patients at home and only insisted on hospitalization when she had no other choice. Like now. She braced herself for pushback from Magdalena, and even more from her husband. She could practically hear Jonas tick off the reasons: not necessary, too costly, she'd had other babies at home, on and on. He had no idea how serious this situation could be.

Jonas was a caring man. Dok saw him around town or on the farm, always a child or two sitting beside him as he worked. Yet in so many ways, he was the opposite of Magdalena. She was a large, round woman, filling her dresses well, even without being in the family way. Maternity clothes weren't part of the culture of the Amish. Their dresses and aprons were big enough that they could just expand the waistline's straight pins as the pregnancy advanced. Jonas was a wisp of a man, no more than five feet five inches, and he couldn't weigh more than one hundred and twenty pounds. Even his beard was wispy—like hay stubble that jutted from his chin. Magdalena was as chatty as a magpie, Jonas's words were few. He scarcely looked at Dok when she spoke with him. So strange, Dok thought, what attracted two people to each other.

Turning onto a winding road that led to the Riehls', she saw the flashing lights of an ambulance already up at the farmhouse. Her heart started to pound. She'd hoped to beat it here. Jonas would be furious; she could imagine him not letting them into the house, sending them on their way. She could even imagine him telling them they had the wrong house, because in his mind, they *were* at the wrong house.

Dok worried that Magdalena's children would be woken by the lights of the ambulance, frightened to see their mother taken away without any understanding of what was going on. It was common for Amish children not to be told that their mothers were expecting a baby. When the time of labor came, they'd be sent off to grandparents at the nearby Grossdawdi Haus or to a neighbor's home. There was a sanctity connected to giving birth in this culture, one Dok understood and respected.

But she didn't have any doubt that this was the right course of action. The lives of mother and baby were at stake.

Dok felt her stomach clench. She wondered now if she should have sent Magdalena straight to the hospital when she last saw her. With Magdalena, she'd been on the fence. What she needed was bed rest, and that's exactly what Dok ordered her to do: Go straight to bed.

Had she listened? Had Jonas?

Dok would never forgive herself if she'd made a mistake that jeopardized the life of a patient, including the life of her baby. These were the moments when she was so pitifully aware of her shortcomings as a doctor. But she'd been in the medical world long enough, and seen enough, to know that no one should put all their trust in a doctor. Any doctor. They were only human. These were the moments she would lift a hand in prayer, for the Lord's protection for Magdalena and this little one who was on its way ahead of schedule.

"Lord, you are the Great Physician. Please protect Magdalena, protect her baby. Be the doctor that I can't be." She swiftly veered to the right, steering onto the lengthy driveway, which was bordered on either side by a yawning trench, a freshly painted white board fence, and a line of gnarled maple trees.

A paramedic met Dok as she grabbed her bag and got out of her car. "Glad you're here. The farmer told us to go away."

"Don't listen to him," Dok said.

The paramedic smiled. "So what are we looking at?"

"Patient with possible preeclampsia," Dok said. "Thirty-four weeks gestation. Patient's labor has started, but I won't know how close she is to delivering until I get in there."

"Just let us know what you need."

Inside the house, Dok was met by Jonas, who looked quite pale, even in the dim lighting. "Which way?"

Jonas's stocking feet padded soundlessly across the cold linoleum as he led Dok to their bedroom.

"Hi there," Dok said softly when she approached her patient in the bed. "I'm here now. And I think your baby is in a hurry to meet you."

Magdalena, relieved, gave Dok a weary smile. "It's too soon."

"It's soon, but not too soon. We're going to do everything we can to make sure the baby gets everything he needs. And you too. I'd like to get you to the hospital."

Jonas jutted out his long beard. "Nee." *No.*

"Nee!" Magdalena grabbed Dok's hand. "Nee! Sis mer bang." *I'm frightened.* She let out a moan as a contraction shuddered through her body.

Dok was prepared for Jonas's stubbornness, but she hadn't anticipated Magdalena's resistance. Insisting on a hospital birth could raise her blood pressure to an even more dangerous rate. Time to pivot, she thought, stroking Magdalena's forehead. "Du brauschscht ken Bang hawwe, die Dok gebt Ach tuff dich." *You need not be afraid, Dok is watching out for you.*

Dok turned to the paramedic who had followed behind her. "Start an IV."

While he traced Magdalena's arm for a raised vein, Dok

pulled out a package of sterile gloves, an obstetrics kit that contained clamps and scissors, a bulb syringe, and a few other instruments. She turned to see if the paramedic had an IV line in yet. In one quick motion, he jabbed the needle beneath her pale skin. *Good.* That would help keep her hydrated.

"Jonas, I need more light." There was one Coleman lantern in the room, giving off odd shadows. "And get Magdalena a glass of water." She turned to Magdalena. "How do you feel? Any headache?"

"Just a little one. Not too bad."

Dok wasn't sure if Magdalena would ever admit how poorly she felt. After checking her BP and pulse, Dok laid a disposable bed pad underneath Magdalena, and did a quick exam. With the telltale bulge of the perineum, she knew delivery was imminent.

Jonas went to the other room and brought back two more lanterns and a glass of water.

"Drink up," Dok said.

Magdalena refused the water. "I can't."

"Drink it," Dok said firmly. "It'll help your body get rid of excess fluids." While Magdalena's blood pressure was high but not alarmingly so, Dok wasn't taking any chances with preeclampsia. She examined Magdalena again and wondered why labor wasn't making much progress. That baby needed to arrive, for his mother's sake as well as his own.

Dawn had barely broken when Annie's dad came into the kitchen to tell her Dok had left a message on the machine in the shanty. "She's on a house call," Dad said. "She said she'll be coming in late to the office today."

Buttering toast, Annie looked up. She wondered whose house she'd gone on a call to. Whatever problem someone was having, Dok would fix it. She always did. "Did she say how late she'd be?"

"She said she's hoping to be there by nine," Dad said.

Oh boy. Annie knew what that meant. Nine o'clock with Dok meant ten o'clock, if not eleven. She pulled on a winter coat and went down to the phone shanty with the day's appointment book in hand to leave messages for the first patients of the morning, asking them to call the office after ten or eleven o'clock to reschedule.

Since she had a little extra time this morning, she offered to help her mother hang laundry. It was a cold, windy day, terrible for laundry, terrible for conversation. She should have known it was the wrong time to bring up something as serious as this topic. "Mom," she said, "I've been enjoying my work at Dok's."

"Good, good," her mother said, distracted by a wet towel that kept falling off the line.

"So much so that I've wondered about doing a little more at Dok's."

Her mother stopped short in surprise. A flapping towel slapped her in the face, and she grabbed it, reclipping it with hard, jerky motions. Her short fuse with the towel should have tipped Annie off to stop right there. "Your hours at Dok's are plenty long. I don't like this Saturday work. How will you ever meet someone?" She stopped to face Annie. "Since we're on the topic—"

Ugh . . . *that* was a topic Annie was eager to dodge.

"—I spoke to Cousin Gloria. She wants you to meet a boy from her church. He's supposed to be real nice. Likes to help people, she said."

No thank you. Cousin Gloria was the world's worst matchmaker. The last boy she set up for Annie to meet with, cleverly coordinated by her mother, wasn't a boy at all but a middle-aged widower with seven children, eager to find a stepmother for his brood. *No thank you, Cousin Gloria.* As her apron flew up, she smoothed it down and pinned a clothespin to the bottom edge to weigh it down in the wind, using the interruption to change the subject. "Mom, I didn't mean more hours at Dok's office. I meant doing more."

"Well, Dad's counting on you to help plant the fields come spring. Be sure to remind Dok that you're only working through March. She needs to start looking for someone to replace you." She turned her head to look at the fields, covered with hard frost. "If spring ever comes, that is. Dad thinks it'll be April before the ground isn't so frozen solid that a plow gets stuck." She reached down for another wet towel and stopped suddenly, clutching her heart. "I think I might have that . . . that racing heart syndrome."

"Tachycardia?"

"Yes! That's exactly it. Cousin Gloria told me she thinks she might have it too. Those things can be genetic, you know."

Of course. Gloria always handed Mom something new to find, then fret over. "Where does Gloria hear about so many terrible things?"

"From her neighbor's son, she said. He tells her all kinds of stories."

Annie rolled her eyes.

"I should probably make an appointment at Dok's, don't you think? Could you fit me into her schedule today? All those canceled appointments this morning must mean there's some openings. Nicht waahr?" *Isn't that true?*

Annie took in a long breath. She had wanted to test the waters about becoming an EMT with her mother before she went to her dad or the bishop or Dok, but she should've given more thought on how to address it. Or when. Her mother seemed particularly distracted from Cousin Gloria's call this morning.

Annie forged ahead. "Some Amish have gotten more skills. Ruthie Stoltzfus, for example. The bishop's own daughter."

Her mother paused and turned toward her, a look of repulsion on her face. "You want to be like Ruthie and draw blood out of people? What's that job called, anyhow?"

"A phlebotomist. But no, that's not exactly the kind of job I'm interested in." A gust of wind blew the towels sideways, nearly right off their pins. A shiver ran down Annie's spine, but it had more to do with this conversation than with the cold. "There's a position called an emergency medical technician. An EMT."

Mom's lips tightened into a straight line. She returned to hanging another towel, her movements sharp, fitful, irritated.

"Mom, there are Amish who are EMTs. Do you remember when Sarah cracked through the ice and fell into the pond? An Amish EMT arrived in the ambulance."

Mom picked up a towel and forced a clothespin on it. "I knew it was a mistake to have you work at Dok's. I just knew it."

This wasn't going well. Annie should've changed the subject, right then and there. But she didn't. She'd already put a toe in the water . . . she might as well step into it with her whole foot. "That's what EMTs do, Mom. They learn skills to help people in emergencies. They're not doctors. They're not even paramedics. But they provide an important service. Like, when Sarah fell in the water, this EMT was the one who pulled her out, and got her into the ambulance, and got her out of her cold wet clothes and—" Perhaps that had not been quite the right thing to say.

Her mother looked at her, eyes wide with horror. "Annie, are you trying to put me in an early grave?"

"No! Of course not. It's just something I've been interested in. I thought, maybe, one day, I might have a talk with the bishop about it." Though the very thought of approaching the bishop about such an unusual topic was terrifying to Annie. Frankly, talking to the bishop for any reason at all was something she avoided. As nice as David Stoltzfus was, and even though he was Dok's brother, Annie could never forget that he was still the bishop.

"You'll do nothing of the kind." Mom jammed the clothespin on the last towel.

"But why? What is so wrong with wanting to pursue work that you love?"

"Family comes first. That's that. Let's have no more talk of this." Mom picked up the empty laundry basket and started toward the house. Halfway there, she turned and put a hand on her heart. "Don't forget to make an appointment for me. First thing. This tacky card is really acting up."

Annie wasn't ready to give up. "I don't see why I can't do both. Love my family and love my work."

Her mother put a fisted hand on her hip. "Annie, not a single boy in our church would be interested in a girl who spends her days riding around in an ambulance, encountering all kinds of evils and horrors. Not a single boy in our church. Not *any* Plain church." Mom turned and went up the steps into the kitchen.

Annie sighed. Frankly, there was some truth to her mother's remark. Most of the young men she knew would frown on it. But on the other hand, she wasn't interested in getting to know any young man who'd squelch a God-given calling to want to help people in need.

The kitchen door opened again and Mom's face appeared. "Edith Lapp said that Hank thought he saw you riding Buster through his yard the other day. Could that be true?"

Annie opened her mouth, then shut it. She couldn't lie. "Mom, when the boys lived at home, I used to ride Buster a lot."

Her mother looked like she was about to explode. "That was when you were a girl. You're a grown woman!" The door closed behind her with a firm bang.

Exactly, Annie thought. *That's exactly right. That's pretty much what I've been trying to tell you this whole time. I'm a grown woman now.*

Dok massaged Magdalena's back, trying to help her relax. It seemed as if her body didn't want to release this baby.

"Fer was?" Magdalena said. *What's all this for?*

Dok looked up to see the paramedic at the door, waiting patiently with an evacuation crib for the baby. "The paramedic has equipment ready. The baby will need to be in the hospital for a while. The baby's lungs will need a little help until they're completely developed."

Jonas held Magdalena's hand and looked at Dok. "Don't you worry, Maggie. We'll take care of the baby right here."

Dok gave him a sharp look. "The baby will need to be cared for in the hospital. Magdalena too."

"Zammer?" Magdalena whispered. *Together?*

"Ya, zammer," Dok said.

In between another contraction, Magdalena said, "Kann er weckgange?" *Can he leave?*

"Jonas?" Usually, Amish women wanted their husbands by their sides during birth.

"Nee. Der anner." *No. That one.*

Dok caught the paramedic's eye. "Perhaps he could wait outside until I call for him." The paramedic nodded and pushed the crib toward the end of the bed, then stepped outside the room, though he left the door slightly ajar.

Inwardly, Dok cringed. Two signals, loud and clear, and she had missed them both. She should've realized why Magdalena was holding back from delivering this baby. Even though the paramedic was a trained professional, modesty was *that* en-grained into an Amish woman. His presence, standing there with an evacuation crib, gave Magdalena the impression that the baby would be whisked away from her.

Magdalena let out a loud cry.

"Baby's coming," Dok said, guiding the baby's head. "Give me one more good push."

With a whoosh, the baby slid into Dok's hands. Under the white, cheesy coating, his skin was a foreboding dark blue. A silent tension gripped the room. Dok took a cloth and rubbed the baby, and suddenly he gasped, sneezed, and took in a deep breath. Immediately his color changed, brightened to a soft pink. Dok cut the umbilical cord, swaddled the baby, showed Magdalena her new son, and then called in the paramedic to hand him over. "You'll see him again soon." Then she returned to the end of the bed to wait for the afterbirth. Right at that moment, Magdalena's eyes rolled back and her body started twitching.

Dok grabbed a vial of magnesium sulfate from her bag and injected a loading dose into the IV.

"What's that?" Jonas said, his voice up an octave. "What's happening?"

"This is an anticonvulsant," Dok said, keeping her voice low and calm, though she felt anything but. "Magdalena's having a seizure. We're going to get her to the hospital."

The seizure subsided as the medication took effect. Within minutes, Magdalena and her baby were in the ambulance and on the way to the hospital. Walking fast to her car, Dok explained to Jonas that she was following the ambulance to the hospital and would call with an update.

Jonas trotted behind her, still in his stocking feet. "What should I do?" He looked bewildered.

Dok felt a touch of empathy for him. He couldn't leave the house because of sleeping children, yet he seemed to finally understand that the lives of his wife and newborn son were in danger.

Dok put a hand on his thin shoulder. "You pray."

Fourteen

Right on the dot, nine o'clock in the morning, Annie arrived to a locked door at Dok's office. These were the times when Annie wished she could use one of those smartphones, just for work, just so Dok could let her know where she was and when she'd be coming back.

She also wished Dok would give her a key so she could get into the office, but apparently a previous office assistant (who happened to be Lydie Stoltzfus, the bishop's own daughter, of *all* people!) had been sloppy one day and left Mick Yoder unattended in the office while she ran over to the Bent N' Dent. Mick, whom everyone knew was a troublemaker, had stolen a drug out of Dok's supply. Drugs that turned out to be nothing but baking soda, not the recreational type of drug Mick was after, but all the same, Dok said she was not going to let that kind of thing happen again. Ever, ever, ever. Since that near-disastrous experience, she insisted on opening and closing the office herself.

Annie would never be sloppy with Dok's office. Never. Still, she respected Dok's office rules and didn't question them. Besides, Dok assumed she was only working there through March. And if Annie could bring herself to apply to the EMT program that started in March, then Dok's assumption would be right. She wouldn't be there much longer.

She thought about heading over to the Bent N' Dent, but a big group of graybeards had just arrived to play checkers by the warm woodstove. So she sat on the office stoop, shivering, chin down, the wind against her, hoping Dok would come soon. How could it be so sunny and still so cold?

A few minutes later, the bishop came out of the Bent N' Dent and shielded his eyes as he looked over at Dok's office, noticing Annie on the stoop. "Just heard from Dok," he said as he approached her. "She's at the hospital. She'll be a while longer. She said she'd try to get to the office by noon."

Noon? Not until noon. *Oh boy.* That probably meant one or two o'clock. Dok's timing was always off.

"Annie, would you like to come in and get warm at the store?"

"Thank you, but I might come back later." There. It came out in a whisper, but she had actually spoken eight words in a row to the bishop. She was proud of herself.

To her dismay, the bishop sat down next to her. Talking to the bishop was top on her list of things to avoid.

"So, Annie, I haven't had a chance to ask how you're enjoying the work at Dok's. You might not remember but my daughter Ruthie was Dok's first office assistant. She loved it. I think she would still be there if she weren't so busy with her children. And, of course, you know about my daughter Lydie's time working at Dok's. She loved it too. Learned so much about herself under Dok's tutelage."

As he spoke, his eyes were on a bright red male cardinal in a nearby tree, which helped Annie relax a bit. She wasn't really sure if he had asked her a question or not, so she didn't say anything. The bishop kept on talking, not like a bishop but like a family friend. Like a kindly uncle. She glanced sideways at him, noticing how many ways he and Dok resembled each other as siblings. The same strawberry-colored hair, the same warm blue eyes. Even their hands were similar—long, tapered fingers. It surprised her to realize the bishop didn't have big hands like so many farmers, but then again, he'd never been a farmer. He was a shop owner.

He wrapped those hands around a bent knee. "I'm sure I don't need to tell you how important Dok's work is to our people. She makes a big difference in this town. People count on her. And then she's taken on fostering the baby too. Another important job." He bent the other knee and rubbed both calves. The concrete stoop was as cold as the air around them. "Annie, I was wondering if you might like me to speak to your father about letting you stay on during spring planting. I'm well aware that he expects you to stop working soon. Your mother reminds me of it whenever I see her. But I also know that you've been a wonderful help to Dok. She's told me how much she depends on you. Appreciates you. She says you have just the right temperament for handling patients."

Annie sat straight up. Her heart started to pound. Little steps, little steps. This was it! The moment to speak up. *Go for it*, she told herself. *Now's the time! Speak up, Annie Fisher! Spill.*

But how? How could she explain to a bishop that she sensed God had talked to her? That God had told her to become an EMT?

Even if there were some Amish who had become EMTs, no one in their Stoney Ridge church had ever been one. And to tell the bishop—the bishop!—that God had spoken to her . . . how would he respond to *that*? The whole thought made Annie feel queasy.

Time stretched out. Annie said nothing. Words floated through her mind but not together in a sentence. Not in a way that made any sense.

Apparently giving up on her, the bishop rubbed his hands

together. "Well, I guess I'd better get over to the store." He rose to his feet. "If you think you'd like me to speak to your father, just let me know."

Out of Annie burst, "Yes! Please."

The bishop turned and looked at her in surprise. "I'll be sure to do it, then." He smiled. "You know how that saying goes—you can't say no to a bishop."

No? That might be true for Annie's dad, but her mom sure could.

Dok knew going to the hospital with Magdalena would scramble the morning for her patients, for Annie, for her. She'd called David and asked him to get a message to Annie that she'd be there by noon. She wasn't going to leave the hospital until she was able to tell Jonas that Magdalena and the baby were admitted, settled, and stable.

After she spoke to Jonas, she stopped by the NICU one more time to check on the baby's vitals. He was so tiny, only three pounds, hooked up to the ventilator and other beeping machines and monitors. His closed eyes protruded, and his skin was pale blue. He'd need specialized treatments until his lungs developed. She watched him as he struggled to take in labored breaths. Silently, she said a prayer over him, thinking how wanted this little child was by his parents and what a happy life awaited him. Brothers and sisters and grandparents and scads of aunts, uncles, and cousins. By now, the message of his birth would have started to travel, and dozens, maybe hundreds, of people would be praying for this little one.

Her mind traveled to baby Gabe, abandoned by a teen mother who was trapped in a life of drug addiction, with no father to speak of. And suddenly Dok felt a sweeping tenderness for baby Gabe, an overwhelmingly maternal feeling, something she hadn't yet experienced for him. She'd felt responsibility and obligation and duty, but not love. Matt had loved him from the start. But not Dok.

When Matt had first brought up the idea of adopting Gabe, Dok shut it down, hard and fast. *We're too old. We have demanding careers. The baby deserves a family, brothers and sisters.*

Matt couldn't deny that everything she said was true. "Even still, I just feel this is something God wants us to do. A calling."

Not fair. So not fair. How did you argue against *that*? Pulling such a card made Dok mad. "If God wants us to adopt Gabe," she told Matt in a tight voice, "then he's going to have to let me know about that. Because I haven't gotten that call yet."

Typical of Matt, he didn't lash back. He nodded, as if he understood. "I'm praying about it, and I hope you will too. We're in this together, Ruth. If you aren't on board with this, then that's the answer."

Dok knew Matt had been praying fervently that her heart would be changed, just like she'd been praying fervently that the caseworker would find a forever family for Gabe. In that moment, standing in the NICU, watching Magdalena's baby struggle for his life, Matt's prayers seemed to be overriding hers. She might've heard the faint whisper of a call . . . but for now she thought she'd just let it ring.

No sooner had the bishop walked away but Hank Lapp's buggy rolled into the parking lot. He waved at her from the open window. "ANNIE! ANNIE! Just the person I need to see. STAY PUT!"

She watched Hank as he climbed out of the buggy. Was it just her imagination or was he moving a lot slower than normal? Stiff, awkward, like he'd aged ten years in the last week.

Hank finished tethering the horse's reins to the hitching post and came toward her. It wasn't her imagination. He was definitely moving like everything hurt. "Hank, are you okay?"

He stopped to cough, so long and hard that he bent over, bracing his hands on his knees. When the coughing jag ended, he straightened, slowly. His face looked bright red, like he'd just run a mile. "I need some STRONGER cough medicine."

"Hank, Dok won't be in for a while longer. You'll need to wait for her."

"Oh, come on, Annie." He coughed a few times, just to show her how bad off he was. "I don't NEED a subscription."

"Prescription," Annie corrected. "I'm sorry. I can't help. Dok won't be here until at least noon and the office is locked tight."

He brushed that off. "Let me just JIMMY open a WINDOW. Dok'll UNDERSTAND." He stepped off the stoop to head toward a window.

"She won't!" Annie jumped to a stand. "Not a good idea." She went over to him, spun him around, and practically pushed him toward the Bent N' Dent. "You go on over and warm up at the store. I'll be sure to tell Dok you need to see her."

He looked back at her, started to say something, then had a coughing fit and waved a hand in the air, frustrated.

"Hank Lapp, what are you doing out in this cold?" Sarah had come out of the Bent N' Dent and down the steps, clutching a shawl around her shoulders with both hands. "Annie, you too! The both of you, come on over and get warm."

Hank went over to the store, but Annie stayed where she was, calling out to Sarah that she had to do an errand before Dok arrived. Sarah talked nonstop. Hank Lapp talked nonstop. They both spoke at the same volume: loud. No way could Annie handle both of them at once. She grabbed her scooter and dashed off to the public library.

She thought she might use the time to read up on her mother's newest self-diagnosis of tachycardia. She browsed the shelves, looking for her favorite medical encyclopedias. So many books, waiting to be read! Her hand paused on one book's binding, ready to pull it out, when she heard a loud crash coming from the children's area, followed by an eerie quiet. Then a blood-curdling scream for help that put a shiver down Annie's spine. She jammed the book back in and raced around the shelves.

A librarian at the front desk was already on the phone. Annie assumed she was calling 911 because she heard her explain the situation, speaking slowly, in a shaky voice. "I'm calling from the Stoney Ridge Public Library. A toddler has climbed up on a shelf of books and it overturned on him. He's trapped underneath."

Annie headed toward the children's area, now walking slowly toward the accident scene. It was something she had read about in the folder given to her at the informational meeting about EMTs. Approach the scene slowly to make assessments of the situation, to avoid causing more panic for the victims.

Annie saw only the top of a child's head. His body was under the shelf. There was no cry from the child—the only sound was the panting of the hysterical mother as she plowed through a mountain of books to pull her child out.

Annie crouched down and placed a hand on the woman's shoulder. "Help is on the way. It's best not to move your child." She repeated it several times before the woman seemed to hear her. She looked up, her eyes full of fear. Annie grabbed her shaking hands and repeated, "Help is on the way."

Annie saw the fear melt away in the woman's eyes. She would never forget that moment—like she was a vessel of God's peace, flowing through her to help the woman.

Just then, a little voice said, "Mommy?"

Annie and the mother looked down to see the child's eyes wide open. "Billy! Stay right where you are. This lady says not to move," the mother said in a voice flooded with relief. "Help is on the way."

And it was. Annie could hear the sound of a siren stop as it arrived at the library. She could hear the doors open and the librarian's tense voice pointing them to the children's area. She heard the sound of heavy footsteps coming toward them.

"Clear the way, please."

Annie stepped aside to let the workers crouch down beside the child. One of them questioned the child to assess his condition while the other one examined the bookshelf. That one wore a black hat.

A black hat. Annie's heart started to pound.

Him! It was him! The Amish EMT.

She recognized the other worker as the older paramedic. So they were a team—an experienced paramedic and a rookie. A wonderful rookie. Mr. Wonderful.

Mr. Wonderful walked around the tipped-over bookshelf. As he came around the other side, he glanced up and stopped abruptly, locking eyes with Annie. She could see recognition dawning on his face as his eyes homed in on her. Her stomach did a flipflop.

"What do you think?" the paramedic said.

Mr. Wonderful startled, looking away from Annie as his full attention returned to the crisis. "Nothing bolted down."

"Everyone stand back, please," the paramedic said. "Ma'am, we'll get your child out of here, but you need to get back." The mother wouldn't budge. He looked at Annie. "Can you help get her out of here?"

Annie bent down and whispered to the mother. "Come with me." She put her hands on the mother's shoulders and steered her several feet away.

Trembling, the mother said to Annie, "He'll be all right, won't he?"

"It's a very good sign that your child is talking," Annie said.

The paramedic and the rookie stood on each side of the heavy bookshelf. "On the count of three, lift. One, two, three." As soon as the bookshelf was upright and stable, the paramedic returned to the child's side, checking for injuries as Mr. Wonderful went out to the ambulance to get the stretcher.

Annie had to hold on to the mother to keep her from running

to her child. "They need to assess his condition. The best way to help your boy is to stay right here with me."

The paramedic and the rookie spoke to each other in low voices. Carefully, they hoisted the child onto the stretcher and strapped him in. The paramedic came over to the mother.

"Is he hurt?" she asked. "Will he be all right?"

"Your son doesn't seem to have any obvious injuries," the paramedic said. "We'll take him to the ER to see about a concussion. You can ride with him in the ambulance or drive behind us." He noticed how she was still trembling. "On second thought, maybe you should ride along in the ambulance."

The mother hurried to her child's side as the rookie pushed the boy on the stretcher. As he walked past Annie, he leaned toward her slightly with a wink and a whisper. "We have to stop meeting like this. People will start talking."

Annie's heart soared. She might love this man.

The librarian watched the ambulance crew leave with the little boy on the stretcher and the mother trotting alongside. "Unbelievable. Just unbelievable. I'll bet that mother was texting on her phone while her son was climbing up a shelf. The amount of paperwork for another accident report will take me all afternoon." She let out a long-suffering sigh. "I know, I know," as if Annie had said something. She hadn't. "I should just be glad that it wasn't worse. That boy could have been killed. It's a miracle."

Yes it was, Annie thought. A miracle. All of it.

That afternoon, Bee dropped by Fern's and discovered her kitchen was full of Amish women. "I'll come another time," she said to Fern, standing at the door. "I didn't realize you had company." But she thought Fern had asked her to come today. In fact, she'd been very specific about the time.

"You come right in," Fern said. "I wanted you to meet my friends."

"Where are their . . . buggies?" Bee almost said cars.

"They all came in one." She pointed in the direction of the barn.

Bee turned to see an open-topped wagon by the barn. It looked so cold! "Where's the horse?"

"In the barn, visiting with its friends." Fern pulled her into the house and closed the door behind her. "Come. Meet everyone." She clapped her hands. "Everyone? This is Bee Bennett. She's the widow lady I've been telling you about."

At the words "widow lady," Bee felt her typical knee-jerk bristle. She wished Fern would stop calling her that! She turned to her with a frown, but Fern had already dashed off. Bee stayed by the door, tongue-tied, glued to the spot. Overwhelmed by the sight of eight prayer-capped Plain women staring at her as if she'd been plucked from the future and dropped into this kitchen. Bee noticed the long kitchen table was covered with parchment paper, and on the paper were freshly baked cookies.

One woman came forward, extending her hand to Bee's. "Welcome, Bee. I'm Carrie Fisher. I live up the road, not too far from you. I've seen your horses grazing in the fields. They're beautiful animals."

Bee shook her hand, liking Carrie immediately. Her warmth, especially. "Fisher. Are you related to Annie Fisher? Dok's assistant?"

Carrie smiled. "Distantly related. You'll find most everyone around here has some kind of family connection." She squeezed Bee's hand. "Come. I'll introduce you to the others. We're baking cookies for a bake sale. An elderly woman in our church fell and broke a hip recently, so we thought we'd raise some money to help with the medical bills." She tucked a hand around Bee's elbow and scooped her into the clutch of women. There was only one, Edith Lapp, who looked at Bee as if she didn't belong here. The others couldn't have been kinder. They spoke in English, all but Edith, and gave her tasks to do. They even complimented the way she rolled out cookie dough, insisting she was a natural. Ha! She'd been taught by Fern.

An hour passed like a minute, and soon the women were putting their coats on to leave. Dishes and baking sheets had been washed, rinsed, and put away. Cookies were packed in Tupperware for the upcoming bake sale. All that remained in Fern's kitchen was the lingering sweet smell of baked goods.

That, and a few things Bee had learned today from listening to these women.

To them, community was profound. It bound these women together. They counted on each other, supported each other, leaned on one another. They raised their families together, worked together, cooked together, shared things, and asked for help when they needed it. Community, Bee learned today, was a give-and-take relationship.

On the drive home, she had no doubt that Fern had invited her over today to drive home a point. Bee needed community. That was probably the reason Fern kept introducing her as a widow lady. A woman alone, identified by sorrow and loss. In Fern's own blunt way, she was pushing Bee to understand that it was up to her to change that moniker, to find that community, to build her own support network by getting involved. Give-and-take.

As Bee rounded the corner to her home, she decided that the next time her path crossed with Dok, she just might ask her which church she and Matt attended. Maybe, just maybe, she'd give it a try one of these Sunday mornings.

Late that afternoon, Dok finished with the last patient and called it a day. She didn't even tidy up her office but locked up and left. Not only was she exhausted from the early and dramatic start to the day, but she wanted to get home and see Matt and the baby. Today, she missed them. Both.

As she walked into the kitchen from the garage, she smelled curried lentil soup simmering on the stove—Dok's favorite. She heard Matt's melodic voice and tiptoed toward the family room. Matt sat on the couch, the baby in his lap, reading *Don't Let the Pigeon Drive the Bus*. Dok's heart melted at the sight. She leaned against the doorjamb, watching them, trying to sear this memory in her mind.

Matt had been right when he told her that they needed to make their marriage more of a priority. Their busy careers took the best from them, often leaving them with a marriage that felt more like two roommates than lovers.

These last few weeks had changed them. So many things had changed. Matt might be worthless during the night in providing help for the baby, but he was an outstanding family man during the day. He made wonderful weekday breakfasts and dinners for them, not just on Sunday anymore. Once or twice, he and the baby had delivered lunch to Dok at the office. The house remodel was getting worked on, little by little. Last Sunday, they'd even taken a day trip to Philadelphia, all three of them, just to see an exhibit at a museum that Matt knew she wanted to see.

With Matt not working, even with an infant, there was just more time. And with that margin came more contentment. What a gift to discover, rather late in life, that less was more. It dawned on her that baby Gabe had brought that gift to them. Other gifts too.

She looked at her husband, at how tenderly he held the baby in the crook of his arm, and listened to the made-up voices he used to narrate the pigeon, and she felt such an overwhelming wave of love for him.

When he finished the last page, he closed the book and looked up to see her standing there. He smiled at her, a tender look in his eyes for her that she realized, just now, she hadn't seen in a while. She hadn't even noticed that look had gone missing.

"When did you get home?"

"A while ago. I didn't want to interrupt the pigeon's temper tantrum." She bit her lip. "Matt, I think it can be . . . on the table."

"The soup? I know. Your favorite. But it gets better. Gabe and I have been improving our sourdough bread and we think today's batch won't crack a tooth." Matt rose and set the now sleeping Gabe in a bassinet. He crossed the room to where Dok stood. "I'll plate up. Maybe we can actually eat a whole meal while he's still asleep."

She put a hand out to stop him. "Matt, I didn't just mean dinner, though it smells wonderful and I'm famished. I meant that adoption can be on the table. Up for discussion."

Matt froze. He took a step back and reached out to put his hands on her elbows. "Ruth, are you sure?"

"Absolutely, positively sure that . . . we can talk about it. For now, that's as far as I can go. Pros and cons, short view, long view. What's best for the baby, what's best for us. All of it. Just talk. No promises."

He couldn't come close to hiding the smile that blossomed on his face.

Fifteen

After work on Friday afternoon, Dok popped into the Bent N' Dent to pick up a few things for the baby, and that was when she heard Hank Lapp coughing. He was sitting by the fire, playing checkers with another graybeard, and he coughed once, twice, then a few more times. There was something about the sound of it that bothered her—a dry hack, almost like a dog's bark. She finished paying Sarah for her items and crossed the room to see Hank.

She crouched down beside him. His eyes looked clear, his face had good color. In a low voice, she said, "Isn't the cough any better?" A few days ago, after Annie had told her that Hank had been complaining about his cough, she sent her over to the Bent N' Dent to give him a little stronger over-the-counter cough medicine.

"HELLO, DOK! Care to JOIN us for a game of CHECK-ERS?"

"Thanks, but I need to get home. I just wanted to know about your cough."

"WHAT COUGH?" His face grew more and more red as he tried to hold back a cough, then finally it burst out of him.

Hmm. "Hank, it's been a while since I've seen you."

"You SEE me ALL the TIME!"

153

"No, I see Edith. I'd like to give you a checkup."

Hank scowled. "Can't. Too busy." And then he barked another cough.

"Monday morning," Dok said in her no-nonsense voice. "Eight o'clock."

Hank let out a loud harumph. "You don't even OPEN until NINE."

"For you, I'll make an exception."

She went to the door, opened it, and turned around. "Monday. Eight o'clock."

The look on Hank's face! Like a mad little boy.

On Saturday morning, Bee stayed in bed later than usual, luxuriating in the reprieve of a daily radiation appointment. From daily drive time in the truck with Damon. She went into the kitchen to make coffee, and as it was brewing, she glanced out the window to see Damon lead Willow—one of her favorite mares—into the arena. On a Saturday morning! Seriously? That man! He had no life outside of horses.

But then, neither did Bee.

The coffeepot beeped its ready signal. She poured a cup and sipped it, watching out the window as Damon started to exercise Willow on the lunge line. The mare started and stopped, moving uncertainly, nervously. She lifted and tossed her head, broke into a fast-moving canter, before settling into a rhythmic, relaxed trot.

Bee cringed, embarrassed. Willow could be a nervous Nellie, but this skittish behavior revealed how inconsistent her training had been. Just basic green horse training. Not enough. And that was on Bee.

Watching Willow settle under Damon's clear cues was mesmerizing. Even without an arm, he moved with such gracefulness, such agility, sheer athleticism. He must be a wonderful dancer, Bee thought, before shaking that unbidden thought right out of her head.

Her husband Ted had been a two-left-feet dancer. The best he could do was to jog in place. She took another sip of coffee, thinking how those two men couldn't be more different.

Both attractive, though Ted's appeal had been in a boy-next-door sort of way. His shaggy golden-grayish hair was thinning and he leaned a bit on the heavy side, but those characteristics only added to his approachability. He exuded warmth and friendliness, with a winning smile that put his patients at ease.

The only creature at ease around Damon was a horse.

Damon was handsome like a James Bond actor, long and lean, perfectly toned. So unlike Ted's roundness. Not a single gray wisp in his perfectly groomed head of dark hair. Bee knew. She had looked.

Damon finished warming Willow up, unhooked the lunge line, and left the mare standing, untethered, in the center of the arena. He walked about ten to fifteen feet away from her and then stopped, keeping his back to her. Willow stared after him for a long moment, then trotted right toward him. Just like she should have. It was a trust-building exercise called the Join-Up. The goal was to gain the horse's willingness to cooperate. Damon was doing everything right.

Bee thought she'd better head to the arena to warn Damon that Willow spooked easily. The mare was born with a sensitive nature, but the horse's high anxiety had ratcheted up several notches after a heavy thunderstorm rolled through Stoney Ridge last summer. It was one of those storms that shook the earth when the thunder cracked. Bee had gone out to the barn to settle the horses, walking up and down the aisle, talking to them in a calm, soothing voice. Willow seemed particularly upset. Bee went into the stall with her and discovered a leak in the roof was sending a stream of rainwater onto the poor horse.

She was standing in a puddle. Ever since that storm, Willow had been afraid of standing water. Loud noises too.

Bee meant to address Willow's skittishness with specific training methods last summer, but she hadn't gotten around to it yet. She knew she needed to—water jumps were a part of every obstacle course. There was no way Willow could ever be sold as a competition horse without working out those fears.

Bee hurried to her bedroom, pulled on her jeans, and slipped a turtleneck over her head. By the back door, she grabbed a coat and stuck her stocking feet into green Wellies. A hand on the door, she stopped. The scent of freshly brewed coffee still filled the air. She refilled her mug and, at the last minute, filled a second mug to take to Damon.

Outside, she walked to the arena gate and stopped to watch. By now Damon had reattached the lunge line to Willow's halter and was cantering her in a wide circle. Now and then, he would shake an empty Clorox bleach bottle that had been filled with pebbles. Bee could see Willow's tolerance of the noise increased with each pass around the arena. Somehow, Damon had already picked up on the mare's problems and was working on them.

Embarrassment flooded Bee. She should've started that kind of conditioning for Willow last summer, right after the thunderstorm. Conditioning wasn't a complicated training experience. She knew better than to let so much time pass by. Why had she? The fog, no doubt. It had descended on her with Ted's death, an oppressive weight that made simple tasks seem insurmountable. Still, that was no excuse to have neglected Willow's conditioning.

When Damon noticed Bee standing by the gate, he released the lunge line from Willow's halter to let her rest. He walked over to Bee. "She's got a lot of potential."

"That she does." She handed him a mug of coffee, which he gratefully accepted.

He took a few sips before saying, "What were your plans to get her past spooking at water?"

Ah. So he'd already discovered Willow's fear of water too. This man didn't miss much. "I thought I might ride her in the rain."

From the look on his face, he wasn't impressed. "I might set up a small water jump in the arena. Get her accustomed to it."

Oh wait. No, no, no. "Damon, we've already had this conversation. No higher-level training."

"Why not?"

"Because . . . she's too young."

"She's not too young. In fact, she's late for it. So are the others."

"Show jumping horses aren't like racehorses. They don't peak early."

"Bee, are you really serious about being a horse breeder?"

"Of course I am." Her spine stiffened. "Higher-level training brings its own problems. Stress on the joints, on the tendons and ligaments."

"I'm not talking about putting stress on a horse. Do you really think I'd train like that? I treat horses well."

"I know you do." She did know. "Still, things can happen. The last thing I want to do is to bench a horse."

"There's a long way to go between starting to train and the show jumping circuit."

She felt herself digging in her heels. "Higher-level training belongs to the horse's next owner."

One of his eyebrows lifted. "Next owner? And just how many horses have you sold?"

None of his business. She cleared her throat. "One."

"Out of how many?"

"Eight."

"And I'll bet you my last dollar that you sold that one because she didn't have enough of Ozzie in her."

Right again. So annoying. And to be perfectly honest, she

didn't even sell that mare. She gave her to a friend who owned an athletic Dutch Warmblood stallion with a perfect temperament for show jumping, in exchange for receiving artificial insemination on demand. A fair deal, Bee thought. But she couldn't deny that she only parted with the mare because there were little signs of Ozzie in her. The mare took after the stud in looks and temperament.

Genetics. Such a mystery.

"Bee, you're never going to have another Ozzie." His voice was gentle, but the words were hard to hear.

This conversation had sailed past uncomfortable for Bee and was now heading into very personal territory. The memory of Ozzie belonged to her and her alone. "I can try."

"A successful breeder retains the best and sells the rest. You're keeping all of them." He pointed to Willow. "She should've been on the market last year." His gaze shifted to the barn. "Others, too. Echo, Marigold. You should've been preparing them for market by age two. You've got three horses that are four, five, and six years old."

Bee frowned. She felt a fresh appreciation for how Ted used to let her do whatever she wanted to do with the horses. "Damon, you said you came to help me, so help me. Stop trying to change things. I'm happy the way things are."

"You might be happy, but your horses aren't."

"Seriously?" She lifted a hand in exasperation. "You think they're not happy? These horses are pampered! They have the best food, the best vet care, the best of everything. I play classical music for them in the barn. I even use aromatherapy on them. Ted once said that if one of my horses ever sneezed, I'd hear it and run out with a tissue."

"I never said they weren't treated well. You treat them just fine. Better than fine. But these horses are born to do more than circle an arena and graze in a pasture. If you aren't training, you're untraining. If you're really in the business, you need to be fully committed." He polished off the last of the coffee and handed the empty mug to her. "Thanks for that." He walked back to the center of the arena and clucked his tongue. Willow, the traitor, trotted right over to him like a puppy. He stroked her long neck, clipped the lunge line to her halter, and went back to the conditioning work.

Damon the Demon was getting on Bee's last nerve.

One little step toward becoming an EMT had been solved for Annie. After church, the bishop had sat next to her father for lunch and told him he'd like Annie to continue working at Dok's. When her mother found out that Dad had said yes, she turned bright red, sputtering away with objections. For a long moment, Annie thought her mom was going to have the final say. But then her dad repeated what the bishop had said. "Sally, you just don't say no to the bishop."

That ended the conversation, but not her mother's agitation. She asked Annie to fit her into Dok's schedule on Monday, because she feared she might have an orphan disease.

"A *what*?" Annie said.

"An orphan disease. Very rare. Difficult to pinpoint."

"Mom, did you happen to speak to Cousin Gloria today?"

Her mom didn't answer. Looking out the window at a robin in a tree, she twirled a cap string in a distracted way. "You'll get me in tomorrow, then?"

Annie wished her mother would appreciate the many benefits that came from working at Dok's office. Like getting her mother an appointment whenever she wanted to be seen, which was often. She let out a sigh. "Tomorrow afternoon." She thought she might spend her lunch hour tomorrow looking up orphan diseases at the library.

In the middle of the night, Edith Lapp called Dok to come right over. Edith didn't ask. She told. Hank was having trouble breathing.

Dok checked her bag for antibiotics before she got in the car to drive over to the Lapps'. Most likely, his cough had deepened into something more serious. She planned to start him on some antibiotics to ward off pneumonia. It could set in quickly in elderly patients like Hank.

Her car headlights shone on a new outbuilding where she usually parked, so she turned off the car's engine in the middle of the driveway and decided to just back the car straight out when she left.

Edith met her at the door and led her to their bedroom. Hank looked so frail in the bed, wire-thin. Dok fully expected his lungs to be congested, but to her surprise, his lungs sounded clear. He continued to struggle to breathe, so she had him try an inhaler, just in case he might be suffering from asthma or allergies.

"No point in that," Edith said.

She was right about that. The inhaler did nothing to help his breathing.

Edith ticked off her fingers as she listed Hank's history with this cough. He'd had it for a few months now and it seemed to be taking a turn for the worse. He didn't have any allergies. He'd never smoked. They'd tried humidifiers and home remedies. His energy level had dropped considerably, though not his volume. That remained at full force, which Dok could attest to.

"And that cough is keeping me up at night," Edith said, which might have had something to do with calling Dok in the wee hours.

Dok had to swallow a smile. These two were the most unlikely pair, yet they seemed content together. As her mother used to say: Es is en Deckel for alle Haffe. *There's a lid for every pot.*

160

"Maybe I should take you over to the ER," Dok said, bracing herself for a strong objection.

It came immediately. "I'm NOT GOING," Hank said.

Edith didn't override him, which meant Dok had no chance at getting him there.

Finally, Dok gave him a sedative to help him sleep. As soon as she felt confident that his breathing had improved, she packed her bag and told Edith she wanted to see Hank at the office early tomorrow morning. She needed to find out what was really going on with that cough.

Normally, Dok was able to hand off lingering concerns about her patients to the Lord and leave them there. She worked to keep a healthy detachment, so necessary for a doctor. But Hank Lapp was special. He was one of a kind. Despite his loud volume and his blundering ways, she was fond of that man. She wanted him to stick around for a long, long time.

She wished her own mother had stuck around longer. She would've loved for Mom to have met baby Gabe, to have seen that Dok had taken, at long last, a traditional female role. Mom would've been shocked. Thrilled, but shocked.

Last night, Matt had asked about Bee, and if the grief counseling with Fern Lapp was a help to her. Dok didn't know for sure, but she thought it might be helping. Then Matt surprised Dok by asking if she thought she had fully grieved her mother's death. Of course, she told him, of course . . . but now she wondered. She had just been getting into a comfortable reconnection with her mother when she fell, broke her hip . . . and it was downhill from there. What was hard for Dok to accept was that her mother didn't seem to want to regain her health. She seemed ready to pass.

Right as David was considering a relocation for the church. Right as she and Dok had been finding their way back to a mother-daughter relationship.

Why didn't Mom try harder to get better? Even if David

161

had moved the church to Tennessee, like he'd been considering, Dok would've looked after Mom. It almost seemed as if Mom had already decided that without David nearby, she was done with living. Her own daughter, who had disappointed her in so many ways, didn't give her a reason to want to live. Dok wasn't Amish, she wasn't a mother, she provided no grandchildren. She wasn't enough.

Dok would never share those thoughts with her brother. No doubt David would tell her that only God decided when a life would end. "Seeing his days are determined, the number of his months are with thee," he would quote from the book of Job.

True. But Dok had seen enough of death in her practice to know that someone's state of mind had a lot to do with whether a person recovered from illness or injury, or languished. She believed that people had to participate in their healing. On the flip side, she also wondered if her mother had willed herself to die.

What was the point of thinking about Mom like this? She was gone. The past was the past.

But thinking about Mom's passing made Dok all the more determined not to let Hank Lapp give up on living. He wasn't done yet.

Sixteen

Dok arrived at the office extra early on Monday morning, half expecting Hank Lapp not to show up. He came, though, accompanied by his wife Edith. She followed them into the exam room and sat in Dok's chair.

Dok gave Hank a basic exam and everything checked out. He looked and acted normal, his lungs sounded clear, and he insisted he felt fit as a fiddle.

"NEVER BETTER," he told Dok, coughing through the words.

But something kept nagging Dok, and she'd had enough experience as a doctor to know she needed to heed that gut instinct. She considered it to be a gift from God. As the saying went, "The doctor can treat, but only God can heal." She believed that with her whole heart. As experienced as she was, as seasoned a doctor, she was well aware of modern medicine's limitations. It was one of the reasons she didn't discourage her patients from trying complementary and alternative treatments. Acupuncture, reflexology, homeopathy, home remedies. As long as they were scientifically safe for a patient, she was supportive of nonconventional therapies. And that definitely included prayer. It was on the top of her list.

Over the years, Dok had made a habit of praying for the

day's patients on the way to work each morning. They may not all know that she prayed for their ultimate eternal healing, but the Lord knew.

On today's drive, knowing Hank would deny every symptom of his strange cough, she prayed that God would give her a hitch in her heart if she needed to take tests a step further. He answered that prayer. She felt very unsettled. "Hank, I want to send you to a pulmonologist."

"A WHAT?"

"A doctor that specializes in the lungs and respiratory system."

"OH NO!" Hank shook his head vigorously. "I am NOT going to another doctor. I keep TELLING you that I'm JUST FINE. I've heard how those SPECIALISTS run up the TAB."

Edith frowned at him. "Why do you want to send him to this doctor?"

"To rule out anything serious."

"SERIOUS?"

Dok didn't want to confuse Hank with too much information. "Just to rule out anything more serious. The specialist will probably order an image of your lungs. X-ray or CT scan. That image will tell us a lot."

"An X-RAY of my LUNGS? Eddy, did you HEAR that? Imagine how much THAT will cost. NO THANK YOU, Dok."

Dok turned to Edith, who looked the tiniest bit pale. "I wouldn't ask you to go if it weren't important."

"There's NOTHING the matter with ME," Hank said.

Dok turned back to Hank. "I hope you're right, but I want to be sure. We need to get to the bottom of why you can't shake this cough."

"I'M FINE," Hank said, hopping off the exam table. "I'm not going ANYWHERE."

"He'll go," Edith said with authority.

Good. If Dok could get Edith on board, then Hank would end up doing what she told him to do. "I'll set up the referral so Hank can be seen by the pulmonologist as soon as possible. Annie will call you later with details." If this cough turned out to be something more serious, Dok might be in for an uphill battle. She knew how the Plain People reasoned about modern medicine. Very cost conscious. Very heavenly minded.

Three weeks down, three to go.

Bee's skin was starting to turn red from the daily radiation treatments, like a mild sunburn, but she was smothering herself with lotion afterward, as had been recommended by Dr. Google. She felt a little more tired than usual, but so far, it wasn't too bad.

On the way to the appointment, she looked at Damon, her chauffeur. "I'm supposed to see the radiologist after treatment today. Apparently, that's going to become a once-a-week thing. Probably means a wait, too, so feel free to head back to the house. I'll get an Uber."

"I'll wait," Damon said. "I need to return a phone call, anyway. There's someone who's interested in one of your horses."

"Excuse me?" Bee gave him a look. "Why would you be representing my horses?" What she really wanted to say was: *How dare you! Who do you think you are?!*

"I'm not. I got a call from a client who's interested in buying a fresh competition horse and I thought of showing her Echo. That's all. So she wants to make an appointment and see her."

"Oh no," she said. "I am *not* selling that horse."

"Why not?"

"Because . . ." *She's one of my favorites. Because there are moments when she gets a look on her face that's so Ozzie-like that my breath catches.* But she couldn't say any of that to Damon. "I want to keep expanding Ozzie's line. Echo has just the right qualities I need."

"But you're a hobby breeder, right?"

"Yes." Though that label sounded a bit patronizing, considering her horses were top-notch.

"Which means you breed horses to sell. I've been working at your place over a month now and I've not seen any clients show up. Not one."

"Well, that's . . . it's, well . . ." She sputtered the words, trying to string her thoughts together. "There's been a lot going on in my life. Plus, it's winter. This isn't the season most people go shopping for horses."

He lifted an eyebrow. "You know what they say about breeders, don't you?"

"What?"

"Breeders are hoarders."

Her lips tightened. "Hoarders," she said in a flat voice.

"They hoard genetics. They can't let go of horses, even if they can't afford to keep them."

His words slapped Bee with surprise. Her mouth opened and shut, opened and shut, like a fish out of water. Her finances were *her* business, not his. She was amazed at his audacity. Cornered by it too. He was spot-on about her expenses. They were exorbitant.

"Most of the breeders I've known are very stuck."

"You're saying you think I'm stuck? Me?" Bee clapped a hand against her chest. *Ouch!* Her chest was tender from the radiation.

He pulled into the building's driveway and stopped the truck by the front door. "Do *you* think you're stuck?"

"No!" She put a hand on the door handle, deliberately looking away from his penetrating gaze. "No. I do not think I am stuck."

"Then why won't you consider selling your horses? At the very least, the *very least*, why not use Strider as a stud? Think of the stud fees you could be getting on that stallion. Think of his foals. Think of how quickly Ozzie's line could be reproduced.

166

Instead, you've got that poor boy spending his prime grazing in a pasture."

They stared at each other, a standoff. He leaned across the center console and started to say something, then shook his head. Bee closed the door firmly and walked away, all the while feeling Damon Harding's stare burning into her back.

On the morning drive into town, nothing much was said between Annie and her dad. Too cold to talk. Too irritated with Annie's mom, though for different reasons. Dad was annoyed with Mom because she said she might be allergic to *him*. Annie had been washing and drying the breakfast dishes in the kitchen, but she'd heard the whole argument going on in their bedroom build to a crescendo.

"I never heard such foolishness!" The bedroom door opened as Dad stomped through the kitchen to the back door. "We've been married nearly forty years. Forty long years." He drew out the word *long*.

Mom trotted behind him. "It's not foolishness! Cousin Gloria knows all about it. It's called mast cell activation syndrome. I wrote it down to get it right. Think about it, Eli. Every time you're near me, I break out in rashes. Gloria said that's the first sign."

"Phooey," Dad said, yanking his hat off the wall peg. "Annie, I'm heading to town if you want a ride." He glared at Mom. "Sally, you know what you're really allergic to?"

"What?"

He opened the door. "Yourself." His voice was thick with frustration. "You're allergic to your own self." He slammed the door behind him.

Wide-eyed, Mom turned to Annie. "Could that be possible?"

"No. Dad's only trying to make a point." Annie put the last bowl away and draped the dishrag over the sink faucet to dry.

"Annie, I want you to get me in to see Dok today."

"Can't." Annie shook her head. "Dok has a full load. With truly sick people."

"I *am* truly sick." Mom started scratching her arms like she was in a roomful of mosquitos. "Please, Annie. Get me in to see Dok. I'm suffering."

There was no talking her out of it. Dad was waiting and Annie needed to get to work. "I'll see what I can do."

"Good. Also, Cousin Gloria brought up the young man again."

Annie pulled on her coat and buttoned it. "What young man?"

"I told you. A fine young man she knows. She says he's the perfect match for you."

Annie shook her head. "No. Tell Gloria I'm not at all interested." The only man she wanted to date was the elusive Mr. Wonderful.

Over the years, Dok had experienced a few patients with symptoms of hypochondria, but Annie's mother took the prize. Sally Fisher was a raging hypochondriac.

Dok paused before she walked into the exam room, silently praying for patience while bracing herself for Sally's latest complaints. She knew exactly how this appointment would play out. Dok would listen, examine Sally's supposed symptoms, and find nothing wrong. Sally would ask for a referral to see a specialist. The only specialist Dok would refer her to was a counselor at Mountain Vista, a nearby facility that dealt with all kinds of mental health issues while respecting the traditions of the Plain People. And Sally would leave her office, offended. Until the next appointment, when she'd arrive with a new symptom, another suspected disease.

But Dok also knew that ignoring hypochondria wasn't effective; if casually dismissed, it would only worsen. While its root cause was health anxieties, it was often accompanied by other mental illnesses—depression, obsessive-compulsive disorder, to name just a few. There was so much help to be had, and Dok continued to recommend that Sally seek out counseling. That's when Sally would leave the office in a snit.

Dok plastered a smile on her face and went into the exam room. "Good morning, Sally. What brings you in today?"

She held out her left arm. "I have a rash on my arm."

Dok pushed Sally's sleeve up and looked at her arm. "Where?"

"Look closer." Sally jiggled her arm, annoyed. "It's plain as day."

Dok turned on the surgical light and drew it close to Sally's arm, examining it carefully. As expected, she saw nothing out of the ordinary. "Tell me about the rash on your arm. How long have you had it?"

"Let's see, at least a day. Maybe two."

"And how does it feel?"

Sally lit up. "Red-hot itching. Like ten million mosquitos have bit me."

"Sounds awful."

"Oh, it is, Dok. You can't imagine how bad it hurts. I can't sleep. Can't stop itching it." Just to prove her point, Sally started to scratch her arm. "My cousin Gloria wondered if it might be mast cell activation syndrome. She thinks I might be allergic to my husband."

Dok had to swallow a smile. "That would be very unlikely. It's extremely rare."

"Is it? What should I be looking for?"

Dok cringed. Open the door a crack and Sally would jam her foot in to keep it open. If she listed off signs, Sally would be in the office next week, detailing out her symptoms. She decided to try a different tactic. She clicked off the exam light and sat on the stool. "Gsundheit is der greescht Reichdum." *Health is the greatest wealth.*

"Ya ya." *Yes, indeed.* Sally peered at her arm. "So what do you think?"

"Sally, put your arm down for a moment and look at me. Could anything else be bothering you?"

Sally lifted her head with a frown. "Well, I sure don't like you talking my Annie into becoming an EMT."

Dok's eyebrows shot up. "Pardon?"

"Annie told me all about it. I think it's a terrible notion to put into a girl's head. Just dreadful." She had a look on her face like she'd sniffed something sour.

"Annie said that I was talking her into it?"

Sally's mouth worked from side to side. "She never thought about such foolishness before she started work as your assistant. I was against her working here in the first place."

"Why? Other Amish girls have worked for me."

"But Annie . . . she's different from other girls."

So true. Annie *was* different. She had more on her mind than most girls her age. She soaked up knowledge like a dry sponge. She read every medical magazine that came in from cover to cover. Dok had even caught her reading medical textbooks when the office was empty. No other girl, even Ruthie Stoltzfus, found medical textbooks to be of interest. Yes, Annie was different from most Amish girls. Such single-minded focus was rare. In some ways, Annie reminded Dok of herself.

But that would be the worst thing to say to Sally Fisher. No doubt Sally was already worried that Dok was tempting Annie away from the church. Not true, not true at all, but Sally Fisher relied wholly on her feelings, never on facts.

In Dok's coat pocket was a sample tube of moisturizer that a salesman had dropped off the other day. "Sally, I'm going to give you a special cream that should stop the itching." She opened a cupboard drawer and took out a small unused jar. Turning her back to Sally, she squeezed all the moisturizer into the jar and hid the empty tube back in her pocket. She handed the jar to Sally, who seemed delighted that Dok took her itching seriously.

While Dok wasn't exactly proud of giving Sally a placebo, she was pleased that she left the office today in a completely different frame of mind than she usually did. For the first time, Sally didn't leave in a snit.

Today, she'd left Dok in a snit.

Sally Fisher had been the last patient appointment for the day, so Annie finished stacking patient files for tomorrow. She went back to Dok's office to let her know she was leaving for the day and knocked lightly on the doorframe. "Hank Lapp's pulmonology appointment is scheduled. If you don't need anything else, I'll be leaving. Mom's waiting for me out in the buggy."

Dok glanced at her. "Sit down for just a moment, Annie."

Annie walked into Dok's office and sat down. Her mind flashed through the day's events as she wondered what she might have done wrong. Like, squeezing her mother in to see Dok after a full day? She wouldn't blame Dok for being annoyed by that. Annie was annoyed by it.

"So . . . you want to be an EMT?"

Annie's eyes went wide. That was the last thing she'd expected from Dok.

"Your mother mentioned it during her visit."

Cringing, Annie tightened her fists.

"Please don't be upset with her." Just then Dok's cell phone rang and she glanced at the caller's name. "It's Matt. I'd better take it. But, Annie, I'd like to talk about this another time."

Embarrassed, Annie darted out the door. She should never have tried to test the waters of being an EMT with her mother! Dok probably thought it would be laughable for an Amish girl like Annie—one whose mother was the informant—to consider becoming an EMT.

And yet, she just couldn't stop thinking about being one. Buttoning her sweater, she felt as if she was starting to understand her mother's fixation on all her crazy sicknesses. Annie was obsessed.

It had taken some time, but Bee now felt comfortable stopping in at Windmill Farm whenever she was in need of a little Fern-fix. And those moments happened more and more frequently, at least two or three times a week. She wouldn't stay long—Fern was hardly the type to encourage lengthy visits—but she always left Windmill Farm feeling better than when she arrived. Emotionally better.

It was strange about grief. Some days, Bee would feel as if she accepted Ted's death although she didn't like it. Other days, like today, she felt as if time had backed up and she was still in that first month of heavy, debilitating sorrow.

She knew what had triggered today's feeling. She'd been in the garage, looking for something, and happened upon a box of Ted's sweaters. They still smelled of his cologne—and Bee picked one up, held it to her face, and wept. When would she get past this kind of thing? She hadn't even started to clean out his closet. His shampoo remained in the shower, as if he'd be coming back soon.

Maybe she was stuck.

So she drove over to Fern's and found her sitting in the front room near the fire, mending somebody's clothes. Bee sat down on the couch and picked up something to mend—though she really didn't know how to sew anything, but this was the way things worked with Fern.

Fern glanced up at her. "You look tired."

"I am tired." She was too. More tired with each passing day.

She couldn't wait to be done with radiation treatments and get on the other side of this. She longed to get her energy back. "I'm tired of radiation and tired of cancer. Mostly, I'm so tired of the heavy weight of grief." She blew out a puff of air. "Fern, I need your help. How do I heal from grief?"

Fern didn't even blink. "Heal from grief?"

"It's been almost a year and a half now since Ted passed away. I should be healing by now, don't you think? Instead, I miss him so much, every day. Damon thinks I'm stuck."

"Who's Damon?"

"He's the trainer who's been helping me with my horses while I'm in treatment." When Fern lifted her sparse eyebrows, Bee was quick to add, "That's a whole other story that I'll save for another day. Right now, I need your best advice. How did you heal after Amos's death?"

"So you think not missing someone means you've healed from grieving for him?"

Was this a trick question? "I . . . think it must be part of it. I haven't been able to bring myself to clear out any of Ted's things. His reading glasses are still on the nightstand." Just thinking about those glasses brought tears to her eyes.

Calmly, Fern threaded another needle, as if Bee weren't sitting on the edge of the couch, waiting impatiently for an explanation. "Maybe you need to rethink grief."

Rethink grief. How? "Are you saying that I will never stop missing Ted?"

"Probably not."

This felt like the worst piece of grief advice Bee had ever received.

Fern glanced at her. "Not what you wanted to hear."

"Well, to be honest, no. Missing Ted makes me feel terrible. A constant ache. I can't help but feel bitter that I lost him. He was too young. It was too soon. It's just not fair."

"You should flip that over."

Bee looked at her. What in the world did that mean?

"You should remember to feel grateful you had him at all."

Bee stiffened. She wanted empathy, not a scolding. "Easier said than done."

"That's because you're always separating grief from faith."

"I'm not! I believe in Heaven. I believe Ted is there."

"Faith should infuse grief," Fern said, attention still mostly on her work, "the way a tea bag steeps in hot water." She finished the last stitch, knotted the thread, and snipped it off, then packed up her sewing basket. She took the unmended clothing from Bee, folded it, and tucked it in the sewing basket, a signal that this visit was over because she had other things to do.

Or so Bee thought.

Apparently, Fern wasn't done. She wasn't about to let Bee descend into self-pity. She looked right at Bee, pinning her to the couch. "The day my Amos died was the hardest day of my life. I learned something important on that day. You can't separate faith from grief and expect to find peace after such a loss. 'When I sit in darkness, the LORD shall be a light unto me.' Micah 7:8." With that, Fern disappeared upstairs, leaving Bee to find her way out. Leaving her with that image to take home: Faith infuses grief the way a tea bag steeps in hot water.

On the drive back, Bee rolled the thought over and over. Fern always, always astonished her, always left her wanting more.

In the back of Bee's mind, she'd expected Fern to give her some guidance about accepting the reality of her situation. Ted was gone. Some things in life couldn't be explained, they couldn't be changed, they could only be accepted.

That's what she had expected. Maybe even what she had sought by going over to Fern's this afternoon. An Amish pep talk: Grin and bear it. Tough it out. Come to terms with it.

Instead, Fern had found the core of Bee's problem with grief, the reason she felt as if she couldn't keep from being swallowed by the quicksand of sorrow. Fern had hit the nail on the head.

Whenever Bee felt a day like today of intense grief that left her unmoored, her thoughts were earthbound, pulled down like gravity. She didn't correct her thinking with promises from Scripture, she didn't lift her thoughts to dwell on a loving and sovereign God, she didn't lean on the doctrine of resurrection. To be perfectly truthful, if she even thought about God, it was only to blame him. To accuse. How dare he take Ted! It wasn't fair, it wasn't right. God had made a terrible mistake.

Bee shivered, though the car's heater was going full blast. What would please the enemy more than accusing God?

"When I sit in darkness, the Lord shall be a light unto me."
Bee had continued to sit in darkness and keep the light off. Something had to change.

For the last week, Dok had made it home in time for dinner. She handed Annie the file for the last patient of the day, pleased that the day had gone so smoothly. If she hurried, she might be able to get home early. Matt liked to bathe the baby in the late afternoon because he thought it calmed him and helped him sleep better at night—which was amusing to Dok because baby Gabe was always calm and slept soundly—but she didn't want to miss his bath time.

And then Annie handed her a slip of paper. "The pulmonologist's office called with results about Hank Lapp's X-ray. They said to call back as soon as you can."

Dok squeezed her eyes closed in frustration. "Annie, how many times do we have to go over this? You have *got* to interrupt me when another doctor calls with test results. No matter what. Knock on the door. Barge in. Whatever it takes!" It was the only complaint she ever had about Annie Fisher.

"I know!" Annie's eyes went wide. "I do! I offered to get you, but his assistant said the doctor wasn't in the office yet. She was just relaying the message."

Dok cringed, sorry she had snapped at Annie. She knew she'd been trying hard to overcome her hesitation to interrupt. "Oh. Well, then, you made the right decision." She went back to her office, closed the door, and sat down at her desk. She had a pit in her stomach about this call and tucked her chin for a brief prayer. "Lord, let this be good news for Hank."

Two minutes later, she hung up the phone and tucked her chin again. "Oh Lord, please help."

Seventeen

Dok drove right over to talk to Hank and Edith. Halfway there, it occurred to her that she should've thought to bring her brother David along. It was tricky—she always felt a little caught between doctor-patient confidentiality and doctor-bishop privileges. But David was good at delivering difficult news.

In the gloaming, as she pulled into the Lapps' narrow driveway, she could see that the new outbuilding she'd nearly rammed into in the recent middle-of-the-night house call was a new henhouse, with a large wire cage that covered the small lawn. Odd. Such a big cage for chickens. As she parked, a large white-feathered fowl burst out of the opening of the henhouse to honk at her car. Ah! So it was a goose house.

Edith answered Dok's first knock on the front door, as if she'd been watching for her car. Hank sat at the kitchen table. As Dok took off her coat and gloves, she took a quick assessment of Hank's pale coloring, the dark circles under his eyes. He had aged markedly in the last few weeks. Edith brought a cup of coffee to Dok and sat down with them. From the somber look on their faces, they were prepared for something serious.

"So," Dok started, "I'll get right to the point. The X-ray scan showed nodules on Hank's lungs."

Hank's good eye showed a spark of interest. "NODULES? What are they?"

"They're a type of growth."

"What kind of growth?" Edith said. "Cancer?"

"CANCER?" Hank looked at Dok in alarm.

Dok's hands tightened around the warm coffee mug. "We won't know until after Hank's biopsy."

"OH NO," Hank said. "Nothing doing. I'm not letting ANY-ONE cut into me."

Dok expected this kind of reaction. "Hold on a minute, Hank. A biopsy isn't the same thing as surgery."

"DOESN'T MATTER. I'm NOT doing it."

"Take a day or two to think about it. You might feel differently." Dok leaned her elbows onto the table. "Hank, Edith, this could be very serious."

"So you do think it's cancer," Edith said, a tremble in her voice.

"We won't know for sure without that biopsy. But if it is cancer, there are treatments."

"SOUNDS EXPENSIVE."

Argh! Dok had to bite her lip not to argue that point. "Please, Hank, Edith, don't think about the costs. Not now. It's just a biopsy."

"NOT doing it, Dok."

She took in a deep breath. "I can't let you ignore this."

"I'm NOT ignoring it, Dok. We've already been PRAYING the HEZEKIAH prayer."

"What do you mean?"

"King Hezekiah," Edith said. "In the Bible. He was dying and prayed for fifteen more years. God answered his prayer. That's what Hank's been praying. Me too. And we're going to get the prayer going with all our people."

"PRAYER WORKS," Hank said.

Yes, prayer did work. Over the years, Dok had observed healings that seemed miraculous, ones she knew did not come from modern medicine. But she also believed God used modern medicine to bring healing. "Hank, I want you to live a long, healthy life. But I think there's a better chance of that happening if you undergo the biopsy and face the results. If it does turn out to be cancer, then you can make a better decision about next steps."

"Can't. Won't. I've got TOO MUCH living to do."

"Yes! That's right. That's why you need to get this biopsy."

He shook his head. "Dok, I APPRECIATE your concern. I truly do. I KNOW your heart is in the right place. BUT if this is my TIME to GO, then so be it. I'm not going to INTERFERE. There's a TIME for all things, including a TIME to die."

Dok's cell vibrated in her pocket. She glanced over at the grandfather clock and felt a thud in her stomach. She'd completely missed the baby's bath time, and if she didn't hurry, Matt would have already put him to bed. As she rose to go, she said, "Please don't shut the door to a biopsy right now. Think it over. Talk to each other. I'll check in with you in another day or so." She could tell from the look on their faces that they weren't going to change their minds. She held out a slim hope that Edith might be able to talk some sense into Hank, but if not, then she'd ask David to intervene.

"DOK, I am going to live EVERY DAY to the fullest doing what I love doing." For just a moment, Hank's shoulders drooped, and he said in a sad voice, "Life just goes by so fast."

Walking to her car, Dok pondered Hank's remark about the swiftness of life. He was so right. It flew.

Ignoring the honking goose that found her parked car to be such a threat, she sat in the car for a long moment.

Life just goes by so fast.

She let out a defeated sigh. Hank hadn't shouted when he said it.

Before she started the car's engine, she remembered to check her phone. There were some incoming texts from Matt.

Caseworker called. We're nearing the mark
without the baby's parents able to be located
or identified. Court is starting the process to
terminate parental rights. Caseworker needs to
know if we are serious about adoption.

Another text came in.

Ruth, I'd like to tell her yes.

Dok looked over at Hank and Edith's home. *Life just goes
by so fast.*

Tell her yes.

Eighteen

The more time Bee spent with Fern, the more affected she felt by her pragmatism. Fern kept only what she used and used what she kept. She made do without things that most people felt were essential. She heated water for tea in a saucepan instead of a teakettle, for example, because the handle on her kettle had broken off with use.

Bee could not have had a more opposite perspective about things. If her kettle had lost its handle, she would've ordered a new one that same day. The Amazon Prime truck rolled up nearly every other day. Her kitchen cupboards held every imaginable gadget. Air fryer, Instant Pot, you name it, she had it. And she hardly ever cooked from scratch.

After spending time with Fern, Bee found herself less interested in shopping therapy. New things didn't give her a brief respite from gloom the way they once had.

"What are you doing with your husband's things?" Bee asked one day.

"Doing?" Fern looked at her as if she hadn't heard her correctly. "I'm not doing anything with Amos's things. They're gone."

"Everything? Clothes, shoes, hats?"

"We had an auction not long after he passed. Sold everything he owned, all except the farm."

"You sold all of your husband's belongings?" It sounded so . . . coldly practical.

"That's how we do things. Everyone gets a chance to buy what they want. It all gets auctioned off. Proceeds got divided up among his children."

"So . . . you even sold Amos's clothes?"

Fern's chin went up a notch. "No point in having them sit in a closet, getting dusty. Amos doesn't need them."

Bee felt like she'd been given a swift kick. Everything of Ted's was still in its place, right where he'd left them. Every single thing.

"Why are you holding on to your husband's things?"

"Because . . ." Why was she? She had to stop and think about it. "Because holding on to them feels like holding on to a piece of him. Because if I let them go, it feels like I'm losing him. Piece by piece. And once his things are gone . . . then he'll be gone."

"You'll never lose him," Fern said, patting her heart. "He's safe." She tipped her head. "Tell me, what made you stay here in Stoney Ridge?"

"You mean . . . since the boxes were still packed, why didn't I just go someplace else? Start fresh?"

Fern nodded.

Bee didn't even have to think about the answer. "Because of the horses. This is their home."

Later that day, as soon as Bee got home, she went to the garage and rummaged around until she found a few empty boxes.

It was time.

Bee took advice from organizing guru Marie Kondo and began with the items that held little sentimental value to her. Ted's baseball caps, old running shoes, surgical scrubs. Next, she tackled Ted's closet.

Much, much harder.

Inside the closet was a set of drawers. She pulled out the top drawer and froze. An ache shot through her. It was the first time she'd opened this drawer since he had died. She'd forgotten how he liked his rolled socks to line up in tidy rows, all color coordinated. Ted was fastidious like that. With both hands, she scooped up all his socks and clutched them to her chest as a sob broke out of her. He had touched these.

She had to let go. It was time.

She squeezed her eyes shut and dumped the socks in an empty box for donations.

Did this task make her miss Ted? So much so that she had to stop every few minutes to get a fresh tissue to wipe away tears. Like the socks, each shirt or jacket brought a memory.

One navy blazer still had a tag on it. Bee had gotten it as a present for Ted for what turned out to be their last Christmas. As she folded it, she realized that she had no memory attached to it. Ted had never worn it. She picked it up and took it out to the barn to Damon. "I'm cleaning out my husband's closet and thought you might want this blazer. He never wore it. You can see the tags. I just thought maybe . . . you could use it."

An odd look crossed his face.

"I'll set it here and you can decide later." She laid it down on top of a saddle. At the barn door, she turned to say, "Just leave it if it doesn't fit." Or feel right.

Later that evening, after Damon had left for the day, Bee went out to the barn. The blazer had been left exactly where she'd put it, untouched. She picked it up and took it to the garage, placing it in the donation box.

She kept going. Whenever she filled up a box, she'd taken it out to the garage. Tonight, she realized the boxes were lining up, and it was getting harder to walk around the garage. Of course, it would probably be wise to sell Ted's car. She never drove it. But that felt like a step she wasn't ready for. Coming out to the garage and seeing his car gone . . . that felt too final.

Little by little, Ted's closet emptied. She took an armful of her own clothes and hung them on Ted's side, and then she realized she needed to stop thinking of it as Ted's side. Fern was right. He didn't need it. When she was done, she felt . . . at peace.

Maybe she should have started to clean out the closet sooner.

The next morning, Damon seemed quieter than usual as he drove Bee to radiation, and that was saying something. As he stopped the truck in front of what she now thought of as the Zapping building, she said, "I think I made you feel uncomfortable by offering Ted's blazer to you."

He didn't disagree. "Did you give it to me because I accused you of hoarding?"

"No." She sighed. "Maybe." She opened the door. "I've been spending time with an Amish woman and she's kind of . . . teaching me a few things about life."

He kept his face forward. "Maybe I could help get those boxes in the garage to wherever you want them to go."

Bee's first instinct was to say no, that she didn't need anyone to pressure her to part with her husband's belongings. But then she thought of Fern, and how she wanted Amos's clothes to be used by someone who needed them, because he certainly didn't. "Thanks, Damon. I might take you up on that." Maybe someday.

Spring teased Stoney Ridge with a few days of warm weather and blue skies, only to have gray clouds close in like someone up there was putting a lid on the sky. Turning the furnace way down too, Dok thought, rubbing her hands together to keep warm as she hurried across the parking lot to the Bent N' Dent.

Inside, she noticed Hank was missing among the graybeards as they played checkers and ate peanuts, rockers inched close around the woodburning stove. Waving a hand to Sarah, she went straight to her brother's office and sat down in a chair.

A pleased look covered David's face. "My favorite sister has come for a visit."

She grinned. She was his only sister. The connection Dok had with her brother David was one of the highlights of her life. While their paths had taken very different turns from their childhood, they had plenty of things in common that bound them together.

She saw him as often as she could, especially if she was bothered about something, or if she needed advice. Or sometimes just to talk. She'd bring her high energy and renegade ideas to the conversation, and he'd bring his quiet sensibility and thoughtful insights. Sometimes she'd get all fired up about something, and David would listen patiently in that way he had, nodding his head now and then. He would let her finish her rant, and only then would he offer a gentle word of wisdom to defuse her. He was a fine listener.

"Where have you been?" Dok said. "I was hoping to talk to you yesterday."

"I was at a meeting for bishops over in Gordonville. Glad it was yesterday and not today. We spent the entire day in the barn."

"Do you remember this saying of Mom's? 'The sign of a big storm was one which began with small flakes.' I wonder if that's how today will end. A big storm."

David tipped his head in that thoughtful way of his. "Funny. I always thought Mom meant it as a metaphor. A warning. You know, nip a problem in the bud. That kind of thing."

A surprised laugh burst out of Dok. "So typical of us. I always took Mom so literally and you had a way of reading between the lines."

Leaning back in his chair, he smiled. "So, what's on your mind?"

Dok clapped her hands on her knees. "What have you heard about Hank Lapp's health?"

David pushed a pen back and forth on his desk. "Hank's been having trouble breathing. He has a cough. And he has nodules on his lungs."

So, he knew. "I need your help to convince Hank to undergo a biopsy. Just that one test. Just to see what's going on with those nodules. It might be nothing at all."

David held her gaze. "It's probably not nothing."

Dok sighed. "Probably not." She could tell her brother felt as heavyhearted about Hank as she did. "He'll listen to you. So will Edith. Well, maybe not Edith. But Hank will." Edith, Dok knew, could be very hard on David. She was hard on everyone, but particularly on the bishop. Edith was disappointed in David for all the reasons that everyone else loved him. Most of all, she complained he was too progressive, which Dok found to be laughable. To her, David was ridiculously conservative.

David kept rolling his pen on the desk. "You've mentioned how medical school trains a doctor to keep a body going at all costs. Death is considered to be a failure."

"True."

"But you know as well as I do that the Plain People don't view death in the same way."

She knew where this was going. The Amish believed a person's days were numbered by God. They felt modern medicine tried to push beyond God's intended biological end. She leaned forward and put her elbows on his desk. "But if it is cancer, it isn't necessarily a death sentence. It can be cured, or at least managed, so that Hank has more good years ahead."

"If Hank were twenty years old, or forty or even sixty, I'd be more inclined to put some pressure on him. But he's had a long life, and it sounds like he's at peace. I can't force him to undergo treatments that can take a hard toll on a body, especially on an older man."

"But there's all kinds of treatment available. It doesn't have to be hard on him."

"Like what?"

"One example is an integrative medicine center. They focus on building a person's immunity to let the body kill the cancer."

"How do they do that?"

"Through a series of tests to see what a cancer patient's body might be deficient in. Then they create a program of supplements to strengthen the body. And there are other facilities, other alternative treatments. But nothing can happen without a biopsy first. We have to know what we're dealing with."

"Do you really think Hank is avoiding the biopsy because he's worried about cost of treatment?"

"Yes. No. I don't know." She shrugged. "I think he wants to keep living. He said he's been praying the Hezekiah prayer."

David's eyebrows lifted. "Fifteen more years?"

"That's what he says he wants."

"Not long ago, I gave a sermon on King Hezekiah. It's nice to know someone was listening." He lifted his shoulders and dropped them. "Ruth, I'm going to have to give this matter some prayer."

Dok noticed the time on the large round wall clock. "And I'd better get back to the office." She stood and went to the door, then turned around. "Would you at least consider talking Hank into a compromise? If he would just get the biopsy, then we'd know so much more about next steps. The pulmonologist set up the order for him with a thoracic surgeon. The best surgeon in Lancaster. The biopsy would be done as an outpatient. He wouldn't have to stay the night. He might be a little sore, but he'll feel better in just a day or two."

He took it all in. But he didn't say anything. Didn't look at her.

"David, this is Hank."

Sadness covered him like a blanket. "I know, I know."

She knew exactly what was running through his mind. What would life be like without Hank Lapp?

Bee met Damon as he brought Echo in from the arena. "I can do the cool down."

He handed the horse's reins to her. "That buyer I was telling you about. She definitely wants to see Echo. Sounds like just the horse she's been looking for."

Bee's eyes went wide. "I told you I wasn't ready to sell her."

"You aren't thinking about the horse's needs. Only your own."

There was the Damon Harding she remembered from thirty years ago. Good with horses, not so much with people. "When the time is right, I'll sell."

"Bee, the time is right. You've got a customer with an open wallet, a horse that's way overdue for higher training, and you need the . . ."

She waited for him to finish. When he didn't, she said, "The what?"

"The money."

She stiffened. "I don't *need* the money."

"No? Then why are you running in the red?"

Bee narrowed her eyes. How did he know what her finances looked like? Why was he poking around in her business?

He lifted up a hand, like he was reading her mind. "Hey, I didn't ask anyone for information, if that's what you're thinking. Your vet, your hay feed guy—they all volunteered that you keep running behind on payments."

She blew out a puff of air. It's not that she didn't have the money. She did, but she'd been so overwhelmed with her own health crisis that she'd let things slide. She'd let everything slide. And maybe she just didn't want to face the facts of how expensive this breeding business was getting—so much more than she had expected. Artificial insemination, mare care, baby care. Her vet bills were astronomical. She was in over her head, collecting horses.

"Look, breeding is a costly business. A fresh competition horse can bring in over six figures. If the horses received some training—"

Suddenly Bee felt exhausted. "Damon, I just can't—I won't—consider higher-level training for my horses. End of conversation."

"Why not? Just tell me why not? The horses need it. Your business could sure use it. You've got everything you need, right here. You've even got me to help train them. I can build a course. It doesn't have to be a Grand Prix course—just a few obstacles. A couple of jumps. You've got the space for it." He looked past the arena to a large open field.

That field was where Ted's large garden was supposed to be planted. He'd mapped it all out.

She couldn't do it. She couldn't wipe out everything Ted had planned, yet she couldn't seem to take any step forward.

"All you need to do is to ask, Bee. I'm only trying to help you."

She spun around to face him. "Then help me! And stop trying to change everything."

They stared at each other for a long moment. Why did Damon keep pushing her? Why couldn't he just do what she asked and leave it there? She couldn't wait until she felt better and could ask him to leave without feeling as if she might be jeopardizing the welfare of her horses. Because what irritated her the most was that she could see how extraordinary he was with horses, how he brought out the best in them. Everything he was saying made at least some sense.

"Fine," she snapped. "Fine. You can do some higher-level training. But not in that field. Only in the arena."

"Good." A shadow of a smile crossed his solemn face, there and gone so quickly she might've imagined it. "Good."

Years ago, as an adult, Dok had been diagnosed with ADHD. It had helped so much to know what was going on with her, why life seemed more difficult for her than for others. And in some ways, easier too. She'd learned how to put systems in place to manage her distractibility and poor follow-through. She'd had helpful counseling, and she took medication. All in all, there were gifts that came with ADHD. High energy, a strong will, creativity, out-of-the-box problem-solving.

There were weaknesses that came with it too.

She was pretty sure Matt had an undiagnosed case of ADHD. His version was different behaviors than hers—the *H* for Dok meant hyperactivity but the *H* for Matt meant hyperfocus. Not official or approved, but that's how she interpreted the *H*, anyway. She had hummingbird energy, easily distracted, while Matt could zero in on a task and never hear a bomb going off. Kind of like how he slept.

They shared some more common ADHD behaviors, though. They were both great at starting things and poor at finishing them.

The house remodel, for example, which was going on five years now. Matt had so many unfinished projects around the house, started and set aside when his interest moved on to another project. Most of the projects could be completed pretty easily if he would just stay focused and make some decisions. Small things, like choosing outlets for the light switches. Or what color to paint the trim around a window.

But Dok didn't nag Matt about their unfinished house. Not much, anyway. She was so rarely home that most of the uncompleted things went unnoticed by her. Things like, their bedroom had only two walls with drywall and two walls of open two-by-fours. Their unfinished house had really never bothered her until she spent more time at home. Lately, it bothered her quite a bit.

The very next day after Dok agreed to pursuing Gabe's adoption, Matt got serious about finishing up the house remodel. He was concerned that the caseworker might not think the house was in good enough condition for a growing child. He painted the spare bedroom a pale blue, with plans to turn it into Gabe's room. At long last, he drywalled the two walls of studs in the master bedroom. He painted the window trim. He screwed in all the light switches. He found a subcontractor to install wood flooring in the kitchen, and then he decided to extend wood flooring through the entire downstairs. Much better than carpet, he told Dok, for cleanliness and allergens. Worth the extra cost, he said.

Since when did Matt care about allergens and cleanliness?

Dok was so happy that the house remodel was finally getting some traction that she didn't object to any additional costs. It was endearing to see how much Matt cared about Gabe's well-being. This is what every child deserved, she thought. Parents who fussed over them.

Matt's leave would be ending soon, and they'd need to consider childcare. Dok knew of several Amish girls who hired out, who'd provide good care. Wonderful care. In fact, you couldn't get much better. The only childcare that could be better for Gabe would be if she and Matt were home full-time. Or pretty close to it.

Lately Dok had been kicking around the idea of reducing her office hours to just four days a week from five and a half days. Her patient load was packed, so it would probably mean four very long days. Matt, who worked shifts, could work a thirty-two-hour workweek and still get full benefits. If he were to stay home with the baby at least one or two days a week, and if she were home another day, then childcare would only be necessary for two days. Her eyebrows lifted. Tonight, she might just bring up that idea to Matt. She almost laughed out loud, thinking of how shocked he'd be.

Seeking margin in her life brought such calm, such contentment. How had she missed that piece? Why didn't other doctors talk about the benefits of a balanced life? Probably because they were all alike. Starting as residents, right off the bat, they were conditioned to be thoroughly consumed by their careers. No wonder the home lives of so many doctors crashed and burned.

Even in her late fifties, Dok felt like she was still learning the basics, as if she'd missed a stage of development. And maybe she had. Leaving home to go to college like she did, only eighteen years old, and the tension that lingered for decades with her mother—it all had an effect. Dok had something to prove. Maybe that's the real reason she had come to Stoney Ridge to practice medicine—to keep proving to her mother that she'd made the right decision and was a successful doctor.

Even after Mom's death last year, she found it hard to shake off a lifetime of habitual pressure. She worked tirelessly to care for her patients, to the point where she was in danger of burning out or jeopardizing her marriage. Or both.

But that was changing.

That dear little baby boy was teaching her about the most important things in life.

What if the birth mother hadn't left him on Dok's office doorstep? What if Matt had said no to fostering him? Think of all they might have missed. Their life together was better with this baby boy.

Days passed yet nothing had been said. Annie had been waiting for Dok to bring up the conversation about becoming an EMT, but she didn't mention it. Nothing was happening to move things forward. On Dok's end, anyway.

On Annie's end, she had gone to the public library and found a Saturday EMT course that would create minimal disruption in her work schedule. She felt pretty sure that somebody could fill in for her on Saturdays. She needed Dok's support, though. She needed Dok to talk to the bishop, and for the bishop to talk to Annie's parents. That path seemed to have the greatest chance for success. The roundabout path.

Finally, during lunch when the waiting room was empty, Annie went back to Dok's office. Dok was at her desk, staring out the window, with that preoccupied look on her face . . . and Annie lost her nerve. She turned around, but Dok must have heard her.

"Annie, what's up?"

"I, um, wondered if we could, um, if sometime we could talk about . . . me becoming an . . . um . . ."

Dok's eyes went wide. "Oh no. The EMT! Oh Annie, I completely forgot. Yes, let's talk. Come in. Come in and sit down. Tell me all about it."

Annie sat across from Dok, prepared to explain her interest, yet as she tried to gather her thoughts and start, her mind went blank. There were no thoughts to be gathered. Every passing second felt like a minute.

"Annie," Dok said in such a gentle voice, "I realize you are shy, but if you are truly interested in becoming an EMT, I need to know more. Do you even know much about what it means to be an EMT?"

"I do." Annie nodded. "I went to an informational class over in Gordonville."

Dok's eyebrows lifted. "So why do you want to do this?"

For God hath not given us the spirit of fear; but of power, and of love, and of a sound mind. It was another verse from Dok's list. Keeping her eyes down, Annie repeated it to herself again and again, then she lifted her head and said the most important thing she'd ever said to anyone, other than the vows at her baptism. "I feel . . . the Lord has called me to it."

That, she could tell, was not the answer Dok had expected.

"A calling." Dok's eyes bored into her. "You're sure? You're absolutely sure you heard a calling from God?"

Annie nodded.

Dok watched her for a long while. "Well, it's hard to argue with *that*. I can say that from personal experience." Then she smiled. "I have to say that I think you'd be wonderful as an EMT. You're very calm in a crisis. Unflappable."

Unflappable. That's exactly what Sarah and Hank had said about Annie. She liked to think that's how people would describe her. She could not be flapped. And suddenly an entire paragraph came together in her brain like puzzle pieces finding their proper position. "Dok, I don't know if someone from our church can be an EMT. I mean, I know there *is* an Amish EMT, but he's not in our church. As far as I know, there's never been an Amish EMT out of Stoney Ridge. Even if the bishop agreed to it, I doubt my parents would allow it. My mother, especially." Phew! That was the most she'd ever said to Dok at one time.

Dok lifted her hands in the air. "There's only one way to find out. Let's start with asking the bishop." She went to the window. "In fact, I see that he's just arriving at the store now. I need to talk to him about a few things myself." She grabbed her coat and opened the door. "Come on, Annie. No time like the present. Let's go talk to David."

Annie's eyes went wide. *Now?*

Nineteen

Annie trotted behind Dok as she marched straight through the Bent N' Dent and into the bishop's office. Sarah, at the register, dropped her mouth wide open. She hurried over to Annie and grabbed her arm. "What is going on?"

Annie kept her eyes down, shook off Sarah's grip, and slipped into the bishop's office behind Dok, quietly closing the door behind her.

Dok sat right down across from his desk, paying no mind to the fact that he was in the middle of something. "David, we've got something we want to discuss with you."

Annie had to hand it to the bishop. He never seemed bothered by interruptions. She wondered if he was like that before he became a minister, then a bishop, or if he'd always been that way. She had a hunch he was just born patient.

The bishop leaned back in his chair. "How can I help?"

Dok looked at Annie. "Annie's interested in doing a little more in the world of medicine."

"Yes, yes, I know. I spoke to your father, Annie, about staying on as Dok's office assistant. He said he'd be agreeable to it, so long as he can get your mother on board." The bishop leaned his elbows on his desk. "Is there a problem with that? Would you like me to talk to your mother?"

Dok waved that off. "I can handle Sally Fisher. That's not what this is about." She turned to Annie. "Go ahead. Tell him what you told me."

The bishop's eyes were on her. Dok's eyes were on her. Annie felt like she was a child again, in some doctor's office with her mother. All eyes on her. Anxiety mounting, she began tugging more urgently at her apron hem. Her chin went down, her eyes went to the top of her shoes. Her thoughts went from clear to fuzzy, wispy, hard to grasp and hold on to. They floated through her mind like fast-moving clouds. Then one clear thought emerged from the fog, a verse from Dok's list that she had just memorized:

Have not I commanded thee? Be strong and of a good courage; be not afraid, neither be thou dismayed: for the LORD *thy God is with thee withersoever thou goest.*

Dok cleared her throat. Once. Then again, a little more forcefully.

Be not afraid. Be not afraid.

Annie took in a deep breath, let it out, and lifted her head. "I'd . . . like to . . . get qualified as an EMT."

The bishop's eyebrows shot up. "You *what*?"

Annie opened her mouth to say something, but no words came out. She closed it and tried again.

"Annie, I might have misheard you, but I thought you said you wanted to get qualified as an EMT. Did I hear you correctly?"

She bit her lip.

"Annie," he said softly, "can you explain why you'd like to be an EMT?"

"Annie," Dok whispered. "You can do this."

But she couldn't.

Yes, she could.

196

Be not afraid. Be not afraid. The Lord thy God is with thee.

Annie straightened her shoulders. "I heard . . . or maybe I felt . . . a clear call from God."

The bishop thought for a moment. A protracted moment. Painfully long. He cast a glance at Dok. "Ruth, is there much of a need for EMTs in the county?"

"Oh yes," Dok said. "A huge, huge need. A desperate need."

That was a significant piece of information. Annie could see it in the bishop's eyes. Tipping the scales kind of information.

"David, I am confident that there's nothing contradictory to the church for an Amish person to become an EMT. Nothing. Other Amish have done it."

He tipped his head slightly back and forth, as if to say yes and no. "Other . . . Amish men."

"Yes, mostly men. But I've read about some Amish females who are EMTs."

Annie's eyes went wide. So she wasn't alone in this desire? There were others? Her toes started tapping.

"Personally," Dok said, "I think it's similar to the church allowing volunteer firefighters. Same thing."

He seemed unconvinced. "But EMTs aren't volunteers."

"No, that's true. It's a job. It will require weeks of training. Then there's a qualifying exam."

"What about a high school diploma?"

"Got it," Annie said. Both Dok and the bishop looked at her at the same time, startled by her admission, and her stomach flipped over. No one, but no one, had known she'd gotten her GED.

Dok burst out with a laugh. "Annie Fisher, you are full of surprises."

Annie dared a glance at the bishop and was relieved to see he didn't seem alarmed or bothered by her confession. His attention was on his sister.

"So, Ruth, I take it you are supportive of Annie's . . . calling."

Dok smiled. "I am. I think Annie would be an excellent EMT. She already has quite a depth of knowledge about medicine, but even more than her aptitude, she has the temperament for it. I've noticed Annie's presence radiates calm in a crisis. And to think she has sensed a calling from the Lord to become an EMT, well, David, that's hard to dismiss."

"You'll lose another good office assistant."

Dok sighed. "I know. But not for a while, at least."

Annie's eyes went from one to the other. She couldn't believe the direction this conversation was taking. Could this really be happening?

The bishop dipped his chin, and Annie had a strange sense that he might be praying.

After a long moment he lifted his head and said, "Annie, I will support you in this, because I believe you. I trust that the Lord has given you a gift to help others in a crisis. As I'm sure you know, no one in our church has ever been an EMT."

Annie's whole body was tingling. It was all starting to add up. Everything except one detail.

"Your parents," the bishop said, "might take some persuading."

Would they *ever*.

"Your mother, especially—"

Bull's-eye.

"—but I can help with that."

"Me too," Dok said.

Annie fought down the desire to leap up and do a cartwheel.

The bishop leaned back in his chair. "I have no doubt there will be criticism in the church that I've become too progressive. I'm willing to accept it, but I want to be sure that you know what you're getting into. There's a young Plain man over in Gordonville who has become an EMT. I'd like to set up a time when the three of us could talk about what the job entails, and the kinds of limitations on a Plain EMT. Would you be willing to take that little step before we do anything else?"

Take that little step?

Meet . . . Mr. Wonderful?

Learn about when and how and why he became an EMT?

Annie could barely hold back from standing on this chair in the bishop's office to jump up and down. Shout for joy. Turn a cartwheel.

She lifted her head to look straight at the bishop. "Absolutely." It came out loud and clear.

Dok didn't see Hank Lapp for another couple of days, which struck her as unusual. Normally, he spent the bulk of his days at the Bent N' Dent, eating peanuts and playing checkers with other older men. It seemed to Dok that many wives of retired farmers sent their husbands there for the day. It was the Amish version of golfing.

One gray afternoon, she was driving past the Lapp house and decided to stop in to check on Hank, see if his cough was better or worse. She'd kept asking David to put some pressure on Hank to get the biopsy, and he would only say that he was praying about it. She had a hunch that her conflict-avoidant brother wasn't going to ever get around to it, especially if it meant butting heads with Hank's wife, Edith. Frustrating! It was just one small procedure, that's all. Just to know what was going on inside Hank's lungs.

A few raindrops hit her windshield as she pulled into the driveway. She got out of the car and looked around, not seeing any signs of Hank or Edith. A noise startled her and she turned to see Hank fly out of the henhouse, chased by that honking goose. Dok had to laugh at the sight of him, high stepping it as fast as he could. She waited until he had managed to get out of the cage without the goose hanging on to his pants leg. "Why would you want to raise such a nasty bird?"

"Hi there, DOK!" Hank locked the cage door behind him. "Eddy and me are in the GOOSE business. Mostly, me. Eddy HATES 'em."

"Really? I didn't know there was such a thing as a goose business."

Hank looked astonished at Dok's ignorance. "BIG business! Steady customers for HOLIDAY supper. RIPE for the PLUCK-ING." He gave her a big wink. "Get it?"

"I get it." It was nice to see Hank up and around. More himself than the last visit.

"They might be PRETTY BIRDS, but they do have a MEAN streak." The goose took offense at that and made a dive near Hank, honking and snapping at him through the wire cage.

Dok laughed. "I suppose that mean streak makes it easier to enjoy the Christmas goose."

Hank joined her in a laugh that turned into a cough. A long, hard cough. Worse than ever. He was doubled over, hacking away, trying to catch his breath between coughs.

After it passed, and he was able to stand up straight, she quietly said, "Not getting better, is it?"

"Alte Fässer rinnen gern." *Old vessels are prone to leak.*

True, older people had lots of ailments. But Dok wasn't going to dismiss Hank's cough as a natural part of aging. She waited until the angry goose settled down. "Hank, I stopped by to ask you to please consider the biopsy—"

Hank lifted a hand to stop her. "NO NEED for it. I've got people PRAYING all over the COUNTRY for me. Those prayers are all I need. Besides, just because folks have a BUNCH of INITIALS after their name doesn't mean they know EVERY-THING. Just look at the weathermen! Sunny today, was the forecast." He held out his palm to capture a few sprinkles.

"Rain HAPPENS even if they don't forecast it." He smiled. "PRAYER WORKS, you know."

"I do know. I keep praying you'll change your mind."

By now Edith had come out the kitchen door to join them. "Only thing we're going to change around here is those geese. They're dreadful creatures." She pointed to the goose who seemed particularly cantankerous. "That one in particular. It's always escaping out of the cage. I'm ready to cook it for dinner."

Hank frowned. "Eddy, these BIRDS are WORTH a LOT."

"Then let's get them in the freezer, where they can't bite us."

"They need FATTENING UP." He coughed, then turned to Dok. "Don't you THINK they look a little SKINNY?"

Dok didn't want to get trapped into this kind of conversation between them, especially with raindrops starting. "Edith, I came to see if you've reconsidered the biopsy. The order is in, ready to go. It would be an outpatient procedure. It's not terribly invasive. Hank will be a little sore for a day or two, then he can get right back to fattening up his geese."

Edith didn't say a word. She kept her eyes on the goose in the cage, who was eyeing her right back. A stare-down.

"Just a biopsy. That's all I'm asking. I can drive Hank to the surgi-center and back home again."

Edith Fisher Lapp did not have a face that was easy to read. As a whole, the Amish leaned toward withholding emotional responses, especially when they were with non-Amish. It was just their way, yet Edith had mastered the look. Even so, Dok thought she caught just a glimmer of shininess in her eyes. Just a tiny bit. And in that look, Dok knew she was worried about Hank.

Go easy here, Ruth, she told herself.

She walked over to Edith and softly said, "All you need to do is to call Annie at the office. We'll take care of getting the biopsy scheduled. And I spoke to David. It will be paid for by the church. You don't have to worry about anything. Not a thing. We'll take care of everything."

Hank stepped between Edith and Dok. "THANKS but NO THANKS, Dok. I know you mean well, but I'll thank you to STOP pestering me."

He spoke so loudly that he startled the goose, and she flapped her wings, honking away at him. So noisy that Dok gave up. She waved goodbye and got in her car. A saying of her father's popped into her mind: Mer kann Vieh ans Wasser dreiwe, awwer mer kann's net saufe mache. *You can drive cattle to water but can't make them drink.*

As she backed down the driveway, she silently prayed for Hank. She lifted a hand in the air. "I've done all I can, Lord. The rest is up to you."

Before she backed onto the road, she turned her gaze forward and burst out laughing. Somehow that angry goose had slipped under the cage and was heading, full speed, right toward Hank.

If Bee were to guess, she would say that Damon's missing arm had something to do with a jump that went horribly wrong. Perhaps the horse tripped, falling on top of him, crushing his arm. Bee had known of terrible jumps gone wrong. Show jumping was a beautiful sport, but it could be a dangerous one.

A show jump horse was a muscular, robust, sturdy animal. Truly athletic, it needed to sail over twelve to fifteen obstacles, which always included a water jump. The tracks and jumps were intentionally difficult, designed to make a horse refuse the jump. It was what separated the bravest horses from the more fearful ones. A horse had to be willing to take the jump.

Anything "off" could risk the horse "going clear"—meaning the horse wouldn't hit any rail or refuse any fence. If the horse became distracted or, even worse, spooked by a tricky jump, a rider could really get hurt. Bee remembered a time when an elite equestrian broke her back in a fall and ended up paralyzed.

That was one of the reasons Bee couldn't let go of her bitterness toward Damon and his misdeed. *Alleged* misdeed, she reminded herself. But when something as simple as a horse's gear was bothersome, even a distraction as small as a hook on a buckle, digging into its chin with its sharp point, it could cause great risk to the rider.

Thankfully, Ozzie kept her wits about her during that Olympic round. Although unsettled by the jab of the hook under her noseband, the mare rode a clear round. She had no faults from knocking or clipping a rail; she sailed over each obstacle. Bee and Ozzie lost because of time. Bee had hesitated slightly before counting down to the jump-off because of the way Ozzie kept tossing her head. Just the slightest distraction—but it cost them the gold.

Bee and Ozzie earned a silver medal for the individual round. It was beautiful, solid and shiny, but it wasn't gold.

Damon had won the gold. No, he hadn't won it. He had stolen it. From Bee and Ozzie.

No proof, no evidence, sore loser.

Bee couldn't let go of that suspicion, but she couldn't confront Damon about it, either. Yet another area where she was "stuck."

That afternoon, cold but sunny, Bee drove over to Windmill Farm and knocked on the kitchen door. No answer. She knocked again, then called Fern's name.

"Out here!"

Bee looked around but didn't see her. "Fern, where are you?"

"On the side of the house. In the vegetable garden."

Bee followed the direction of the voice, and there was Fern, tackling a weed in a long straight row of something or other. "What are you doing?"

"Cleaning the garden patch."

Patch? This garden was bigger than most people's backyards. Fern was peering at her. "You look tired."

So blunt. "I am. A little." A lot. Really, really tired. Bee took two naps a day and still felt exhausted.

"Too tired to grab a hoe and help? Movement is good for you, you know."

"Sure. I can help." Bee walked over to where a few tools were leaning against the fence. She grabbed a hoe and joined Fern. At first, all the winter-weary plants looked alike. She watched Fern for several long moments, until she figured out which leaves belonged to the strawberry plants and which were weeds. "Why are you doing this now? Why not wait until everything starts to grow?"

"Because weeds steal nutrients from the soil that the berries will need." Fern tossed some weeds into a bucket.

Bee pondered that as she tried to pull a big thick weed out. It had a ridiculously long root, though the leaves on top weren't that big. "Look at that!"

Fern lifted her head to see. "That's the problem with weeds. They dig down deep and take all the good things away." She jammed her trowel into the dirt. "Some minds can work that way."

Bee sat on her heels, wiping mud off her hands. *Like my mind.* Which was what Fern was getting at. That woman never missed a chance to drive home a point. "Certain thoughts take hold. Certain memories . . . they take up a lot of space in my brain."

"Bad thoughts can be like weeds. Pull them out quickly before they take over. There's no point in watering the weeds."

And that became the opening Bee had been looking for. "Years ago," she said, "someone stole something from me. Something really important to me. I think he did, anyway. It was something done in secret, so I'm not absolutely, one hundred percent positive. I have no proof. None. Just a pretty strong hunch."

Fern kept jamming the trowel into the dirt to dig up weeds, saying nothing, but Bee could tell she was listening.

"I hadn't seen him for a very long time. And then out of nowhere he burst into my life, uninvited. And now I see him nearly every day."

Fern gave her a sideways glance. "That trainer fellow?"

Bee nodded.

"How does he do with your horses? You seem pretty finicky about them."

Bee smiled. Finicky didn't come close to it. Obsessively over-protective was Ted's description. "He's actually been doing an outstanding job with my horses."

"So, then, does he seem like a thief?"

"No. Not at all. In fact, he's very reliable. Extremely conscientious with the horses. And if he says he's going to be somewhere at a certain time, he'll be there. Not the best listener, though."

"If you asked this trainer fellow if he had stolen something from you, do you think he would tell you the truth?"

Ask him? Just like that? "It's a pretty harsh accusation. If I'm wrong, he would have every right to be offended. I couldn't blame him if he up and left. I need his help, at least for a while longer."

"So that's why you haven't said anything?"

"Yes." That's exactly why. Bee had needed Damon's help, and she continued to need it.

"Seems to me you've already decided he's guilty." Fern stabbed the earth with her trowel. "Then again, if you're wrong, you'll have discovered that you've been spending years just watering the weeds."

Bee's hands froze in the middle of yanking a weed from the cold soil. Another gotcha moment. She stared at Fern. Such a small woman, a pixie, yet her words could strike like the point of a sword.

If Bee wrongfully accused Damon, he'd leave her high and dry. Who could blame him? If she found out she was wrong, she'd have to admit to herself that she had overlooked double-checking the buckle on Ozzie's chin strap. The mistake would belong to her.

But if her hunch was right, if Damon had indeed sabotaged her round, what would that mean? How could they work together with *that* out in the open? She still had one more week of zapping to go, and the radiologist had told her to expect the fatigue to last for as long as the treatment had lasted. That meant she wouldn't fully recover her energy for another six weeks. She knew she couldn't handle the horses without his help.

Fern shook dirt off weeds and tossed them into a bucket. "I get the impression that whatever went on between the two of you, it happened a long time ago."

Bee puffed out a sigh. "Three decades ago."

"Don't you think," Fern said, lifting a sparse eyebrow, "that it's time to find out, one way or the other?"

Bee was silent for a long while. The problem, she decided, was that whether she'd been right or whether she'd been wrong, she had something to lose. Losing Damon's help with the horses was one thing.

But letting go of her carefully nurtured grudge was another.

Early Saturday morning, Annie practically jumped out of bed, eager for the day to start. She hadn't said a word to anyone about the talk she'd had with the bishop and Dok about becoming an EMT. Not a soul. She still had to pinch herself, just to make sure she wasn't dreaming. How could this have happened? Who would've thought Dok would cheer her on? Or that the bishop would support her desire? Not only support, but take on the responsibility to persuade her parents? No one else had the influence over them—Mom, especially—like the bishop did.

This afternoon, the bishop and Annie would head to the Gordonville Fire Station to have a conversation about becoming an EMT. Annie wasn't sure what made her more nervous— spending that kind of extended time in close proximity with the bishop, learning about EMT work from the very EMT who had first lit the spark for her . . . or officially meeting Mr. Wonderful.

She reminded herself that getting better acquainted with the love of her life was not the purpose of today's meeting. *Stay focused. Focus, focus, focus.*

Knowing that her mind hopped on a spinning hamster wheel whenever a "person in authority" put their attention on her, she wrote down a few questions to ask Mr. Wonderful. (Correction! Today she would only think of him as the Amish EMT.) Questions like, how difficult were the classes? What about the qualification test? Could she go on a ride-along in the ambulance before she took the test?

But what she really wanted to find out from the Amish EMT was whether there were conflicts with his church. If there was any criticism of his work from people in his church and, if so, how did he manage it? Most likely, being a male, he wasn't subject to criticism. Annie's test-the-water conversation with her mother gave her a taste of what was to come. She did not manage open conflict well. Fingering her index card of questions, she hoped the bishop would ask the EMT most of the questions.

When office hours ended on Saturday, Annie went back to Dok's office to tell her she was heading out with the bishop.

Dok came from behind her desk to give her a hug. "Good luck, Annie. I hope today provides all the answers you need to become an EMT."

For a few seconds, Annie wobbled, wondering why she was taking this step, unsure of where it could lead her. Why change anything? Working for Dok was a dream come true. It was enough. Or . . . it should be enough.

As if reading Annie's wobbly mind, Dok took her by the shoulders and steered her down the hall and out the front door. "Don't let fear stop you. Go. Learn all you can today."

Slowly, Annie walked over to the Bent N' Dent to wait for the bishop. She would've stayed outside, but the cold wind was whipping her bonnet strings, so she quietly slipped inside. Tried to, anyway. The chimes on the door rang and Sarah looked up from behind the register. "ANNIE! I'm still looking for that EMT for you. I haven't found him yet, but I keep asking customers if they've seen him."

Annie backed up to the door.

Sarah came around the register corner and headed toward Annie. She was one of those people who stood close, way too close, and Annie was now truly cornered at the door. "I'm not giving up. I will find him." Sarah peered at her. "Are you all right? You look pale."

Coming from behind Sarah, the bishop cleared his throat. "Annie, if you're ready, let's go."

Sarah spun around. "Where are you two going?"

"Sarah," he said with a frown, "we've talked about this before. You don't need to know everything."

"But I do," Sarah said.

"No, you don't." The bishop crossed the room. "I'll be back before closing time."

Annie scooted around Sarah to allow the bishop space to open the door. She could feel Sarah's eyes on her as she followed the bishop to the horse and buggy.

The bishop helped her in, then untethered the horse's reins and came around to the driver's side to climb in. "Sarah is a fine worker, and she's learning to not cross the line with her . . . curiosity."

Was she? Annie saw no such improvement. In fact, she

thought Sarah's nosiness was only getting worse since she'd started working at the store. Sarah interacted with so many people throughout the day that she was turning into the town crier. She was getting as bad as Hank Lapp—supplying news that no one wanted, mixing up important details, leaving people confused and upset. Just like Hank Lapp.

As the buggy went along the road to Gordonville, the wind was so loud that the bishop didn't talk, which suited Annie nicely. She was ridiculously nervous enough to meet Mr. Wonderful, who'd held her fascination for months now. Correction. Today he was *not* Mr. Wonderful. He was the Amish EMT.

Twenty

Annie's heart seemed to trip over its next beat. Here he was, standing right in front of her. Mr. Wonderful. The man of her dreams. Dizzy, she stepped back and did her best not to look like she might fall over in a dead faint.

The bishop reached out a hand in a warm shake. "Gus, I'd like you to meet Annie Fisher. Annie, this is Gus Troyer."

"We've met, actually," Gus said.

"Really?" The bishop turned to Annie. "You know each other?"

Her mouth fell open silently, as her eyes shifted to Mr. Wonderful. Correction. Gus Troyer. Such a perfect name. Such a perfect man. She had promised herself that the next time she saw this man, she wouldn't stand there like a mute.

And yet! Here she was. Her thoughts, her mouth, all of her felt like a fast-moving stream suddenly dammed up by a fallen tree.

"We sure have. She follows me around, from one emergency to the next." His grin split wide, and her stomach flipped.

Heat rushed to her face, and probably her neck and chest and legs and every other part of her body.

"I'm just teasing," Gus said. "We've crossed paths a few

times. But we've never been formally introduced. Nice to meet you, Annie."

She dipped her chin in a tiny nod, still fighting a blush. Her eyes went to the tops of her shoes and stayed there, like glue.

"As I mentioned on the phone," the bishop said, "Annie has a few questions about becoming an EMT." He glanced at her. "I might go say hello to the fire chief and give the two of you a moment to chat."

Wait. What? You're leaving me alone with him? Don't leave! Part of her wanted to follow the bishop right out the door. But a bigger part of her wanted to stay.

Gus led her into the kitchen where a firefighter in uniform stood in front of the stove, stirring something that smelled delicious. As Gus took two mugs off a hook and poured coffee into them, the firefighter turned around and noticed Annie. He did a double take, looking startled, recovered, and said hello, then went back to his cooking.

Gus set the mugs on a table and pulled out a chair for her. "So, I hear you're considering EMT work."

Placing her hands around the warm mug, she nodded. But she didn't say anything. Her eyes stayed on the top of her coffee.

"Do you have any specific questions for me, Annie? Things like, what it's like to be Amish and be an EMT? If there might be any conflicts with church? Those were the questions I had, at least. And then, of course, there's the added complication of being female." He leaned a little closer. "Which I think is pretty awesome. Brave. I'm sure you wouldn't be considering it if you didn't feel a real calling to it."

Her eyes lifted to his. Bless him—he understood! She did feel a calling. In fact, she *heard* a calling! Their eyes locked, and she wondered if a tropical ocean was the same color as his beautiful blue eyes. She swallowed once, then twice, trying to clear her throat of her wildly thumping heart.

Patiently, he waited for her to toss him a question. And waited. And waited.

She wanted to say something, anything, but her mind was mercilessly blank. What was that Bible verse she had memorized to help in moments like this? She could remember only bits and pieces, scrambled words that didn't make any sense. She was making a huge fool of herself. If it was possible, her hot cheeks burned an even brighter shade of red. Beet red. Fire-engine red.

And then two firefighters walked through the door into the kitchen. One was telling the other a story, using very colorful language. When they caught sight of Annie and Gus at the table, they stopped short. "My apologies, ma'am," said the one who had used a few unrepeatable words. They exchanged a curious look.

"Bannet." *Bonnet.* Gus reached out to straighten her bonnet, and his gentle touch made her tremble. "They're not used to seeing an Amish woman in here."

Annie had been so consumed by Gus's blue eyes that she hadn't even thought to take off her big black bonnet. She untied the strings and slipped it off, into her lap.

"I'm sure you've got lots of questions, Annie. That's why the bishop brought you here today. So fire away. Ask me anything." When he saw her eyes dart toward the three firemen standing near the stove and refrigerator, he added, "No need to be shy. We're all like family here."

"Oh, I hope not. You haven't met my mother," Annie said. Then her eyes opened wide as she realized what she had said. Mortifying! Absolutely mortifying. Of all the things she wanted to say to him, how did *that* rude remark pop out of her mouth? Her hands tightened around her bonnet, and she thought about bolting out the door to hide in the buggy.

Gus looked as shocked as she was. Suddenly, a chuckle burst out of him, followed by full-blown laughter. He laughed so hard he slapped the table with his palms, nearly knocking over his coffee cup, which only got him laughing again. His laugh wound down and then came back again. Finally, he shook his head, smiling. "Annie Fisher, I don't think I've ever met a girl quite like you."

For several long seconds, it was like everything had ceased to exist around Annie. Her eyes were on Mr. Wonderful, his messy mop of blond hair, his twinkling blue eyes, his gigantic muscles on his arms that looked like he'd dug more than his share of fence posts over the years.

There was something about his laughter—so easy and light-hearted and contagious—that caused her to loosen, to relax, to feel at ease. As if the dam that kept blocking her thoughts from reaching her mouth was starting to break up. As if water was trickling again, finding a downhill path, flowing free and steady.

"I do have questions for you," she said, her voice clear and steady. "Quite a lot of them." Happiness filled her, head to toe.

During lunch on Monday, Dok checked messages on her phone and realized she'd missed a call from baby Gabe's case-worker, Sandra. The voicemail she left said to call back, but she didn't sound like it was urgent—she probably needed yet another paper signed for the adoption—so Dok thought she'd get back to her later. And then she forgot.

Later that day, Dok prepared to stitch up a two-inch gash on the knee of Noah Miller, a six-year-old Amish boy. Solemn Noah had been so brave when she gave him the shot to numb the knee, but as he watched her thread the needle, a tear had leaked down his cheek.

"Es dutt mer so weh!" *It's so painful.*

"Net waarhr," Dok said. *Not so.* A six-year-old Amish boy was just starting to learn English in school. Up until now, he spoke only Penn Dutch. Within a few years, this little boy would be fluent in English and German, as well as Penn Dutch.

Noah was a quintessential Amish boy. Bright blue eyes and a bowl cut of nearly white hair, not unlike baby Gabe, though his hair was just peach fuzz. She wondered if Gabe might resemble Noah in a few years. She hoped so.

Annie knocked on the door of the exam room and popped her head in. "You have a call."

Dok was just about to ask who it was and maybe she could call back later, but she caught herself. Annie was trying to be bolder and Dok should encourage her efforts.

"It's the caseworker for the baby," Annie said. "She said it was important."

"I should take this call," Dok told Noah's mother. "I won't be gone long. By the time I return, Noah's knee will be thoroughly numb." She went into her office and picked up the phone. "Hi, Sandra. I'm sorry I didn't return your call sooner. What's up?"

"I wanted you to know that the baby's father has been in touch with us."

"Hold it. Say that again?"

As Sandra repeated herself, Dok sank down in her chair. "How could this be?"

"He initiated the contact."

"But . . . how do you even know he's the father of Gabe?"

"Well, he's provided a fair amount of proof that he and the mother were involved in a relationship. He's offered to take a paternity test—"

Dok scoffed.

"—we didn't have to ask him for it, is what I meant. And of course we'd do a swab test with the baby. He's also provided evidence that he's clean. No drugs."

"How do you know?"

"He's been painting houses these last few months, and the owner of the painting business requires regular drug tests. Plus he's been living in a halfway house."

"So what does he want?"

214

A long pause. "He's interested in seeing the baby."

Hearing that raised the hair on Dok's arms and made her hands tremble. Leaning back in her chair, she drew in a deep breath. "Why now? Where's he been these last few months?"

"He says he didn't know about the baby. He thought the mother had . . . made a different decision about the pregnancy. They had split up long before the baby was born."

"Then how did he find out about Gabe?"

"Sounds like he heard through a mutual friend at the half-way house."

Oh great. Nice network of friends. "Is he in touch with the mother?"

"He says he doesn't know where she is. He hasn't been in contact with her since they parted ways."

Dok let out a puff of air. "So what does this mean?"

"As I said, he wants to have a visit with the baby. Supervised, of course. And it goes without saying that the paternity test would come first."

"I meant, what could that mean for the adoption? It's still on track, isn't it?"

A long pause. Sandra cleared her throat. "We'll have to see what happens. Most likely."

Dok felt a hitch in her gut. "Most likely but not definitely?"

"Much too soon to say."

"Sandra, surely the courts wouldn't hand a baby over to a father who shows up out of the blue. A guy who's currently living in a halfway house?"

The silence on the phone felt palpable. "The courts lean heavily toward reunification of parent and child. It's just the way things are."

"But what about the best interests of the child? What about making sure he'll be provided with a safe and secure home? What about having two loving parents? Doesn't the court prioritize a child's needs?"

"The data indicates that reunification is in everyone's best interest."

"Data." Dok knew all about data. Statistics didn't take into account human emotions and attachments. "Even if this man is a stranger to his own child." Her voice sounded ice cold. She couldn't help it.

Another long pause. "I trust you would honor the request to provide a swab from the baby's cheek for the paternity test."

"Yes. Of course." Of course she would honor it. "I'll take care of it."

"Thank you. And I'll keep you posted."

Dok set the phone down with a sinking feeling. She remained at her desk for a long time, trying to absorb this news.

She wondered how to break the news to Matt. Would he be angry? Or have mixed emotions? As fond as she'd grown of baby Gabe, her feelings didn't compare to Matt's. He was crazy about the baby.

First things first. Tonight, she'd take a swab from the baby's cheek, a nonpainful, nonintrusive test, and have it sent to the lab for analysis. Maybe this guy wasn't the baby's father, after all. Maybe that's why he and Monica broke up.

Annie knocked on the door. "I'm sorry to bother you, Dok, but Noah Miller's knee is going to lose its numbness soon."

"Oh, right! The knee." Dok hurried into the exam room, apologizing profusely, and sutured Noah's poor knee. It wasn't her best stitching job.

Twenty-One

A few days later, the caseworker called Dok with results from the baby's paternity test.

"So," Sandra said, "the paternity test checked out. No doubt that he's the birth father. And now the birth father would like to meet his son. Spend some time with the baby. Supervised visits, of course."

Visits? So there was more than one visit planned? Dok was trying to get her head around the idea that this young man—barely out of his teens—was actually the father of baby Gabe. "And we have to do this? Don't we have any say-so in this?"

"When you signed on as foster parents, you agreed to comply to the requests of the court. And the court's primary concern is whatever is in the best interest of the child."

Dok scoffed. "How is it in the child's best interests to deliver him into the hands of a man who is a stranger to him?"

"*Supervised* visits, Dr. Stoltzfus."

"And if this plays out the way I think it's going to, this little baby boy is going to be taken from our home and sent to live in a halfway house with his father."

"You're getting the cart before the horse."

"I've been around the block a few times, Sandra. I have no doubt that this father is learning all kinds of things from other halfway house tenants. Things like, it's much easier to receive government assistance if you have a dependent. So please tell me how any of this latest scenario is in the best interest of the child? Because it sounds to me like it's all in the best interest of this father."

"If a parent is deemed to be making meaningful efforts to address his issues, then there is a preference to aim for reunification."

"Meaningful effort," Dok said in a flat voice. "Like . . . showing up out of the blue?"

Sandra ignored her. "I'd like to set up weekly visits for the father to be with the baby. And the father wants to attend the baby's next wellness checkup."

Which would be taking place at Dok's office. She let this absorb in. "Sounds to me like you are making a lot of plans to pave the way for this father."

"If the visits go well, we'll start transitioning the baby to two days a week with the father."

"And then?"

"Then comes overnights. A weekend at first. The goal is to help the baby adjust."

"Adjust to what?"

"If the father can pass these hurdles, then there's a good chance he will be allowed to reclaim his child."

"Reclaim. Even though he never claimed him in the first place."

"Don't overlook the fact that he didn't know that he had a son."

"Why don't you just say it, Sandra? This adoption is unraveling."

Sandra sighed, like she'd had too many of these conversations. "Adoption was never guaranteed, Dr. Stoltzfus. And I'm sure you can imagine that severing parental ties is a very serious step for the court to take."

Right, Dok thought. So was severing the ties of foster parents who loved their foster child. The very ones who had been taking care of this child, day and night, providing nourishment and enrichment and love. Most of all, love. "You keep quoting court policy to me, Sandra. This baby is an individual."

"Dr. Stoltzfus," Sandra said, her voice bristling with irritation, "foster care is intended to be temporary. As I recall, you were the one who called daily to remind me that the arrangement you'd agreed to was for *emergency* foster care. Making it even *more* temporary. The ultimate goal is to return the child to his or her birth parents. I realize you have developed a bond with this child, but that doesn't change the goal."

That was hard to argue away. When Dok hung up, her hand remained on the receiver for a long moment. She felt as if someone had taken her life, hers and Matt's, and shaken it upside down. She felt sick to her stomach.

Later that night, after giving the baby a bath, she was getting him ready for bed and rubbed noses with him. The baby squealed in delight, over and over again. She hugged him to her, breathing in his clean baby smell. How she loved him.

After rocking him to sleep, she came into the kitchen. Matt was at the sink, washing and rinsing supper dishes. She leaned her back on the counter, crossing her arms against her, as if trying to hold herself together. "I had a phone call from Gabe's caseworker today."

Matt paused for a moment, then picked up another dish to rinse.

Dok relayed the entire conversation to him. Judging by his calm response, he seemed to have already anticipated this turn of events. "You don't seem surprised."

He looked over his shoulder at her. "I'm extremely disappointed. Crushed." He picked up a pot he was scrubbing and rinsed it out, before setting it on the counter. "And yet . . . there's a little part of me that admires this young man for stepping up and taking responsibility for his son. He's what, only nineteen or twenty years old? There aren't many guys in this world who would do that kind of thing. That might be a good sign of things to come for Gabe."

"Is it? Is it really best for Gabe? He will live in a tiny room in a halfway house, Matt. With other recently reformed addicts. Think about it! What kind of life is that for our beautiful baby boy?"

Matt lifted his shoulders in a slight shrug. "I just think we have to trust God about this." He wrung out the sponge in the sink, calm as a man could be. Infuriatingly unruffled. "We don't know the future, Ruth. If Gabe's meant to be with us, then something will change so that he stays with us. And if not, then . . ."

"If not, then we hand him over to a man who didn't even know he existed until recently." Her voice shook and the tears began to roll down her cheeks. Her attachment to this little baby felt profoundly deep. She couldn't imagine feeling any more protective of him than if she had birthed him herself. She felt like she *was* his mother.

Matt wiped his hands on a dishrag and hung it on the sink faucet. "Come here," he said, pulling Dok into his arms. "Our time with Gabe came about unexpectedly. Really, all because Monica left my mother's handkerchief with him. It could be that his leaving will be just as unexpected. I've always said this—I believe that all God has asked of us is to be there for Gabe as long as he needs us."

Resting her head against his chest, Dok tried to get her mind around the fact that they were probably going to have to hand over their precious baby to this . . . stranger. "How can you be so understanding?"

"I've been giving this a lot of thought, Ruth. I don't think Monica abandoned the baby like a throwaway doll. I think she knew what she was doing when she set him on the steps of your office. She was probably watching from a distance when you showed up. Probably still watching as the ambulance pulled away with her newborn baby on board. My guess is that's why she went on a bender afterward. And who knows? Maybe she's the one who sent word to the baby's father about him. It might be just wishful thinking, but there's a part of me that believes she's been trying to do what's best for the baby, even if it doesn't look that way."

She breathed out a long, slow sigh. "I wish I had your optimism."

"I think it will all turn out for the best," he said again, more quietly, more urgently.

"You can't know that," she whispered. She stepped back from him slowly, swiping the tears from her eyes. "I'd feel better if Monica's parents would step up and take custody of Gabe. I know they live in Florida, but they've made no effort at all to see the baby. He's *their* grandson."

Matt put his hands on her shoulders. "I feel responsible. I'm the one who wanted to provide foster care for the baby. I'm the one who brought up the notion of adopting him. Ruth, you've been incredibly supportive. I wish this story had a different ending, but we can't hold on to anger and bitterness."

"You sound resigned to the court awarding custody to the father."

"I have to believe the father won't be given custody unless the court is convinced the baby will be well cared for. If that's the direction that things go, then we're not going to battle for custody. We're going to turn him over to his father and hope that we will still be allowed to remain in his life. The court will have nothing to do with that—it'll be entirely up to the father. Just a verbal agreement between us. Nothing official." He let out a sigh. "We don't have a choice about this situation. Well, we do, actually. We have a choice about how we respond to it.

I want to focus on being grateful that we had time with Gabe to start his life off well. We just can't live consumed with worry for his future and bad feelings toward Monica or the baby's father. That won't do anyone any good. It would jeopardize the relationship we have with this father. We want to continue to be in Gabe's life. He's going to need us."

"I am convinced that Gabe's future will be diminished in every conceivable way."

"That's what it looks like now. And that's one of the reasons we want to stay in his life. But I also hope this young man will surprise everyone."

Dok sank into a chair. She knew Matt was right, but it didn't stop the sadness from barreling toward her.

Matt crouched down next to her. "Hey. The baby's not gone yet. Let's enjoy the time while we still have him. One day at a time."

There *was* still time. The thought cheered Dok. As long as they still had Gabe, there was hope that circumstances might change with the father. If he was going to fumble, Dok prayed . . . she hoped he might hurry it up.

On the last day of Bee's radiation treatment, she was given a certificate of completion. She nearly danced out the door, so happy to be done. Damon was waiting for her with a huge arrangement of flowers. His truck smelled like a greenhouse.

"They're beautiful," she said, laughing at the ridiculous size of the bouquet. There was barely room for her legs. "Thank you for driving me these last six weeks. You've made it easier. Because . . . radiation, I have discovered, is no walk in the park." Bee's chest and back were bright hot red, tender to the touch. She was so tired that she often put her head down on the table during the day and rested. She slept twelve hours every night, but woke up exhausted in the morning. "And thank you for your help with the horses these last few months." She hadn't thanked him enough.

"It's been my pleasure."

"Damon, I should be able to handle the horses on my own now."

He glanced at her with a look that said *Yeah. Sure.*

"Well, soon." She brushed off a flower petal from her coat. "I was told it takes as long to recover from radiation as the treatments lasted."

"That's exactly right."

Something in his tone gave her a jolt. Her eyes flicked at him. He was tapping restlessly against the steering wheel as he waited at a red light. For all of Damon's sharp edges and angles, she had a hard time not looking at him. Wanting to see more, or understand more. He was such a mystery to her, a complicated mystery. His response to her just now made her think that he understood cancer better than she had thought. "Damon," she said softly, "you didn't lose your arm in an accident, did you?"

He adjusted his grip on the steering wheel. "I lost my arm to a cancer called soft tissue sarcoma. A couple of surgeries, then amputation, then radiation."

"Had it spread?"

"No."

"When did this happen?"

"Nearly two years ago." The light turned green and the car lurched forward. "When Matt told me that you had cancer, and that you were alone with all those horses, well, I wanted to do what I could to help out."

"But how did you even know that I knew Matt?" She'd never been clear about that connection.

He leaned forward to mess with the temperature controls, his eyes avoiding hers. "I sat behind you and your husband at their wedding."

"At Dok and Matt's wedding? We were both there? How did I not see you?"

"I didn't stay for the reception, only the ceremony."

"But why didn't you say something? If you sat right behind us, why didn't you tap me on the shoulder or something?"

"I arrived a little late. The ceremony had started. It just didn't seem like the right time."

Watching his profile, she saw his Adam's apple rise and fall, rise and fall. And suddenly she knew exactly what had stopped him.

Guilt.

Bee was silent for the rest of the ride home. Damon pulled into her driveway and turned off the engine, but Bee remained where she was. Her thoughts kept circling back to the conversation she'd had with Fern. Would Damon tell her the truth if she asked? She had to ask, to hear Damon say no and let this go. "Damon, at the Olympics, just before I started my second round, I handed you Ozzie's reins while I checked the saddle cinch."

His eyes were focused on the dashboard. "I remember." It came out as a whisper.

She glanced Damon's way. "Something wasn't right with Ozzie after that. She wasn't at ease. Later, I saw that the buckle on her chin strap had come undone, and the hook was digging into her chin." Bee took in a deep breath. *No proof, no evidence, sore loser.* That phrase circled her mind. If she were wrong, she was about to insult a man who had gone the extra mile for her these last few months, who had been nothing but wonderful to her. Quite frankly, he had been a godsend.

His head was turned away from her, and she had no idea what was running through his mind.

Did it really matter anymore?

No proof, no evidence, sore loser.

Did knowing the truth really matter? If the last year had

taught her anything, it was to let go of all the things that kept her stuck. To treasure her present life as a gift.

So did it really matter?

It didn't.

She put her hand on the door to open it. "Anyway, I was just thinking about it. That's all."

"Bee, wait."

She turned to the left and saw his face change, something behind his eyes, something like ice cracking in a spring thaw.

"Yes, Bee, I unhooked the buckle to Ozzie's chin strap."

Twenty-Two

Damon's words hung in the thick air as Bee breathed in their gravity. She couldn't believe what he had just admitted to her. "Why would you do such a thing? How could you? You've ridden in . . . what, three Olympics? Four? You were a legend. You *are* a legend . . ." Her words trailed off.

His mouth tightened, and she saw a muscle jump in his cheek. After a few seconds, he cut through the silence, attempting to explain. "I had never won gold for individual. I was this close"—Damon squeezed his thumb and forefinger together—"until you finished your first round. You were not only flawless, but you had something else. Something I didn't have. I was born into the horse business, with parents who pressured me to surpass their own success. Don't get me wrong. I love horses, I do, but it was the family business. But you . . . Bee, you were one of those iconic horse stories. A girl loves a horse. It showed in your riding. I was so close to winning that gold and I knew it was slipping away. When you asked me to hold the reins, I just . . . I just . . ." His eyes grew glassy. "I just gave in to temptation. It's as simple and as complicated as that." He wiped his eyes with the back of his sleeve. "I'm so sorry, Bee.

So, so sorry. I've never done anything like that before or since. That moment has haunted me."

She didn't know how to respond. Not to his confession, not to his emotions. She just stared at him, trying to make sense of what he was telling her. Finally, she said, "Is that why you're here now? You're trying to make up for what you did?"

"I want to make it right. I know what I took away from you, Bee. I've tried, a couple of times, to see you, to talk to you. But I never could bring myself to do it. When I sat behind you at the wedding, it seemed like God's way of giving me a hard kick in the butt. And still . . . I couldn't man up. I left the ceremony before it was over. Then this happened." With his good hand, he pointed to his missing arm. "Things like this change you. I couldn't put it off any longer. I contacted Matt and found out your husband had died, and then heard about your cancer, and I knew I had to step up."

"What were you going to do? I mean, do you really think driving me to treatment or cleaning out stalls was going to make it right?"

"No. Not at all. I was waiting to bring it up until you finished treatment and felt good again." He rubbed his forehead, like he had a headache. "I do want to make things right, and I have a plan." He dropped his hand and looked her in the eye. "I want to return my medal to the Olympic Committee and disqualify myself. It would mean a historic reversal, which is possible because it's all based on a point system. Nothing subjective. You'd be given the gold medal."

This was all too much for Bee to take in. She wished Fern were here. She would know what to do, what to say. "Damon, I'm going to have to take some time to think about this . . . conversation."

He nodded. "Take all the time you need." He looked right at her. "Bee, that part about you being iconic. A girl loves a horse. It showed then. It shows now."

Dok braced herself as she opened the door to the exam room. Sally Fisher sat on the table, one stockingless foot sticking straight out. "Morning, Sally. How are you today?"

"Oh, just terrible, Dok. That cream you gave me isn't helping at all. This rash on my leg is just putting me over the edge. I can't sleep a wink. I can't keep a sock on—it just gets so itchy."

"Well, let's see." Dok washed her hands and clicked on the exam light. Looking closely at Sally's leg, she saw nothing out of the ordinary. No redness. No sign of insect bites. Maybe a little dryness. She clicked off the light and sat in a chair to face Sally. "So what do you think caused this?"

"Bedbugs. My cousin Gloria told me all about them. Practically invisible, so tiny, but they crawl all over you while you sleep and bite away."

Dok had to bite her lip. Amish homes were, for the most part, spotless, uncluttered. And if they weren't, hosting church once or twice a year meant they would be scrubbed clean by neighbors. She had never, ever heard of bedbugs in Stoney Ridge, or in any Amish community.

Closing Sally's chart, Dok felt that sinking feeling again. Something in this patient's life wasn't working. It wasn't unusual for patients to be stuck psychologically. Dok had seen it happen often, especially after a trauma or grief. Bee Bennett, as an example, couldn't seem to move forward in her life after Ted's death. Most people, Dok had discovered, could point right to the experience in their life that stopped them in their tracks. Yet life was meant to move. Physically, mentally, spiritually. Life was meant to keep moving.

If Sally Fisher wasn't willing to go to counseling, maybe counseling, Dok-style, should come to her. "Sally, do you remember when you first started to think that you weren't well? Not just what brought you in today, but way, way back."

Sally looked at her strangely. "Of course I remember. Very clearly. It was right after Annie started school."

"Why then?"

Sally scoffed, like it was obvious. "Because I finally had the time to pay attention to how I was feeling."

Something about her answer seemed too simplistic. "But Annie's your youngest by quite a bit, isn't she?" And hardly a difficult child to raise.

"We had four boys, and then we just couldn't seem to have any more. Not for the longest time. And suddenly, when I turned forty, Annie came along."

"Remind me again . . . where are your sons?"

"They've all moved to be closer to their wives' parents. One in Kentucky, one in Maine, and two in Michigan."

"Do you get to see your grandchildren very much?"

"I'm a mother-in-law, not the mother," Sally said, her shoulders slumping. "You know how that goes."

"I don't, actually. Tell me."

"Well, my sons' wives have their own mothers to turn to. For things like babysitting or helping out when a new baby gets born."

"And that's the reason you don't see your grandchildren?" Dok wondered if the reason had more to do with Sally being a difficult mother-in-law. She was a difficult patient. Dok dreaded these appointments.

"Yes, that, and of course the dairy keeps us housebound. Our boys are dairy farmers too. They're pretty housebound too. We keep hoping Annie will marry a man who wants to take over the dairy. My husband's not getting any younger, you know." She let out a long-suffering sigh. "But Annie says the boys in our church don't interest her."

Dok moved on to more general questions: what kinds of things Sally liked to do, who her friends were, what brought meaning to her days. And that's where she learned something she wouldn't have expected. To her surprise, Sally wasn't as involved in the church community the way most Amish women were. Other than church, she didn't participate very often in the typical female gatherings, like quiltmaking or canning. "Why do you think that is, Sally?"

"Those are mostly mother-and-daughter gatherings. Granddaughters too. I wouldn't feel comfortable going without Annie, seeing as you've got her working so much."

Dok ignored that dig. "But others participate in those events without family. Fern Lapp, for example. She never had children of her own and yet she is completely invested in the community."

Sally didn't like Dok to push her. In fact, the more questions Dok asked, the more reluctant she became to answer them. She would pause slightly, narrow her eyes as if she was trying to figure out why Dok was poking in her business. Her entire body had grown tense. Her back stiffened, she crossed her arms against her chest, and her hands gripped her elbows. She looked anywhere but directly into her eyes.

That was when Dok knew she was onto something.

One more question. "Sally, do you feel needed?"

Sally snapped. "What does that have to do with the rash on my leg?" She gave Dok a look that made it clear she didn't like the direction this appointment had taken.

But from Dok's perspective, this question had everything to do with the source of Sally's continual ailments. "Tell me. Do you really want to live the rest of your life this way?"

They locked eyes in a stare-down until Sally dropped her chin.

"I'm asking you again. Do you feel needed?"

Sally didn't say anything for a long moment. When she did lift her head, her eyes had grown shiny with tears. "No. No, I suppose I don't. I used to. But nobody needs me anymore."

Her voice dropped to a whisper. "Sometimes, I don't think I have anything to live for."

Okay. Okay, maybe now they were getting somewhere.

Driving home that night, Dok rolled the conversation with Sally over and over in her mind. Bee kept popping into her thoughts. The two women were nothing alike, and yet Dok had a feeling that they were both suffering from the same core issue.

Nobody needs me anymore.

Sometimes, I don't think I have anything to live for.

Bee had never expressed those exact thoughts to Dok, but she had a pretty good hunch that she had them.

But they were both wrong. They couldn't see it, or maybe they'd forgotten, but they were part of something bigger than themselves. Sally was part of the lives of her family, she was part of the church. Bee had a stepson and a stepgrandchild on the way, if she'd only reach out. She had a stable full of expensive horses that depended on her. She had this "amazing lineage" of her Olympic horse to protect.

They felt done . . . but Dok knew they weren't done. Their lives weren't over. Not by a long shot.

Bee caught Fern on her hands and knees, scrubbing the linoleum kitchen floor. She sat back on her knees and waved Bee inside. "I'm in the middle of tidying up." From the looks of it, she had embarked on a serious spring cleaning. Curtains had been washed and were hanging on the clothesline to dry. Rugs had been rolled up and pushed to one side of the room. Windows had been polished so squeaky clean it almost seemed like there was no glass in the frame.

"Fern, have you done all this yourself?" At her age!

Fern rinsed a rag in the bucket and returned to her task. "I want things to be nice for Luke and Izzy. They're coming home tomorrow."

"I wish you would've asked me for help. If you'll show me where you keep the rags, I'll join you."

Fern glanced at Bee's outfit. "You're not really dressed for scrubbing the floor."

Bee looked down. She had on cream-colored wool pants, a soft teal cashmere sweater, and new suede booties. No, she wasn't dressed for housecleaning. "I could run home and change."

Fern waved that off. "I appreciate the offer, but I'd rather do it myself. There's just a certain way to do things."

Bee knew all about *that*. "Would it bother you if I stayed? There's something I'd like to talk to you about."

"Not if you don't mind that I keep going. I want to get the whole downstairs cleaned by noon."

Bee squinted. Fern was a widow, like Bee. Her husband Amos had died suddenly, like Ted. But, unlike Bee, Fern hadn't stopped living her life. The more time she spent with Fern, the more inspired she became to pick up where she had left off and get life moving again.

Fern Lapp was the perfect grief counselor—because she had lived through it all. Bee would have to remember to thank Dok for connecting them.

After refilling the bucket at the sink with warm, sudsy water, Fern went back to scrubbing. There was no chair to sit on, as every piece of furniture had been pushed against the wall. So Bee leaned against the wall near where Fern was scrubbing. "Damon and I had a long talk."

Fern glanced up. "Damon the horse trainer?"

"Yes. And it turns out that my hunch had been right. I wasn't just imagining it. He *had* done something to distract my horse during the Olympics."

"Is that why he's here?"

"Yes. Yes, that's exactly why he's here. He said he wants to make amends." She still couldn't believe that he had offered to return his gold medal to the Olympic Committee and ask for a historic reversal.

Fern leaned back on her haunches. "Isn't that what you wanted from him?"

"Yes. I guess it is. But it doesn't seem quite so important anymore."

"A week ago, it seemed pretty important to you. What's changed?"

"I suppose . . . the fact that he admitted what he'd done. He even asked for my forgiveness. Do you think I should give it to him?" Fern scoffed, just a little, but enough to make Bee narrow her eyes in a question. "What? Tell me what you're thinking."

"I thought you should have forgiven him thirty years ago."

Bee dropped her jaw. "It took him thirty years to confess that he had stolen something from me."

"And look what not forgiving him stole from you over those thirty years."

That stopped Bee short. What exactly had not forgiving Damon stolen from her?

Quite a lot, actually. She'd given up competing. By not competing, she gave up any future possibilities to be chosen for the Olympic team. She'd given up the circle of friends that went along with show jumping.

And bitterness gave her nothing in return. It had been cold comfort. Bee tapped her forefinger against her lips. "So you're saying I should've forgiven Damon long ago, whether he asked for it or not?"

"Isn't that what it means to be a true Christian? God forgives us for our sins and we forgive others for their sins." Fern spoke with quiet conviction. "Otherwise, a person remains stuck."

Stuck. There was that word again.

Annie tidied up her desk as the workday came to an end. She went back to Dok's office to tell her she was leaving. "If you don't need anything else, I'll say good night."

Dok looked up. "David told me he spoke to your folks. Have they made a decision about you becoming an EMT?"

"My father has agreed to the bishop. My mother has said no. To quote her directly, she said, 'Absolutely not. Never, ever, ever.'"

"But why? If I'm in favor of it and the bishop is and your father is . . . so what's stopping your mother?"

"She's convinced that it means I will remain a Maedel." *Old maid.*

"And that will mean no local grandchildren for her. And no one would need her."

"Graad recht." *Exactly.*

"I promise I'll help," Dok said. "There's a way to break through your mom's resistance. Don't give up hope."

On, no worries there. Meeting her future husband had only boosted Annie's determination. "Good night, Dok." She put on her coat and bonnet, opened the door, and her mouth fell open. There stood Mr. Wonderful. "Gus!" Her heart rose in her throat. "What brings you here?"

"We had a call down the road that turned out to be a false alarm. My partner wanted some hot coffee to drink so I mentioned that little Amish store . . . and . . ." He tipped his head in the direction of the Bent N' Dent.

Oh! There was the ambulance. Annie had been so taken by the sight of Gus that she hadn't noticed it parked right next to a horse and buggy.

Gus's hands were tucked in his pockets. "Annie, I was, uh, hoping to see your name on the list for the upcoming EMT class. It's nearly full."

See that? Not just handsome, but so incredibly thoughtful. Was there anything about this man that wasn't wonderful? She felt tingles all through her body. "I still have to get my mother to agree to let me take the class. She's not in favor of me becoming an EMT."

"It's going to work out. I can sense these things."

Annie hoped he was right. "So there's that."

"Exactly," he said. That dazzling smile broke across his handsome face. "So there's that."

That apology from Damon? It didn't magically fix everything, but it did leave Bee thinking a little differently. Feeling a little differently. Hearing his story changed things for her.

The more she thought about it, the more convinced she was that he shouldn't return the gold medal to the Olympic Committee and reverse the result. Her life wouldn't change one iota with a gold medal.

But she did want something.

They were in the barn one morning, feeding the horses. "So here's the deal," she said. "I'm not really interested in that gold medal. But I would like to see you up on a horse."

He'd been filling a bucket with oats and stopped mid-scoop. "Let me get this straight. Instead of getting you the gold medal you deserve, you want me to ride a horse."

"Yes."

"Doesn't seem like a fair deal."

"To me it's more than fair. I think it's something you need to do, Damon. You're an incredible rider."

"That was before." He started down the aisle to Willow's stall.

"And it can be again." She followed him down the barn aisle. "I don't need the gold medal. It wouldn't change my life. But if you got up on a horse, I think . . ."

He spun around. "You think it would change my life?"

"Yes. I do. I think it would help you heal."

"Heal."

"From the experience of having cancer. From its effects. Cancer isn't like breaking a leg or getting a hip replacement. It stays with you. It grabs you by the heel. There will always be the threat of recurrence hanging in the shadows. But if you get on that horse, it's like you're telling cancer where it stops. You're telling it that it can't take everything from you. It can't take your love of riding." She paused her lecture. "There must be a part of you that longs to sit in a saddle again."

His gaze grew intense for a brief moment. Then, with a blink, the intensity vanished, giving way to a deliberate air of indifference. He shook his head. "Bee, it's not going to happen."

"Why not? I don't understand why you won't try. You love being around horses. Your life still revolves around them. I've seen how you've adjusted to not having an arm. If anyone can do it, you can."

His forehead furrowed. "It's the same thing as you being a breeder who can't part with horses."

She tipped her head. "What does that mean?"

"It means . . . it's easier for someone to give advice when they're not in your shoes."

"Maybe it's easier to see what someone needs to do when you're not in their shoes."

He turned to her. "I'm going to up the ante. The day you sell a horse is the day I'll get back in the saddle."

"What about the gold medal?"

"Too late. I already notified the Olympic Committee."

"But I told you I don't need it. I don't want it. In fact, just the opposite. What I really need to do is to let things go." All kinds of things, from unused items to old grudges.

"You do need it. Your breeding business would get a boost from it. There'll be publicity about it. Reversing a medal doesn't happen very often. You need to make the most of the media attention."

"It also means you'll be disqualified. What will that do to your reputation as a trainer?"

He lifted a hand. "It's already done, Bee."

Later that afternoon, Bee went to Fern's and explained the whole story. Being Amish, she expected Fern to not understand Olympic competition, much less to know about it. She almost expected her to frown on the whole notion of medals and competition. An Olympic gold medal was far outside the scope of being Amish. "I wish he would just keep it. I don't need it. I don't even think I want it. I don't understand why he went ahead and just disqualified himself."

Typical of Fern, she surprised Bee. "You said you wanted him to be healed from the experience of having cancer. Maybe it's not cancer he needed to be healed from."

"Then from what?" It took a moment to sink in. "Oh. Oh, I think you're right." Fern was always right.

Dok couldn't believe how calm Matt was, sitting in the exam room with the baby in his arms, waiting for the baby's biological father to arrive with the caseworker. He had met the father yesterday, when he had delivered the baby to him for the first supervised visit. Dok grilled him after he returned home, and his only comment was that the father seemed okay.

"Okay isn't good enough," she had said.

"He's not a bad person, Ruth." Matt sounded like he was pleading with her.

Her gut twisted. "Not bad isn't good enough, either."

Dok really had no desire to meet this young man. She glanced at her wristwatch. "He's already late. Maybe that's a sign that he's not all that serious about the baby."

Not ten seconds later, Annie knocked on the door and opened it. "They're here. They got mixed up and went to the Bent N' Dent."

Dok exchanged a look with Matt. "Thanks, Annie. Please send them back."

A minute later, Sandra came into the room with a young man behind her. Neither of them was what Dok had imagined them to be. She would've thought Sandra was a giant of a woman. Instead, she was barely five feet tall, with long bleached-blond hair that didn't at all match her gruff voice. She wore a silver fleece vest, black jeans, and cowboy boots. And the young man, whom Dok had imagined with devil's horns, was nothing like that. He was on the bottom end of an average build for a male, had fine features—quite a beautiful face, actually. A head of curly brown hair, and vulnerability in his eyes. His demeanor, unlike Sandra the caseworker, was quite gentle. And he looked so, so young. He was a boy-father.

He reached out to shake Dok's hand, then Matt's, and then his eyes went straight to the baby.

"May I?" he said, holding out his arms.

Carefully, Matt handed the baby into his father's arms. Dok caught sight of the resemblance Gabe had with his father—the finely shaped ears, the dimple in his left chin, the shape of his eyes. It was as if she were looking at a split picture—Gabe as a baby, and Gabe as a young man.

She sensed Matt's eyes on her, but she didn't want to look at him. She knew what he was thinking: *Look at them, Ruth. They belong together.*

"I've already weighed and measured the baby," she said, shifting into her professional voice. "He's up two pounds from his last checkup. Everything looks good. He'll be getting some vaccinations today, which will probably make him a little fussy tonight."

"Will it hurt?" the father said.

Dok looked up, surprised at the concern in his voice. "The vaccines? They're just a quick prick. But within a few hours, he'll be feeling their effect. Last time, Gabe had a slightly raised fever and acted a little fussy. Didn't he, Matt?"

Matt nodded. "He was back to his fine self within twenty-four hours."

"My mom always said I was an easy baby," he said.

Dok listened to the baby's heart, though she'd already done it before the father arrived. "Are you in touch with the baby's mother?"

She could sense Matt frowning at her. She probably shouldn't have asked that question. But why not? She wanted to know.

The father's eyebrows lifted, surprised. "No. I haven't seen Monica for at least six months. I don't know where she is. No one does. I tried to find her after I heard she'd had a kid—" He paused, as if he didn't want to think of Gabe as somebody's kid. "After I heard my son was born."

"What about the person who told you about Gabe? Is she able to get in touch with her?"

Sandra cleared her throat. "Dr. Stoltzfus, the purpose of this meeting is for the father to be appraised of his child's health. To learn of his vaccination status and to be prepared for what comes next."

In other words, Dok thought, not to grill him. "Well, the baby is clearly thriving." *Because he's in our home. Because we care for his physical, emotional, and intellectual needs. Because we provide enrichment and stimulation.* She didn't say all of that out loud, but she wanted to. "My assistant, Annie, will give you a copy of his vaccination record and a pamphlet of what's still to come."

Sandra headed to the door. "Next visit will be in two days. Officer Stoltzfus, I'll expect you to bring the baby to my office at ten o'clock. This visit will last six hours, so plan to return at four o'clock."

"Actually, my last name is Lehman," Matt said. He had to

remind her of that detail every single time. "You can count on me to be at your office."

The father handed the baby to Dok. "I'm . . . grateful. For everything you've done for my son."

Dok could hardly look at him. *Don't be nice. Don't be a good guy.* And mostly, *don't make this harder than it is.*

Twenty-Three

A week later, Sandra the caseworker called Dok to say that the court had decided to reunite Gabe with his father. Dok wasn't surprised. She had foreseen the path to be unrolling in that direction.

Reunite.

That was the court's language, not Dok's. It was the court's decision, not Dok's. If anyone has asked for her opinion, she would've said the court was moving way too fast, handing over the responsibility of a child to a man who hardly knew him, a man who hadn't proved himself as a father other than showing up to a few appointments. The court should just slow way, way down. Give this young father time to understand what fatherhood meant, what it truly required out of a person. The need for consistency, for stability. For sacrifices.

The caseworker kept insisting that the court was only concerned with what was in the child's best interests. So the baby, Dok kept repeating, was leaving a loving home with two parents to go live in a single room in a halfway house with one parent he'd barely met more than a few times. So Dok kept insisting, "How exactly is that in Gabe's best interest?" Her voice might have sounded a bit testy.

Dok knew this turn of events wasn't Sandra the caseworker's

fault. She was only following the protocol. But Dok still wanted to push back at it. She was ready to hire a lawyer.

To her shock, Matt said no. No legal battle for custody of Gabe. He insisted that they comply with the court's decision. "We want to stay in Gabe's life. There's no point in stirring up bad feelings between the father and us. Or between the caseworker and us. Sandra's going to be watching this father closely. If he messes up, if the court has to intervene, then we want Gabe back. Let's not jeopardize that in any way."

Matt had a point.

So when Sandra called to inform them of the date of Gabe's transfer, Dok had become resigned to the situation. Defeated. By the morning of the actual transfer, as she finished packing up Gabe's clothes and toys to send along with him, she felt numb.

"You don't have to go with me," Matt said. "I know you have to work."

She would never let him do this hard thing alone. "We're in this together."

He reached out to take her hand. "Thank you."

"For what?"

"For being willing to take the baby in the first place. For all the night feedings that I slept right through. For accepting the change that came with having a child . . . at our advanced age." He wiggled his eyebrows. "And mostly for being gracious about how this chapter in our life is ending."

She leaned into him and he wrapped her in his arms. As hard as today was—and it might be one of the hardest things she'd ever had to do—she and Matt had never been closer. Another gift that this baby had brought to them—the realization of how blessed they were to have each other. How quickly time was passing. "Matt, I want to hang on to some of the changes we've made in our lives because of Gabe."

"Let me guess. You want me to finish the remodel."

She pulled back, smiling. "There's that. And then . . . there's other things."

"Like what?"

"Like . . . slowing life down a little."

"What does that mean for your work?"

"I'm not sure yet." But she had a few ideas.

Since Dok had cleared the morning of appointments, Annie thought she might treat herself to a few delicious hours in the public library, reading up on the Heimlich maneuver. Gus had told her about a recent event in which a teenager had choked on a hot dog while watching a high school football game. Gus and the paramedic had been at the game, a standard practice, so they could immediately respond to the boy. The Heimlich maneuver had saved his life.

Annie's longing to be an EMT doubled as she listened to this story, and other ones from Gus. He had all kinds of fascinating stories. What a privilege—to be the hands and feet of God's healing touch. She couldn't wait to take the EMT classes. One week left before they started. Gus had promised to save a spot for her on the list.

But Annie's mother hadn't budged an inch. Nothing was going to change her mind, she said, after Annie had made another appeal last evening. "Nothing," Mom said, "and no one."

Dad had lifted his shoulders in a helpless shrug.

Annie tried to give the whole thing up to God—her calling to become an EMT, her longing to get to know Mr. Wonderful—only to snatch it back again. She did her best to set aside her disappointment, but it kept creeping up on her, covering her like a blanket. She just couldn't believe that God would give her the call to be an EMT without paving the path that led to it. Step by step, it seemed like things were working out. But this last step wasn't a little one. It was huge. It was her mother.

By the back door, Annie tied her bonnet strings under her chin as her mother came looking for her. "You said you didn't have to be at Dok's 'til noon."

"I don't, but I thought I'd go to the library."

"You read too much as it is." Her mother shook her head. "I need you home. Cousin Gloria is coming for coffee."

Annie's heart sank. That would mean Gloria would describe another gruesome disease and Mom would spend the rest of the day perseverating on it.

"And she's bringing someone."

Annie narrowed her eyes. "What kind of someone?"

"That young man! The one she wants you to meet. Honestly, Annie, sometimes I don't think you listen to a word I say."

Annie's heart hit the floor. "Mom, I'm sorry, but I can't stay. I just can't."

She opened the door and took a step outside. Cousin Gloria had already arrived. The horse and buggy stood by the hitching post. Beside the post was Annie's red scooter. She cringed, knowing she was trapped.

"Yoo-hoo!" Gloria said, climbing out of the passenger side of the buggy. "Annie, I brought someone special I want you to meet!"

That someone was looping the horse's reins around the hitching post. When he finished, he turned around.

Annie squinted. Something about him seemed familiar. He took off his hat and shook a hand through his hair. Then he looked up and saw Annie. Their eyes locked. Then his face broke into a huge smile.

Her heart skipped a beat. Maybe two. Gloria's young man was Gus Troyer. Mr. Wonderful.

"Maybe," she told her mom, "I can stay for coffee after all."

244

Bee's fatigue hadn't ended with radiation, but that oppressive feeling of being dogged by a cancer diagnosis had left her. She had her life back, and now she just had to figure out what her life was going to look like—because she knew changes were needed.

Actually, change had been underway. Thoughts of Ted still brought a deep ache. But the sharp edges of grief had softened a little. Their jab wasn't quite so severe.

Over these last few weeks, Bee had spent the afternoons packing up a box or two of Ted's belongings and taken them, one at a time, to a donation center. She sold his car. Her garage was nearly cleared out and she could actually drive her car in—something she hadn't been able to do since moving in. Little by little, the house was getting organized. Lived in, the way she and Ted had planned for it.

Maybe it was Fern's doing, or maybe it was Damon's, or maybe it was both of them, but Bee didn't feel quite so stuck anymore. Taking a step made the difference. It might've started with cleaning out Ted's sock drawer, but that simple action created a trickle-down effect on her entire sense of well-being. Movement. It was huge.

Yesterday, she'd asked Damon to help her hang some framed artwork. That task took a little maneuvering, considering he was one-armed. In the end, she had to hold the nail while he hammered it in. "Now here's a trust exercise that can rival a Join-Up," she said, and he laughed. Really, really laughed.

She couldn't remember ever hearing Damon laugh. He hardly ever cracked a smile. It was nice, that laugh. She'd like to hear it more often.

After the last picture was hung on the wall, he asked her if she felt up to working with Echo in the arena.

She tossed the hammer in the toolbox. "That's not what you're really asking, are you?"

"Bee," he said softly, "that horse is ready for more. She learns so fast."

Bee already knew. Despite her objections, Damon had set up obstacles and fences to get Echo accustomed to navigating a course. She'd seen how quickly the horse responded to his training. "You want me to sell her."

"Honestly, I don't care if you keep Echo or sell her. What I want is for that remarkable horse to be in training. To be challenged. Otherwise you're just keeping her . . ." He stopped short of saying the word.

"Stuck."

"Stuck," he repeated. "It isn't fair to her, Bee. Not to any of them." He handed her a business card for the client who had been waiting for word on Echo. Then he picked up the toolbox to take it out to the garage.

Fingering the business card, she knew he was right.

So maybe more change was still needed in Bee's life.

The formal transfer of baby Gabe into his father's custody was anticlimactic. Oddly quick. It occurred in Sandra's office, with interruptions coming every minute or so. Sandra's mood was authoritative and efficient as she handed them papers to sign—as if to ward off any emotional outbursts. And then the boy-father left with his infant, who'd slept through it all in his carrier.

Sandra looked at Dok and Matt. "Thank you for all you've done." And goodbye, she meant.

"And you'll let us know when our visits will be scheduled with Gabe, right?" Matt said.

"I'll be in touch," Sandra said. And goodbye. She closed Gabe's file and put it on top of a stack.

"That's it?" Dok said. "File closed."

Sandra sighed. "Not closed. We will be monitoring the situation. I'll call with updates if there are any." And goodbye.

Matt rose from his chair and Dok took his lead. He was about to shake Sandra's hand, but her phone rang and she picked it up, lifting one hand in a wave.

They didn't say much on the way home. There wasn't much to say. They walked into the house and Dok hung up her coat and her breath hitched as she noticed a little stuffed bunny on the ground. It must have fallen out of the diaper bag.

Matt saw it too. They stood there, staring at it.

"His favorite," Matt said, his voice raspy. He reached down and picked it up, and then his shoulders started to shudder. A sudden, guttural sound escaped from his throat, and he covered his face with his hands, succumbing to sobs.

Dok wrapped her arms around him and cried along with him.

Twenty-Four

Dok knew Annie was quiet, but today's quiet seemed different. During lunch, she asked Annie if anything was wrong.

"Today's the last day to register for the EMT class. But my mother . . . she will not change her mind."

Dok cringed. She'd been so preoccupied with Gabe's situation that she'd completely forgotten her promise to help persuade Sally Fisher to let Annie take the course.

"She's said that no man would want to be with someone who rode in an ambulance for a living. But then she met Gus . . ." Annie paused, cheeks coloring.

"Gus?"

"He's . . . an Amish EMT in Gordonville. The bishop introduced us."

"I'm still lost. Why would he change your mother's mind about you becoming an EMT? You just met him, didn't you?" Hold on. Wait just a minute. "Unless the two of you had met before . . ." Dok started connecting the dots. "Is he the same Amish EMT who arrived here on the morning the baby was left here?"

Streaks of red started up Annie's cheeks. "We've only met a few times."

Bingo. "Annie, is he the reason you want to be an EMT?"

"No! Not at all. He's the reason I discovered that Amish can be EMTs."

"So why did you think meeting Gus would change your mother's mind?"

"Because . . . well . . ." Annie's look of mortification grew.

Dok figured it out. "Never mind." She swallowed a smile. "So, Annie, why do you think your mother is still so opposed to the idea?"

"I think it's because . . . when her children move on, she feels left behind."

For whatever reason, Sally Fisher had trouble believing she was part of a bigger whole. Baffling to Dok, because Sally's feelings were so opposite of most Amish women, who grew up with an engrained sense of belonging. But everyone deserved to feel as if they were needed. Everyone had lessons to learn and gifts to share. Everyone was here for a reason.

A light bulb switched on in Dok's head. "Annie, would you mind calling your mother and ask her to come to the office this afternoon?"

Annie's brow furrowed. "Are you sure?"

"I'm sure."

A few hours later, Annie let Dok know that her mother had arrived and was waiting in the exam room. "She thinks you're going to tell her that she's got a terminal illness."

Dok had to stifle a laugh before knocking on the exam room door and opening it. Sally was lying down on the table, hands twisted together in a tight knot. "Go ahead and tell me, Dok. I'm ready."

Expecting that reaction, Dok sat calmly in a chair at the end of the table and waited. Sally's head poked up. "What are you waiting for?"

"I'm waiting for you to sit up. It's hard to talk to a pair of feet."

Sally pushed herself up on her elbows to face Dok.

"I understand you're still a little reluctant to let Annie start the EMT coursework."

Sally's face tightened. She rose to a stiff sitting position. "Dok, there's nothing you can say that will make me change my mind."

"First hear me out, Sally. I'd like you to come work for me on Saturdays while Annie is taking her EMT class. We're supposed to close by noon, but it usually spills into the early afternoon."

Sally blinked several times. "Me?"

"Yes. You. I've been thinking about who to get to replace Annie on Saturdays and I feel confident you're the right one. You certainly have heard of more illnesses than most folks—"

The tiniest of smiles began in Sally's eyes.

"—and I have no doubt that Annie's amazing organizational skills came from your housekeeping—"

Sally tucked the back of her hair up into her prayer cap.

"So would you be willing? To be perfectly frank, I really need your help, Sally."

Sally took her time answering. "I suppose," she said, sounding pleased, "that we could give it a try."

Bee hung up the phone with Tyler, Ted's son. She called to check in, to let him know she'd weathered a bout of breast cancer, and he was so concerned that he asked if he could come visit. Or maybe she'd like to come to New York and stay with them for a few days?

"Soon," she told him. "Maybe I could even come and help out after the baby arrives. That is, if you could use the help." She didn't want to trespass in his mother's orbit. Ted's first wife could be territorial with her son. A bit like Bee with her horses.

"We'd love the help," Tyler said. "Count on it."

Pouring herself a second cup of coffee, she chided herself

for waiting so long to call Tyler. She shouldn't have waited so long for a lot of things.

One of these days now, Damon wouldn't arrive early in the morning to help Bee with the horses. Every few days, her energy level rose a notch or two. She was on her way to a full recovery. And Damon was in high demand as a trainer. She knew because the client he had sent her way had told her that very thing. The woman wanted to buy Echo and hire Damon to train the mare in show jumping for her daughter to compete. "He's the best, you know," the client said. "The very best."

Yes, Bee knew. Over the last two months, she'd seen him take her horses to a level she'd never introduced to them. She was also aware that he had never cashed the paychecks she'd given him. Not one. She had no idea of his financial status, but this arrangement couldn't keep going much longer.

The client upped her offer on Echo, but Bee couldn't bring herself to seal the deal. Her reluctance sent the wrong message to the woman. "Name your price."

"It's not about money," Bee said.

"Then what is it you want?"

That's the thing. Bee really didn't know, not until the client made a parting shot.

"You can't just keep Damon Harding all to yourself, you know."

And in that sentence, the future became crystal clear to Bee.

She poured two mugs of coffee and took them out to the barn. At first she couldn't find Damon. He wasn't in the arena or the barn. She opened the back door of the barn and saw him walking in from the pasture where he'd turned out Strider. The fields were carpeted with Kelly-green grass. Birdsong filled the air, trees had begun to leaf out. The sky was blue as a robin's egg, with white fluffy clouds skirting along. She took in a deep breath. At long last, spring was coming.

Damon met her at the back barn door. "Strider needs to

work, Bee," he said, taking the coffee from her without a hello or thank you.

"I know," she said. At the sound of her voice, Echo and Willow stuck their heads over the stall doors, as if trying to eavesdrop.

He took a sip of coffee. "They all want to work."

She knew, she knew. "I thought we could make a deal."

"We did make a deal. You didn't keep your end of it. I heard you turned down the buyer for Echo."

"That's because I want to up the ante on our deal." Was Bee really going to do this? She glanced over at Echo, who nodded her big head up and down, up and down, as if she knew what Bee was thinking and was all for it.

Yes, she was going to do this. Try, anyway.

He looked at her curiously.

"Damon, I'd like you to stay on. I think we could make a good team. I'll keep breeding Ozzie's line. You provide higher-level training for the horses."

He walked down the aisle of the barn to hang Strider's lead rope on a hook, as if he hadn't even heard what she had just said. He did this to her all the time! Ignored her. Didn't listen to her. Just went about his own business.

So maybe this was a terrible idea. Clearly, they couldn't work together. Maybe it was time to part ways.

But she didn't want to! For her horses' sakes, for her own sake. Damon had grown on her, much the way Fern Lapp had grown on her. He'd been an instigator to help her start to heal—from cancer, but also from grief. As exasperating as he could be, he was also remarkable. He'd treated her so well these last few months, shockingly tender and kind. He gave outstanding care to her beloved horses. Skilled training beyond anything she could give them. No, she didn't want to part ways. But that didn't mean he didn't make her mad. "Damon, did you hear me?"

He finished his coffee and walked back down the aisle. "I heard you."

"Really? Because it's hard to tell. Sometimes I don't know if you have a hearing problem or just an ignoring problem."

A slight grin started.

"So? What do you think about my offer?"

"What do I think?" He scratched his jaw, his eyes narrowing. He didn't say anything for a long time. Way too long. Finally, he spoke. "Bee, do you really think you can part with the horses after I spend months training them?"

Two months ago? No way. Not a chance. But now, she thought she could. It was the right thing to do, both for the horses and for herself. "I do. I really do." Imagine if one of Ozzie's horses made it all the way to the Olympics one day. What a way to honor Bee's magnificent mare. "And when a horse *is* sold, we split the profits sixty-forty."

Damon walked over to the open barn door to look out at Strider in the pasture. "What about him?"

"We can use him as a stud." She waited. And waited. "So what do you think?"

He considered her words another long moment. "They are beautiful horses." His eyes were still on Strider.

She followed his gaze. "I know. They're magnificent horses."

Abruptly, he spun around to face her. "Split the profits fifty-fifty and I'm in."

She'd expected as much. "Fine." She let out a sigh, like it hurt. "Fifty-fifty."

He held out his hand. "Partners?"

"Hold on. Not so fast. There's one more condition. You've got to get back up on a horse and ride."

His eyes snapped to hers. "You're kidding. You're holding me to that?"

"I sure am. I've been researching what adjustments are needed for a rider like you to maintain balance. There's lots of ways to make it work, like a specialized rein grip. Echo is the perfect horse for you to get started again. She's got a calm temperament and smooth gait." She rubbed her hands together in delight. "Somewhere in the tack room is a mounting block. I'll get it in the wheelbarrow and haul it into the arena." She was about to launch into all the other helps she'd discovered to adapt riding for a handicapped rider, until she realized the color had drained from his face.

In Damon's dark solemn eyes was naked fear. "Bee . . . I don't . . . I don't think I can." The words came out strangled and rough.

A laugh bubbled up inside Bee. Well, she had some experience here! "We'll start slow. One step at a time." She walked toward Echo's stall and plucked her bridle off the wall peg. "Coming, partner?"

The next time Dok saw Hank Lapp, he appeared much worse. He lay on the couch in the kitchen, limp and hollow-faced. His voice sounded a bit reedy, as if he wasn't getting quite enough air to fill his lungs. Dark fatigue lines rimmed his brow and face. There was a vagueness in his eyes that filled her with dread. She'd seen that same look in terminally ill patients. She'd seen it in her mother's eyes. It was a look of giving up.

"He won't eat," Edith said. "I fix his favorite foods and he just won't eat." She let out a weary sigh. "So darr as er rappelt." *He's so lean that his bones rattle.*

Everyone knew Hank Lapp had a hollow leg. The man could outeat anyone. "Hank, if you won't consider a biopsy, what about some other tests?"

He shook his head. "Dok, no point in beating around the bush. I'm about done."

Done living, he meant.

What worried Dok most was seeing Hank lose his will to live, because when a person lost it, he or she started to die. "What about the Hezekiah prayer?"

"Seems like the good Lord is saying no to that request." His eyelids drooped. "Die Dode lost mer rughe." *Let the dead rest in peace.*

She gave him a stern look. "Hank Lapp, *you* are not dead yet." She left him with some medications to try, hoping one or the other might help with his cough and fever, but it was like playing darts in the dark. If this were lung cancer, no medications from her bag would stop its advance. He would need serious intervention.

Driving home in the dark, the only tool she had left was prayer. So all the way home, she prayed for Hank Lapp.

Through Dok's office window, Annie saw an ambulance pull into the parking lot. The driver hopped out and ran into the Bent N' Dent. Smiling, Annie grabbed her sweater and hurried out the door. Gus was already walking toward her with a big smile on his handsome face.

"We were in the neighborhood," he said as he drew close to where she stood on the step. Grinning, he added, "I might have reminded Pete how much he likes the Bent N' Dent coffee."

"Sarah makes good coffee."

"That she does." His eyes had a teasing look. "Speaking of Sarah, she's the reason I let Gloria talk me into meeting her cousin's daughter."

"What?"

"Gloria had been hounding me to meet this girl named Annie Fisher, but she's tried her matchmaking on me before and, well, it's been painful. Then a couple of weeks ago, Pete and me, we stopped in the Bent N' Dent for coffee. Pete had a call so I paid for his coffee. That Sarah asked me if I happened to know of any Amish EMTs. I wasn't wearing my hat, and she just assumed I was Englisch. She said there's a girl who works for the doctor who's looking for an Amish EMT. She's a bit chatty, that Sarah. She gave me the impression that this girl Annie was sweet on the Amish EMT." He wiggled his eyebrows.

Sarah! Annie could feel her face heating up. Soon it would be scarlet red.

"The very next day, you and the bishop came into the fire station. That was when I connected the dots and realized you were Gloria's Annie. *And* that Sarah had it wrong. You weren't looking for the Amish EMT because you were sweet on him but because you wanted to become an EMT."

Both, actually. Annie's face was cooling down. She tried to act like a just-fine person.

He glanced back at the Bent N' Dent. "Before Sarah releases Pete and his coffee, I have a question for you."

"What's that?"

He turned to face her. "Now that the weather is warming up, would you like to go on a hike someday? Maybe a picnic at Blue Lake Pond?"

Annie had already decided that she wanted to marry him.

"What do you think?"

What did she think? She thought they should name their first baby girl after Gloria. Second baby girl could be named Sarah.

That said . . . she hesitated.

He shifted his weight.

She was taking too long.

"I would love to go on a picnic with you but . . . ," she said, "not until after I finish the EMT course. In fact, it might be best to wait until after I pass the test and qualify."

His face scrunched up in disappointment. "That could take a long time."

"I know. But I think it might be best if I didn't have any distractions right now."

He nodded slowly, like he understood. "Maybe, then . . . I

could help. Study with you. Prepare you to pass the exam." He wiggled his eyebrows. "Do I *ever* have stories." Then his face sobered. "Only if you want to, of course."

She could feel a smile take over her face. "Oh, I definitely want to."

Dok woke in the night with a start. She had a bizarre dream that a life-size goose was at her front door. Honking to be let in. Honking, honking, honking.

She lay on her back, looking up at the ceiling. Suddenly, it dawned on her.

Geese!

She bolted out of bed and dressed in a flash. She drove to her office to find a certain medication, hoping that Annie had remembered to refill the cabinet when the drug rep had been through recently.

And yes! It was there. Bless that Annie! She kept Dok's medicine cabinet in meticulous order. Dok grabbed the right medication and flew to the front door, then remembered she hadn't locked the medicine cabinet and hurried back to secure it. She had learned her lesson about carelessness from Mick Yoder. A saying of David's popped into her mind: Even a saint is tempted by an open door.

Ten minutes later, she was knocking on the door of Edith and Hank Lapp. "Edith! Wake up! It's Dok. Open the door!"

It took steady rapping on the door before Edith finally opened it up, pointing a flashlight right in Dok's eyes.

"Edith! Put down the flashlight! You're blinding me."

"I didn't call for you to come."

"I came because I think I know what's making Hank sick."

"It's the cancer."

"No! It's the geese! He's been inhaling their feces."

"He's been *what*?"

Dok walked past Edith into the kitchen. "I think he has valley fever. It's a fungal infection he's caught from the geese." She looked at the empty couch where Hank had been spending most of his time lately. "Where is he?" A terrible feeling came over her. "He's not . . ."

"I'm not quite done yet, Dok!" Hank came out of the bathroom, pulling his suspenders over his shoulders.

"Hank! Thank God. Edith, please get some light in here. Hank, sit down. I brought an antifungal medicine."

He stopped short. "A what?"

Dok pulled a chair out and steered Hank onto it. So frail. She could feel his shoulder bones beneath her hand. "Hank, I think your geese have been making you sick."

"Impossible!"

"Possible. Probable, in fact. The nodules looked like cancer on the X-ray. I didn't consider valley fever. I should have. It's on the rise, but we hear more about it happening out west."

"But how did I get this . . . valley fever?"

"Spores. From geese feces. You breathed them in when you were in and out of the goose house, and when the spores got into your lungs, the fungi reproduced. At first, it probably presented more like a bout of flu."

"He was under the weather back in the fall," Edith said. "Not long after he got those vicious geese."

Hank looked hurt. "They're not vicious, Eddy."

"They are. They're horrible creatures."

Dok prepared the vial. "I'm going to give you an injection of an antifungal medication. We should know pretty soon if I'm right about what's been causing you so much trouble."

Hank eyed the needle. "Not too bad. Cured in just one shot."

"Not hardly," Dok said. "It'll take three to six months of treatment."

His bushy white eyebrows shot up.

"I'm hoping that we caught this in time. Normally, people

improve from valley fever after a bout of the flu. But if some-one is immune compromised, or elderly, and if it disseminates, meaning if it gets beyond the lungs, it can cause chronic, de-bilitating problems. Even death."

"Is it contagious?" Edith said, her voice tinged with worry.

"No," Dok said. "It's not contagious from person to person."

"Just goose to man," Edith said.

"Even that is rare, but then again, Hank's a rare bird."

Driving back home, the dawn of a new day was emerging. In front of Dok's car was light, behind her was darkness. It would be a few days until the antifungal medication took full effect, but she had a good feeling about this diagnosis. This was why she was a believer in house calls. Had she not dropped by the Lapps' to check on Hank a few weeks ago, she probably wouldn't have known about Hank's geese venture. It wasn't newsworthy in a farming community to raise fowl or livestock. She doubted that she would've put the puzzle pieces together.

Finding a partner willing to make house calls, she thought, was going to take some work. But it was time to find one. Not just because Matt wanted her to, but because she wanted it also. She'd had a taste of margin and didn't want to lose it. Maybe that was the best gift of all from baby Gabe—to not neglect the most important things.

She felt her eyes start to sting with worry over the baby. Apparently, the birth father had even changed his name from Gabriel. It seemed like a metaphor—the baby was drifting fur-ther and further from their grasp, their influence, their love for him. It was such a slippery downward spiral—fear for the baby's daily well-being, fear for his future.

But she knew better than to marinate in those troubling thoughts. She took in a deep breath and asked God to bless Gabe's day today. Something about that specific prayer, a blessing for this day, shattered fear's grip on her thoughts. And it turned her mind toward other blessings too.

Through her windshield, she looked up at the brightening sky as a flock of red-winged blackbirds passed overhead. Spring had taken a long time coming this year. "Thank you, Lord, for breaking through my subconscious with a silly dream about a goose." She let out a relieved sigh of content. "And thank you for answering Hank's Hezekiah prayer."

Because one thing Dok knew without any doubt—a doctor can treat to the best of her ability, but only God can heal.

Discussion Questions

1. Setting aside Dok Stoltzfus's commitment to keep up the practice of house calls, what made her such a good doctor? And why do you think, besides knowing the Amish culture and language, she was so accepted by the Plain People?

2. Dok was a wonderful doctor to her patients but seemed to have missed some important cues from her husband. What was your reaction as you read that her husband thought they needed counseling? What did Dok seem to be missing?

3. On the face of things, Bee Bennett could be considered a bit prickly. Reclusive. Introverted. Better with horses than with people. As you learned more about her, did she grow on you?

4. A theme in this book was getting stuck. Sally Fisher, for example, was psychologically stuck. She felt her purpose in life was gone after her season of full-time

motherhood ended. Dok reminded her that she was part of a whole, and was still very much needed.

Bee Bennett was stuck for a different reason. After her husband died, Bee couldn't move forward. Fern Lapp, her grief counselor, kept talking about the importance of movement. She didn't mean just physical movement. When do you think the turning point out of heavy grief came for Bee?

5. Annie Fisher had to get to a point where it was worth the effort to give up her "default" shyness. When do you think Annie realized that her shyness was holding her back from living the life she was meant to live?

6. At first, Dok felt pressured by her husband Matt into taking on emergency foster care for the little baby left on her doorstep. How did her feelings change about the baby? Would she have felt different if he hadn't been such an easy baby? What else did she seem to learn from the experience of saying yes to foster care?

7. Fern Lapp's comments felt like a sharp arrow to Bee. Wise and beneficial, but they came with a jab. Here's one example: Fern reminded Bee that by not forgiving Damon, she had given up more than a gold medal. She had walked away from all competition, including any chance for a spot on a future US Olympic Equestrian Team. Turn Fern's sharp point around. Are there people in your life you haven't forgiven? Have you ever considered what unforgiveness might have caused you to give up?

8. Letting go was another theme in this novel. Bee had to let go of her heavy grief, Dok had to let go of the baby

to his birth father. Is there something difficult in your life that you've had to let go of? Or need to?

9. As the novel ended, things were just beginning for Annie and Gus, as well as for Bee and Damon. How would you write their next chapter?

TURN THE PAGE FOR *a sneak peek* **AT THE FIRST IN A NEW NOVELLA COLLECTION FROM SUZANNE WOODS FISHER**

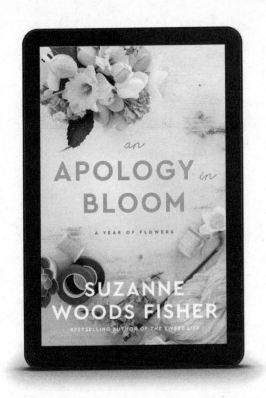

AVAILABLE NOW

One

You're only here for a short visit. Don't hurry, don't worry.
And be sure to smell the flowers along the way.

—Walter Hagen

Jaime Harper stepped back to examine the bridal bouquet she'd created for the Zimmerman-Blau wedding. She had to get this bouquet right today. Did it seem balanced? Was anything sticking out? A bridal bouquet was the most photographed floral piece of an entire wedding. Nail it down and everything else would fall into place.

This was the sixth mock-up. All previous ones had been shot down by the mother of the bride. These mock-up meetings were critical steps in the planning process. And Mrs. Zimmerman was a critical customer. She had a way of making Jaime feel like a rooster one day and a feather duster the next.

The Zimmerman-Blau wedding was going to be the highest-profile wedding yet for Epic Events. Sloane, the project manager, reminded her that it was such an important wedding that Epic's owner Liam McMillan was leaving an initial design consultation with a prospective client to be at this flower mock-up with Mrs. Zimmerman. "Liam asked me to make lunch reservations at his favorite restaurant," Sloane said. "A congratulations lunch," she added, crossing her fingers. "Today's the day." Final approval from Mrs. Z, she meant.

"Let's hope so," Jaime said, but she wondered. She'd been tinkering with the arrangement all morning. Her mind kept wandering, and she had to keep tugging herself back to the here and now. When she was distracted, she missed things. When she missed things, bad things happened. She knew that for a fact. "Do you think it's too, too . . ." Too much? Too little?

Sloane rolled her eyes. "Stop sounding so pathetic."

"I can't help it," Jaime said. She had a better sense of the terrible things that could happen in the world than most people did.

"Hurry and finish and clean up your workshop!"

Jaime looked at her and sighed. "I don't know why y'all are always in a rush."

Sloane turned from the door and winked. "My little Southern belle, have you still not realized we have only one speed? Express."

Jaime listened to the sound of Sloane's staccato heels doing their fast-walk down the hallway. Why did New Yorkers go through life like their hair was on fire? And for what? She got the same results by taking her time.

In the mirror, she examined the bouquet one more time. Was it as good as Sloane said? She hated that her first thought was no, that she never thought her work was good enough. She didn't know what took a greater toll on her sense of well-being—her own self-deprecating thoughts or high-maintenance clients with way too much money. Something was still cattywampus with the bouquet, and Mrs. Zimmerman would notice that indescribable *something* and reject, yet again, the design.

For most weddings, flowers took about 10 to 15 percent of the total budget. Clients were delighted to cut down on costs and waste by letting the ceremony flowers do double duty at the reception space. The welcome arrangement from the ceremony could be reused at the table seating display. Or the bridal bouquet could be put in a vase and used as the sweetheart table arrangement. But there was no such skimping for the Zimmerman wedding.

Flowers, Mrs. Zimmerman insisted, were to be the main décor for her daughter's wedding. She loved flowers and wanted lavish displays to fill every space in the venue, the New York Botanical Garden—a beautiful oasis in the middle of the Bronx. All in all, the flower budget for the Zimmerman wedding came to a staggering sum. That was the reason there was such heightened concern at Epic Events to get Mrs. Zimmerman's approval on the flowers. Sloane couldn't start billing until Mrs. Z signed off, and Jaime couldn't order the flowers without paying a sizable deposit up front. So today was the day. She had to get the mock-up bouquet right today.

She took a picture on her phone of the bouquet and sent it to Liam. A minute or two later, Liam texted back *Subtract*, and of course he was right. He was always right. Jaime had a tendency to jam-pack so that blooms competed for space as they expanded in the heat of the day. What looked to be a perfectly balanced floral arrangement in the cool of the morning would look stuffed and tight by evening. So she subtracted by pulling stems and removing materials, until she thought it thoroughly resembled Liam's recipe.

That man had some kind of superpower in how he could read his clients' minds. He was able to visualize and articulate what the clients wanted even if they didn't seem to know themselves. This was the sticky-floral-tape thought for Jaime: How to put into reality the creation Liam had imagined. That was the secret sauce for everyone at Epic Events—to think like Liam McMillan thinks and execute like he executes. He *was* the brand.

She went over to the mirror again to hold the bouquet low

against her belly, the way a bride would. She rotated the bouquet to see it at every angle, examining different viewpoints to make sure it looked balanced. Photographs exaggerated the depth of field, so it was wise to note whatever might jut out.

Everything looked good. Better than good. Jaime exhaled a sigh of relief. Time to stop. Knowing when to stop was critical.

Jaime taped the stems and set the bouquet in water in the walk-in cooler to keep it as fresh as possible for the meeting.

Before closing the cooler, she breathed in deeply the perfume of fresh flowers, letting their scent calm her nerves. Whenever she paused to soak up the fragrance of flowers, she was instantly transported to the sweetest, happiest time of her life. Back in high school, working afternoons and weekends in Rose's Flower Shop in a tiny town in North Carolina with her two best friends, Claire and Tessa. Mentored in the art of flower arranging by Rose Reid, the shop owner, who had the patience and kindness and generous nature to teach the three girls everything she knew. Flowers were the business of happiness, Rose had often reminded them. They brought joy and comfort to people.

Rose Reid had been on her mind all morning. She was the reason Jaime felt as if tears kept threatening. The reason she felt emotionally wobbly. It was hard to squeeze shame back into its box. Even harder to keep it from spilling out again.

When Jaime had arrived at work this morning, a registered letter was waiting for her. Instantly, she recognized the elegant handwriting, the pale pink stationery. She hurried to the workshop and sat right down on a stool, her chest stinging with pain. How had Rose found her? It was the first time there'd been contact between them since that terrible August day. She cringed at the memory she'd tried so hard to forget. Hands trembling, Jaime skimmed the letter once, twice, then read it again more thoroughly. *All is forgiven*, Rose wrote. *It's time to come home.* And then she outlined a plan for Jaime to return to live in North Carolina, to run Rose's Flower Shop.

Run a little flower shop in that off-the-beaten-track Southern town? Was Rose serious? After all that had happened between them, that offer took gumption. But did she really think Jaime would give up all *this* . . . for *that*?

Because *this* included quite a bit. A floral dream job led by a remarkably creative boss. And when it came to Liam, there was potential for romance written all over their relationship. Well, sometimes it seemed to be written all over it. Scribbles, maybe. They had "moments" now and then that made her think something was brewing. She hoped so. Oh boy, did she ever hope so.

Then again, so did most every female who worked at Epic Events. So did every female client.

Jaime closed the cooler door—pushing with two hands because it had a tendency to stick—and grabbed a broom to clean up the stems and leaves and petals strewn over the floor. As she gathered the excess flowers to return to the cooler, she glanced at the large wall clock. An idea had been tickling in the back of her mind for a unique bouquet—a contemporary take on a cascade style. Why not? She had time. Sitting in the cooler were leftover Zimmerman flowers, plus some unusual flowers she'd picked up on a whim this morning at the New York City Flower Market.

First, she began with a dense center: clusters of color for focus. The showstoppers. Café Latte roses, Cappuccino roses, Café au Lait Ranunculus as big as roses. She built intensity by adding pops of color: Black Parrot tulips and Hot Chocolate calla lilies. The black tulips were the color of an eggplant (Mother Nature doesn't make truly black flowers), petals glossy with a dark luster, tops fringed like feathers—hence the name parrot tulips. The calla lilies were a deep chocolate burgundy bloom.

She brought in texture with trailers of creeping fig woven in through the roses. Next came gradients, accent flowers to bridge

the colors—mini Epidendrum orchids, ruffly Lisianthus. Then
foliage to fill the gaps. A light hand, though.

She stood back to assess. It felt like it still needed more, but
she hesitated, thinking of Liam's text: *Subtract!* A phrase from
Rose popped into her mind: *"Let the flowers speak."* So Jaime
added layer upon layer, letting the flowers do the talking. She
stood in front of the mirror, just as she had done with the Zimmerman bouquet, and felt a deep sense of satisfaction.

The door opened and Sloane stuck her head in. Her mouth
opened, closed, opened again, then stopped. Her eyes and at-
tention were on the bouquet. "Jaime, it's an absolute stunner."
She took a step into the workshop. "It's like an oil painting."
Adding in a warning tone, "But . . . that's *not* the bouquet that
Liam wanted—"

"No, no. Don't worry. This isn't the Zimmerman bouquet.
That's in the cooler."

Sloane crossed the room to examine the bouquet in Jaime's
hands.

"Sometimes . . ."

"What?"

"Sometimes . . . I wish I had your job."

Jaime's eyes narrowed in surprise. Sloane was a phenomenal
project manager. So smart, so capable. She kept the team on a
strict timeline. "I thought you liked doing what you do."

"I do. Sure I do. I mean, if I want my own company one day,
this is the best path. But there's just something about flowers."

Sloane bent over to inhale deeply from the bouquet and
Jaime understood. There *was* just something about flowers.
"I'll tell you *what*! After the Zimmerman wedding, maybe I
can teach you some flower basics."

Sloane smiled. "I'll tell *you* what." She liked to mock Jaime's
Southernness. "You're on." She tipped her head. "Are those
black tulips?"

Jaime nodded. "Tulips symbolize eternal love."

"Get a picture of that one. I want it for my wedding." Sloane rolled her eyes upward. "If Charlie will ever get over his allergy to commitment." They'd been engaged for seven years. She pointed to the large clock on the wall. "I just heard from Liam. They're on their way."

More than on their way. Through the large warehouse window, Jaime could see an Uber pull into the parking lot, followed by Mrs. Zimmerman's white Tesla. She took a few steps over to the large window, watching Liam, her heart humming like a contented cat. She enjoyed observing him unawares. Stolen moments, she thought of them.

"Checking out Mrs. Z's latest ensemble?"

Not hardly. Jaime's eyes were on Liam. He hurried over to open the door on the Tesla for Mrs. Zimmerman. *Such a gentleman.*

Sloane came up behind her to join her at the window. "What's she got on today?"

Mrs. Zimmerman, somewhere in her late sixties, had memorable taste in clothing. Today, she wore an orange pantsuit—radiation, glow-in-the-dark orange—and her hair was hidden under a yellow and purple scarf, its tail resting on her shoulder. Sloane whistled, long and low. "I'm still amazed that the flowers for the wedding are subdued colors."

"She wanted everything in pink, all shades, especially hot pink, until Liam told her that pink was requested all year long."

Sloane coughed a laugh. "He's got her figured out. Mrs. Z wants nothing more than to stand out from the crowd." She gave Jaime a pat on her shoulder and started toward the door.

Jaime was barely aware of Sloane's departure. Her eyes were still glued on Liam. Mrs. Zimmerman was giggling at something he was telling her. Mothers of the brides seemed especially vulnerable to Liam's charms. Maybe it was his thick Scottish brogue. There was definitely something mesmerizing about it. Or maybe it had to do with the way he looked at you when he spoke, as if you were exactly the person he was hoping to see and he just couldn't believe how fortunate he was to find you. She wondered if that characteristic might be true of all Scotsmen . . . or if it was just part of the Liam McMillan magic.

Add to that musical accent his good looks—finely chiseled features, his deceptively casual appearance—and females became captivated. Jaime, especially. If he were tall, he might have been an imposing figure, but his below-average height for a man only added to his appeal. He was so approachable, so inviting. Today, Liam was dressed in a black merino sweater and olive trousers, Ferragamo loafers. Jaime caught herself calculating how much money his outfit cost—easily between one and two thousand dollars. Right in the range of hers, though everything she was wearing today had been purchased at an upscale consignment store for a fraction of its original cost. It was one of the perks of living in New York City—lots of one-season-wear castoffs.

With that thought, her stomach started turning again. This, she knew, was the core of her insecurity. Pretending to be someone she wasn't.

With a start, she hurried over to the walk-in cooler to switch the bouquets. She pulled at the door with her free hand, but it wouldn't open. "Stupid cooler!" She rued the day she'd bought this cooler. It was a smoke screen—it looked new but broke down regularly. She yanked and yanked, but she'd need two hands to open the stuck door. She spun around to find a place to set the cascading bouquet and there were Mrs. Zimmerman and Liam, staring at her with wide eyes.

Two

Flowers don't tell, they show.
—Stephanie Skeem

As soon as the waiter seated them, Jaime cast a shy glance at Liam. "She liked it. Everything." She was giddy. Overjoyed. She felt as if light beams were radiating off her head. An hour earlier, when Mrs. Zimmerman had appeared at the workshop door with a shocked "What's this?" she had marched straight toward Jaime—who stood frozen like a deer in headlights, her heart pounding, her palms sweating. She shot a glance at Liam. His smile fell and he raised a serious brow, as if to say to Jaime, *What have y' done with m' recipe?*

I can explain, she mouthed back, but suddenly Mrs. Zimmerman was circling her, quietly and cautiously, as if she were watching a rare bird on a feeder.

"What is *that*?"

"That? It's . . . a parrot tulip."

"And that?"

"A calla lily called Hot Chocolate. Even its stems are dark."

"Rare, aren't they? This is one of a kind, isn't it?"

Well, yes and no. Floral arrangers certainly knew of black

flowers, though they weren't commonly used in wedding arrangements. But Jaime sensed what Mrs. Zimmerman was truly asking. Once, after a particularly difficult mock-up meeting with her, Sloane had rolled her eyes and whispered to Jaime, "Nouveau riche," as if that explained everything. Jaime had to google it: "Newly rich. A derogatory term to describe persons who acquire wealth within their generation and spend it conspicuously."

Jaime had never had any money at all, not old or new. But she did understand Mrs. Zimmerman's almost desperate need to "be somebody." So she nodded and said what was true. "Mrs. Zimmerman, I highly doubt any of your friends would be familiar with black tulips or black calla lilies."

Jaime knew that to be true because Sloane had given her the inside scoop to the Zimmermans' social circle. Mr. Zimmerman had warned his wife that not a single friend of theirs would want to schlep into Manhattan for a wedding, and that was the reason Mrs. Zimmerman chose the New York Botanical Garden for her daughter's wedding venue. The opinion of her friends mattered to her greatly. She had high hopes to impress them with this wedding.

Mrs. Zimmerman was beaming. She turned on her heels toward Liam. "Liam, your girl finally, finally got it right."

It was like the sun had come out from behind a cloud. It was like a chorus of angels had started to sing.

The waiter brought some bread and butter to the table. Liam held the bread basket out to her. She shook her head, too excited to eat. Not only did the mock-up meeting go better than she could have expected, now she was having a private lunch with Liam. Just the two of them! She'd assumed Sloane would have joined in as the project manager for the wedding. But she didn't. And she thought Mrs. Zimmerman would also be joining them, but she had lunch plans with her daughter the bride, who seemed as disinterested in this wedding as her mother seemed obsessed with it. Jaime had met the bride only once, at the initial consultation, and was surprised at how bored she had seemed. Bored! By her own wedding.

"So," Jaime said, running a finger around the top of her glass of iced tea, "do you think I can go ahead and put in the flower order?" The flowers should have been ordered weeks ago.

Most flowers came from the Netherlands, the land of flowers. "Such a wee country," Liam often said, yet it provided half of the fresh-cut flower imports to the United States, especially tulips, lilies, and peonies. From Ecuador and Colombia came long-stemmed roses, because the stems grew perfectly straight near the equator. South America was also the source for orchids and anthuriums, and so many other varieties.

Mrs. Zimmerman had insisted on a hard-to-source Café Latte rose. Vanilla-scented, with a copper bronze color and very slight pink undertone, it was definitely a showstopper. But it was also bred and grown on a flower farm in Kenya, and there was only one supplier to the United States. Jaime would probably have to pay express shipping fees to make the deadline.

Liam smiled thoughtfully and picked up his fork. "Aye, order away. Mrs. Zimmerman signed off on yer happy accident, mo leannan."

Normally, Jaime nearly swooned when he called her mo leannan. It was Scottish for "my sweetheart, a term of endearment" (she had googled it). Sadly, he used it quite generously with women. Still, she loved the sound of it.

But calling her bouquet a happy accident popped her giddy-balloon. So she had veered far, far off from Liam's recipe. Why was that so wrong? The original bouquet was waiting in the cooler. She'd followed his instructions to the T.

The waiter interrupted to take their order. Jaime hadn't looked at the menu, so Liam ordered for both of them. After the waiter left them, Jaime said, "Liam, about that happy accident bouquet. I thought I might—"

But she couldn't finish her sentence because Liam's watch buzzed, snagging his attention.

The second half to her sentence was that she had thought she might enter the bouquet in the New York City Blooms to Bouquet competition. Jaime had never thought her work was good enough for that contest, plus the concepts weren't her interpretation. They were Liam's ideas with that special Liam finesse. Today's success gave her a boost of self-confidence. Enough to make her think about entering the bouquet in the competition.

Or maybe it was Rose's letter. In it, she'd outlined a plan for Jaime to run the flower shop—but required winning one of the prestigious flower competitions held around the country. *Just one*, she wrote. *Just to prove you've still got "it."* It being passion, drive, determination.

Jaime had forgotten how Rose loved these contests. Rose considered them to be objective affirmation of a florist's imagination and ambition. She used to enter regional contests on an annual basis, and she won many of them. If she didn't win, she was almost always a finalist, which she considered a win. Plastered on the front window of Rose's Flower Shop were seals of her awards. Claire would tease her by calling it her trophy display. And Rose would blush, insisting it was nothing of the sort.

Claire, full of sass. And Tessa, full of daydreams.

Jaime hadn't thought of those lighthearted moments in the flower shop in a very long time.

"Sorry 'bout that, lass. Now, what were y' saying?" Liam's Apple watch had gone silent for the time being, which meant his attention was turned back to her.

Maybe Jaime was getting ahead of herself. Maybe Liam was right—her design today was just a happy accident. "Nothing," she said, taking a sip of her iced tea. She stopped, mid-sip, surprised by the taste. *Well, I'll be.* Sweet tea? Heavy handed with simple syrup. She didn't think anyone in New York City knew how to make sweet tea. Just then the waiter brought their meals and Jaime lifted her head and looked around. "Where are we?"

Liam snapped his head up, surprised by her question. "Southern Comfort. Best Southern and soul food in Brooklyn. Have y' never come here?"

No. She'd been in New York City for over two years and had never been to a restaurant that served Southern cuisine. She didn't think there were any. On her plate was a heaping pile of biscuits and gravy. And pickles! Her eyes darted to the bread basket. *Corn bread.* Her favorite. Liam had chosen a restaurant that featured Southern cuisine. And she hadn't even noticed! Just yesterday, she'd had a hankering for a real Southern biscuit—buttery, flaky, fluffy, soft like a cloud. How had he known to pick a place like this? *So thoughtful.*

She held up her glass of sweet tea to clink with his. "A toast to celebrate our winning over of Mrs. Zimmerman."

"A toast t' you, lass," he said, holding her gaze in a way that stole her breath.

Breathe, Jaime. Breathe.

Late in the day, Jaime's mind kept circling back to the Blooms to Bouquet competition. Today was the last day to enter, and the application required a photograph of her work. She asked Todd, the intern, to come and take pictures of the bridal bouquet that she'd made with the excess flowers this morning. Todd had more technical skills than anyone else in the company, and they all relied heavily on him to problem solve. "Send them only to me," she told him. Twice, because as savvy as Todd was with tech, as remarkable as he could be with details that interested him, he was equally poor at listening.

Todd went to his computer to edit the pictures and, not thirty minutes later, forwarded the finished photographs to Jaime. She clicked through them, holding her breath. Todd's backlighting enhanced the arrangement, bringing out certain textural elements that might be overlooked. Even to her self-demeaning eye, the bouquet looked exquisite. Dramatic and captivating. Like Sloane said—an oil painting.

She glanced at the big clock on the workshop wall. One hour left before the deadline for the competition. Could she, should she? She whispered a little prayer, filling out the entry form and paying the fee, but her fingers hovered over the send button.

Why was she doing this?

She pulled back from the keyboard. Why? Well, because floral design competitions had been experiencing a resurgence in the last few years, especially in the virtual world. They were a way to have design work evaluated by the best in the industry, to receive feedback from respected judges.

She wasn't entering the competition because she wanted to run Rose's Flower Shop, because she certainly didn't. No way.

Or did she?

No. Absolutely not. She had everything she had always wanted. This was her dream—to live in New York City, to work for Liam McMillan. Why would she want to change her life?

Because something has been left unfinished.

Her head snapped up. Where did that thought come from?

She looked around her office, as if she sensed someone was there. A shiver went down her back, though of course the workshop was empty.

She shook off that unnerving thought, turned back to her computer, took in a deep breath, and pressed send.

Three

*A flower's appeal is in its contradictions—so delicate in form
yet strong in fragrance, so small in size yet big in beauty,
so short in life yet long on effect.*

—*Terri Guillemets*

Jaime was hoping to hit the sack early because she wanted
to get to the flower market when it opened, but her neighbor Harrison caught her in the hallway. As she went past
his door, he burst out of his apartment, just waiting for her to
get home.

"Jaime! I need your help."

She should have tiptoed past his door. She usually did. "Hey
there, Harrison." She smiled and kept walking, hoping he'd get
the hint that she was busy, but he didn't. He never did.

"Jaime, I need another one."

She stopped and turned. "Another Apology Bouquet?" He
looked distraught. Puppy-dog sad with droopy eyes. "What
have you done now?" Or, more likely, not done?

"My mother's been in the hospital. I meant to go visit, but
I—"

"You forgot? Your eighty-year-old mother is in the hospital and you *forgot*?"

"I know, I know. I just get so absorbed in my art." He waved his hands. "Time becomes irrelevant. Please, Jaime. Help me out."

The look on his face! Like he was about to cry. She softened. "I'm heading to the market in the morning. I'll pick up some flowers for you."

"Actually . . . I stopped at a store and bought flowers for you." He scrunched his face up. "I was hoping, maybe, you'd make a bouquet for me to take to my mother tonight."

"Oh Harrison, can't it wait? It's been a long day and I'm worn slap out."

"You're what? Never mind. Please, Jaime. Your flowers always do the trick."

Jaime let out a sigh. She felt like a drug pusher, enabling him to keep neglecting his long-suffering mother. "You have got to stop forgetting about your mother. She's no spring chicken! You're not going to have her around forever. A woman in her eighties deserves a son's attention."

Harrison's face blossomed into a smile. "Don't you worry. I've learned my lesson." He crossed his heart.

That, Jaime thought to herself, was a stray-dog lie. Poor woman. Bless her heart.

She put the key in the dead bolt and turned it. "Go get the flowers and bring them to my apartment." He practically skipped back to his open door. "Bring a vase this time too!" He never returned her vases.

He stopped at his door, his face a puzzle. "A vase? I have an empty pickle jar."

"That'll do. Just make sure it's cleaned out." That's the kind of thing you had to tell Harrison.

An hour later, Harrison left her apartment with the pickle jar full of arranged flowers—the jar was completely covered in satin ribbon, wound and wound around it and tied with a perfect bow. Jaime couldn't let her work go out the door in a jar with a pickle label on it. He'd bought tight bundles of cheap flowers in plastic wrap, unsold leftovers from a street vendor. Lots and lots of inexpensive carnations, some Japanese iris with petals that looked a little worse for the wear. Two red Gerbera daisies, yellow stock, and a feathery bunch of chamomiles, which Jaime didn't even bother to include. All in all, a truly dreadful combination of flowers.

The bouquet wasn't her best work, the colors and textures were difficult to harmonize, but she hadn't chosen the flowers, she wanted to get to bed, and Harrison's serial forgetfulness of his poor mother didn't deserve another hour of her time. But he left happy with his pickle jar of flowers.

Poor Harrison's mama. Bless her heart.

She didn't mind doing a favor for Harrison. He'd been good to her. He looked out for her, and when he knew she had a jam-packed schedule of events, he would offer to move her car to the other side of the street in the early hours (street cleaners!) so that she could sleep in. Now and then, they'd walk to the laundromat together, and he would carry her laundry. All in all, Harrison was a good neighbor, and everybody needed a good neighbor.

Best of all, he loved hearing stories about her hometown. A native New Yorker, he said it sounded like she'd grown up in a foreign country. When she told him that she'd grown up in a "dry town" (if you had a hankering for a beer, you'd have to drive over yonder to the next county) and that the name of her town was Sunrise, he howled with laughter.

As she lay in bed, looking up at the ceiling, she breathed in the fresh scent left over from Harrison's carnations. Rose used to call them gimcrack—substandard to other choices— but Jaime loved their spicy smell, and as cut flowers, they lasted for ages. She had enjoyed creating the impromptu flower arrangement. It reminded her of slow times at the flower shop. Rose would empty out the cooler and give the girls the leftovers, and tell them they had an hour to create something special. "No rules!" she would say. "Just have at it." After an hour's time, she would judge the arrangements and pick a winner.

Their three arrangements couldn't have been more different. Rose would inspect each one, offering compliments and helpful suggestions. It didn't even matter who won—they oohed and aahed over each other's work and learned so much. Looking back, Jaime benefited from some of the lessons that Rose taught in those friendly contests. Working under a time pressure. Handling flowers that might not appeal to you. Finding ways to not waste inventory.

Rose let them take the arrangements home, and somehow all three girls felt as if they had won. But that was back when they were friends. Before Rose's nephew had changed that.

This kind of a morning was worth getting out of bed at the crack of dawn. Jaime had set her alarm for 4:00 a.m. to arrive at the New York City Flower Market when it opened to professionals at 5:30. Located in Chelsea on West 28th Street, between Sixth and Seventh Avenue, you knew you were close when the air started to smell different. Cleaner, fresher, greener. A gem in the jungle. And if she arrived before five a.m., she could actually find a parking spot on the street.

The first time Jaime had gone to the flower district, she thought she'd died and gone to heaven. The abundant variety of plants and cut flowers was a horticulturist's dream. So many different smells, blending and mixing, that she didn't even bother separating them in her mind. When she first moved to New York, she'd tried to find a job at the market, but without connections, no wholesaler would hire her. Two years later, vendors knew her by name and set aside buckets of flowers for her. All because of the Liam McMillan magic. Like fairy dust.

Having found the lilacs she'd come for, she treated herself to a cup of coffee and drove to the warehouse. There was less traffic than expected and she arrived before seven o'clock. The parking lot was empty, so it startled her to open the front door to Epic and hear the sound of music. She closed the door behind her and paused. Was that . . . ? No . . . it couldn't be. But it was. Hezekiah Walker! But who would be listening to gospel music? She walked down the hallway and realized the sound was coming from Liam's office. His door was partially opened, and she peeked inside to find him scribbling on the large whiteboard on his wall, singing at the top of his lungs to "Better," a gospel song. Not just singing, he was rocking out! He knew every word to the song. Jaime stared in disbelief. The lyric at the end of the song, "Things are going to get better 'cause God is in control," rose to a crescendo, Liam right along with it. When it finished, she couldn't help but clap.

Liam spun around, a look of shock on his face. "How long?"

"The whole thing." She laughed. It was fun to catch Liam being . . . a regular guy. "What the Sam Hill is a Scottish lord doing listening to Southern gospel?"

Still frozen, he didn't smile or flinch. "'Tis a Grammy winner, I b'lieve."

True. And to think he would know the music of Kentuckian Hezekiah Walker made her fall in love with him just a little bit more. Was that even possible?

"Y' found the lilacs?"

Not so fast. "So you *like* gospel music?"

She thought she saw his cheeks color a bit. "I'm fond o' all kinds o' music."

Yes, but. "Gospel music is a little more . . ."

He waited for her to finish the sentence. When she didn't, he filled it in for her. "A wee bit more Christian."

Ah, there it was. Religion. A subject she carefully avoided with New Yorkers after making some naive assumptions and getting mocked as a farmgirl sap. Ever since, she studiously avoided assuming people approved of a traditional faith. It was right up there with her efforts to retire some Southern phrases that brought ridicule, like *might could* for "maybe." Or *down yonder* for "over there." Or *bless your heart* for "poor you." Liam was the only one in the office who didn't tease her. He smiled at her homespun sayings, amused but not mocking. There's a difference.

He gave her a thoughtful look. "'Tis a good thing, is it not?"

It was. It was a very good thing to be Christian. Jaime had been raised in a churchgoing home. Her mother sent her a monthly postcard with a postscript: *Have you found a church yet?* But she hadn't. She'd looked around for a church when she first moved to New York, but they were so big! Overwhelming. And then the pandemic hit. After the lockdown ended, when she was newly hired by Liam, her weekends became consumed with the pent-up demand for weddings. Sometimes, during wedding season, depending on the scale, Epic had two to three weddings per weekend.

So no. She hadn't found a church yet. But she did think of herself as a churchgoer. She did, the way she thought of herself as a brown-eyed brunette. It was part of her identity, her DNA. And her mother made sure she remembered it as well, texting her Bible verses. Thinking of her mama, she felt a stab of guilt. She did pray! Every morning and every night, like clockwork. That counted for something, didn't it? "It's harder here, in New York City, to keep faith from growing cold," she said.

"Takes a bit more work, I'll grant y' that. So now and then, I find I have t' borrow faith from the lyrics in a song." He lifted his shoulders in a slight shrug. "Surely there are seasons in life when faith can go dormant. But it can spring t' life again. After all, that's what faith is, is it not? It brings new life."

Startled, she didn't know how to respond. She had never thought of Liam as a man of faith. Not that he seemed like a man lacking a moral compass. Liam was honorable and conscientious in his work. Squeaky clean, Sloane called him. But he acted as skittish as a calf about anything remotely personal. She certainly never expected to have a conversation like this one with him.

His eyes were intense, curious, and staring right at her, waiting for an answer. His look became too much all of a sudden. She felt her cheeks flush and her skin tingle, so she lifted the bundles of lilac. "Speaking of life, I'd better get these into water."

Jaime walked down the long hall to the workshop, located at the far end of the Epic Events warehouse. She had designed this room herself when she first started working here. She considered it a serious workplace for a serious floral designer.

A far cry from Rose's Flower Shop in North Carolina.

But would Rose think this was a place for the business of happiness? Or was it just business?

Jaime pushed that thought right out of her head. She had to stop thinking about Rose Reid! That registered letter she'd sent kept churning up old memories, best forgotten.

When Liam had offered the job to Jaime, he promised her space for a dedicated workshop. She'd come to New York City fresh out of college with a degree in horticulture, inspired by an interview with Liam that she'd read in *Martha Stewart Weddings*. She'd been following Liam on social media for a year or two, just as he was making a splash in the wedding world. In the interview, he said that New York City was the place to break into the flower world, because it has a sumptuous floral scene. *Sumptuous*. Who used that word for flowers? Only some-one who loved flowers like she did. So she took that advice to heart, along with her from-afar crush on him, and moved to New York City without knowing a soul. Her mother thought she had lost her mind. There were many times during that first year when Jaime thought she'd lost her mind too. She sublet a small furnished apartment in Brooklyn from a friend of a friend of a friend in college . . . a dinky four-hundred-square-foot apartment on the second floor of a five-story building. So dinky that her shower was in her kitchen. On the garden level were two retail shops—a cat adoption agency and a shop that sold crystals and incense. (Mama would have something to say about *that*. Ironically, Jaime never saw a single customer go in or out of the shop.)

That first night in her dinky apartment, Jaime wanted to pack up Tin Lizzie and head home. But she didn't . . . and she couldn't. She had scrimped and saved to give herself a year in New York, and knowing she would wobble, she had written down that promise to herself, dated it, and stuck it in her Bible.

And it was a good thing she did, because the wobbling only got worse. She had absolutely no connections to anyone flower-related in the city, no résumé to speak of other than working in a flower shop during high school, and she ended up with no job offers.

Then the pandemic hit. And boy did it hit New York City. She'd never known what lonely was until that time. Desperate for something to take her mind off her loneliness, she started making flower arrangements in her dinky kitchen. Social media was her only means to advertise (free!), so she created Instagram-worthy arrangements and posted them. She had ten followers, one of whom was a cat from the adoption agency below.

Until one day, when everything changed.

Sharing the second floor in her apartment building was Harrison the artist, a weird-but-nice-but-weird man who painted enigmatic oil paintings. Dramatic, colorful, inscrutable. (She could just imagine what her mama would have to say about Harrison's paintings. "Son? What the Sam Hill were you thinking?") He'd seen her bringing cut flowers from the flower market up the stairwell, and one morning he stopped her in the hallway to beg for a bouquet. "I've done something terrible."

"What?" Then, "No, don't tell me."

But he did. "I forgot my mom's eightieth birthday. The date blew right past me. I got all involved, you know, in my work."

"Can't you just admit you forgot it and tell her you're sorry?"

"Tried that. Didn't work. She's really, really mad at me. Won't even pick up the phone when I call. Jaime, I need your help. My mother loves flowers. And flowers have a way of getting the message across."

Wasn't that the gospel truth? Flowers said so much. Of course Jaime said yes. How could she not? So she made Harrison a gorgeous bouquet, one of her best (if she did say so herself). And his mama forgave him.

But the story didn't end there.

Turned out Harrison had quite a following online, and he posted the arrangement, tagging Jaime, crediting the Apology Bouquet for repairing his relationship with his mother. The post went viral and suddenly she had a steady stream of orders. Seemed like a lot of people in New York City had apologies to make.

It was a start in the flower world, but it didn't pay the bills. Not with New York City rent, not with student loans to pay back. So she nannied for a few families over in Park Slope and Brooklyn Heights. Nanny jobs paid well but left her with no time for flowers, plus the children were incorrigible. Absolutely appalling manners. Coming from the South, Jaime thought children should show respect for those who were older than them, like their nanny. Not the children in New York City. When she told them to call her Miss Jaime, they burst out laughing. Jaime started to seriously consider packing up and moving home.

And along came Liam McMillan.

Acknowledgments

Several people provided their insights, stories, knowledge, and wisdom to me as I wrote this book.

Before I began, I asked my friend AJ Salch if I could toss some questions to her about horses. About halfway through our coffee, I realized that I couldn't have chosen a better person to interview. A skilled competitive show jumper, AJ provided a framework for Bee Bennett's personality, for what drove her reluctance to part with her horses. What impressed me so much about AJ was that she didn't try to tell me everything she knew about show jumping—she held back (so hard to do!) and answered the questions that I needed answered. It was a blessed time. I left that coffee ready to start this novel! And so thankful for AJ. Just a side note—Ozzie is the name of AJ's magnificent mare.

Thank you to Jane Womack, a stellar cardiac care nurse at a teaching hospital in New England. Jane has many years of experience in hospital work and radiates a calming authority. I can't imagine anyone I'd rather have by my side in a medical emergency.

A big shout-out to Lindsey Ross, an instructor at a university,

291

who always takes time out of her incredibly busy life to be my first-draft reader. She has an amazing eye for the big picture. For example, as she read through this manuscript, she sent chapter 1 to the cutting floor. It had too slow a start. "Begin with the Amish farmer's finger cut off," she suggested. And she was right.

To Carol Vannerson, my dear friend from college, who shared the story of a beautiful foster baby who entered her life unexpectedly and left just as unexpectedly. Walking through this experience with Carol has been a privilege, and I continue to pray daily for that little child. Thank you for permission to take a few pieces from that story to weave into this novel. While not exactly the same story, there are bits and pieces that reflect Carol's experience with the foster care system.

To the Revell team, thank you for taking a manuscript and turning it into the best possible book it can be.

To my readers, who make writing such a pleasure. I treasure our connection through words.

To the Lord, the first and best storyteller, the spark of all imagination, I thank you from the bottom of my heart for the privilege of this career. May every book bring a reader closer to you.

Author's Note

Please keep in mind that I do not have any medical training. Just a keen interest! I asked some friends trained in the medical profession to read the pages in this novel that described specific medical situations, and they provided suggestions and corrections. Still, any blunders are mine.

That said, I do have a curiosity about health and well-being, and the role of prayer for healing and wholeness. That interest has taken me to several books that I would recommend to you.

Resources

Larry Dossey, *Healing Words: The Power of Prayer and the Practice of Medicine* (San Francisco: HarperSanFrancisco, 1993).

Hillary L. McBride, *The Wisdom of Your Body: Finding Healing, Wholeness, and Connection through Embodied Living* (Grand Rapids: Brazos, 2021).

Gladys McGarey, *The Well-Lived Life: A 102-Year-Old Doctor's Six Secrets to Health and Happiness at Every Age* (New York: Simon & Schuster, 2023).

Bessel Van der Kolk, *The Body Keeps the Score: Brain, Mind, and Body in the Healing of Trauma* (New York: Viking, 2014).

Suzanne Woods Fisher is the award-winning, bestselling author of more than 40 books, including *The Sweet Life, The Secret to Happiness*, and *Love on a Whim*, as well as many beloved contemporary romance and Amish romance series. She is also the author of several nonfiction books about the Amish, including *Amish Peace* and *Amish Proverbs*. She lives in California. Learn more at SuzanneWoodsFisher.com and follow Suzanne on Facebook @SuzanneWoodsFisherAuthor and X @SuzanneWFisher.

Don't miss these sweet Amish romances from
SUZANNE WOODS FISHER

"*A Season on the Wind* overflows with warmth and conflict, laced with humor, and the possibility of rekindled love."

—AMY CLIPSTON,
bestselling author of *The Jam and Jelly Nook*

A rare bird draws Ben Zook back to his childhood home, the Amish community of Stoney Ridge—and back to Penny Weaver.

Revell
a division of Baker Publishing Group
RevellBooks.com

Available wherever books and ebooks are sold.

Find more charming romance from
SUZANNE WOODS FISHER

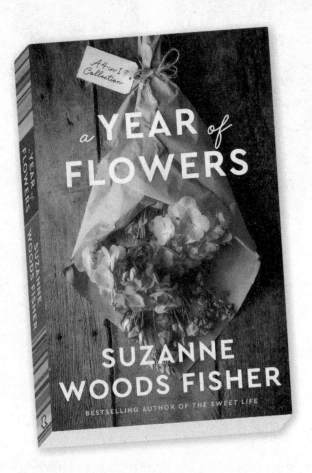

In this collection of four heartfelt novellas, three former friends have found success in the floral industry, but happiness—and love—remain elusive.

Ⓡ Revell
a division of Baker Publishing Group
RevellBooks.com

Welcome to Summer on Cape Cod

Connect with SUZANNE

SuzanneWoodsFisher.com